# Man Down

## A Firefighter's Story of Loss and Redemption

### By

# H. Scott Walker

Man Down by H. Scott Walker

ParkWood Creative
2912 ParkWood Drive
Quincy Illinois, 62305



ISBN: 979-8-9865898-1-7


**Authors note:** This is a work of fiction.. Any resemblance to events, locations or actual persons living or dead, is coincidental.

# Dedication

This book is dedicated to the brave men and women of the fire service who risk their lives, and well being in the protection of others.

*Greater love has no one than this, that he lay down his life for his friends.*

*John 15:13*

# Acknowledgments

The author wishes to acknowledge Tracy Knight. An accomplished author in his own right, his counsel was of great value

In particular, I want to Thank  Dr. Karen Sears, my adviser, my editor, cheerleader, critic and my wife. Without whom my own story would  lack a happy ending.

# Chapter 1

Thunder reverberated through the shabby mobile home. Gusts of wind elicited groans of protest from the thin walls. Nick liked the sound of a storm; it added spice to what had become a life that was far too dreary. The scotch wasn't bad- not really. Not what he was used to, but it was growing on him. He had drank expensive single malts, back when a bottle lasted a month. The *good stuff* got sacrificed when drinking became about the effect, not the experience, and the occasional glass became one a night, then several.

Setting his drink down, he looked at Cat. "I think I'm ready for bed. Care to join me?" Cat raised her head, gave him a dismissive look and laid back down. "Really? We have lived together for a couple of months and you still don't like me? Somebody really did a number on you, huh? Oh well, you know where to find me if you change your mind." Again, Cat ignored him.

Nick threw back the remaining whiskey and staggered down the narrow hallway. He threw his clothes in the corner and collapsed on the bed.

*****

It was unlike any fire he had ever seen. Strange flames tumbled and danced across the hallway ceiling in glowing shades of electric blue and brilliant white. Tongues of vivid red probed the swirling cloud of flame. The effect was mesmerizing - alien - sinister, and as beautiful as it was terrifying. Neither he nor Lou wore breathing apparatus. They didn't need them, the thick, black, choking smoke that should have obscured the fire was absent. Instead, the flames bathed the hallway in shimmering hues of blue and white light. It reminded him of a swimming pool at night. Missing too, was the punishing heat that should have pushed them to the floor.

Lou looked up and laughed. "Fire is like a woman; the prettier it is, the more dangerous it gets."

After so long, it was odd to be working with Lou again; but he found it reassuring. Before his death, the old man had taught him everything he knew about working a fire. Lou had been his department *godfather*; bigger than life, old school, tough, and invincible; at least until cancer ate him alive.

Nick asked, "Lou, you're dead; why are you here?"

The old man shrugged. "You tell me. This is your thing, not mine. Come on, let's get this done." He pushed the hose line down the narrow hall. Nick followed; the absence of heat made progress easy and the bluish light made for good visibility, a rare thing in a fire. Nick could clearly see several doors lining each side of the hall. "*Like a walk in the park,*" as Lou would say.

They reached an intersecting hallway, Lou stopped. To the right, a door stood open at the end of the hall. Nick saw an eddy of brilliant blue flames flowing like a stream from the door. To the left, he saw nothing but the shimmering blue flames dancing on the ceiling.

Nick said, "This is going to be an easy one."

Lou looked at him and shook his head. "No kid, this one is going to kill us. I should know."

"Maybe we should back out then."

Lou glared at him. "I taught you better than that. You can't run from what owns you."

The odd fire grew, and flames gathered closer to their heads. Even so, there was still no heat or smoke. Nick reached for the hose; it was gone.

In a panic, Nick shouted, "LOU, WE LOST WATER, WE REALLY NEED TO BAIL!"

Lou replied, "Christ Nick, what's wrong with you? Wait here; I got something to take care of." With that, the old man crawled down the hall to the left, away from the burning room.

Alarmed, Nick called out after him. "Get your ass back here. You know better than to split up. Didn't you hear me? We need to back out."

Lou waved him off. "Don't be a pussy. Go do your job. I got other stuff to do." He turned and disappeared into the shimmering blue light.

Nick hesitated. He felt his heart pounding, and an icy tightness spreading in his gut. It all felt wrong - sinister. He looked to his right, toward the burning room that somehow wasn't, then to his left, where Lou had disappeared. He knew he should get out, but he couldn't. "No," he said, "not again." It wasn't a sense of duty that held him there, or concern for Lou, not even curiosity. Instead, he felt an irresistible compulsion to follow the old man. He had to face whatever was down the hall. He didn't want to, deep down, he knew what was waiting, there just wasn't a choice. The pull was as relentless as gravity, and so he followed Lou into the blue light.

Someone had piled a stack of ceiling tile in the center of the hall. Nick crawled over them. As he did, he heard laughter.

He came to a door; it disappeared when he tried to push it open.

Thunder rolled in the distance.

A second door waited at the end of the hall. When he opened it, a host of butterflies exploded in his face. As they fluttered down the hall, some rose too close to the blue flames above; they sizzled and fell like sparks to the floor. He peered into a large room bathed in a hellish looking red glow. The flashing lights of the fire apparatus parked outside created a strobe effect in the room; each pulse of light illuminated the men and women standing within.

The gathering was of every age and shape; most were naked, a few wore gray robes. Many were holding cameras. In unison, the congregation turned to him, all with the same blank expression. A short, fat man put a pudgy finger to his lips to shush Nick. In unison, the group turned their attention to an altar like bed ringed with candles, standing in the middle of the room. Nick's chest tightened, a growing lump threatened to close his throat. Becky lay naked on the bed, a man cradled between her legs. A wave of revulsion coursed through him; the man was rail thin, with long oily hair. His face was completely featureless; as if an unfinished sculpture of molding clay,

Nick screamed, "Becky, what the fuck are you doing?"

She turned and smiled at him. "Hey, baby, I've been waiting for you. We're making a movie, come join the fun."

"Stop this, what's wrong with…"

The pudgy man interrupted, "He's right, this doesn't work. She should be on top."

A woman added, "And the dumb ass let all the butterflies out. We need more butterflies."

Another voice chided her. "Enough with the butterflies already, they were stupid."

Becky climbed on top of the faceless man. The pudgy director clapped and said, "And go!" Becky started riding the stranger.

Again, Nick yelled, "Get off of him! Stop it, what's wrong with you?"

A mouth materialized on the stranger's face, and with it came a malevolent grin. He stuck a long tongue out at Nick as he roughly pawed at Becky's breasts. A tattoo picturing two snakes wrapped around the man's left forearm caught Nick's attention. The tat was familiar, but Nick couldn't remember from where. A wave of nausea rolled through his gut.

From the corner, he heard Lou say, "Hey, relax kid, this ain't no big deal. This whole thing is your doing, so relax."

Becky added, "Yeah Nick, this is on you. If you don't like it, just go away. That's what you do, isn't it? You just bail, right?"

Nick half whispered, "No, that's not true."

Becky sat still on the stranger. "You bailed on me. And you bailed on her."

"I had to. I had no choice."

Becky resumed rocking on her new lover, but with more enthusiasm. A look of pure lust spread across her face. Almost panting, she breathed, "Bullshit… (moan)… you cut and ran… (moan)… you pussy."

"Becky," he pleaded. "Please stop, why are you doing this to me?"

"You know why. This is how it is now. Why are you here, if you don't want to play?"

Nick groaned. "The building is on fire. We have to get out. I am here to save you."

Thunder again rolled in the distance.

Becky smiled at her husband. "I think we both know that I'm not the one needing saving. Dominick, honey, you don't need to worry about me. My new friends and I will be okay. Just go do what you need to do."

Intent on dragging her out, he tried to crawl to Becky, but a large nude woman blocked his path. His throat tightened, and he could feel tears gathering in the corner of his eyes. "Becky, stop this. I don't deserve this."

"Yes — Yes, you do. You let me down, Dom. You're not the man you used to be."

Thunder rolled in the distance again.

His stomach turned, and the building despair turned to rage. "Fuck you. I don't need this; I don't need you," He spat.

She shook her head. "You're wrong about that. You reek of desperation. Now, shoo honey, you need to go."

Lou shook his head solemnly. "Sorry, you had your chance kid. It's too late now."

The blue flames poured into the room. Unfazed, Becky waved them away like hovering gnats. No one else seemed to even notice them. A sudden wave of heat pushed Nick back into the hall.

He heard a woman's voice call out, "Come back when you have some butterflies!" The sound of laughter filled the hall as the door slammed shut.

"They were right, you know. It is all your fault."

Nick turned and saw a beautiful little girl standing at the far end of the hall. She wore a white dress- a communion dress. Blonde curls flowed from underneath her veil. The electric blue and white flames were swirling around her feet, snaking up her bare legs; she ignored them.

"What's my fault?"

She stared at him. "Everything. It's all your fault. She waited for you, you didn't come; I waited for you, but you didn't come."

He heard thunder again. "I'm here now."

She frowned. "It's probably too late."

He watched her dress ignite. Without flinching, she held his gaze as her porcelain skin blistered, then charred. In horror, he watched the flames transform her into a grotesque abomination.

Neither of them had moved, but somehow, they were now face to face. The girl held out the smoldering corruption that had once been her arm. She said, "Take me out of here. I don't belong here."

Bile rose in his throat; he didn't want to touch her. A far-off voice called; it was Lou. "Time to get out, Kid."

Nick tried to look at the girl but couldn't. He said, "Sorry, I have to leave."

The thing that had been a little girl, grabbed his hand. "No," she said. "Take me out of here. You owe me that much."

In revulsion, he yanked his hand back, pulling her arm off. She screamed as her body crumbled into a pile of smoldering ash. It was the scream of a wounded animal.

Searing heat pressed down from the ceiling, pushing him down flat to the floor. With it came black, suffocating smoke obscuring the blue flames. Gasping for air, he reached vainly for a wall to follow out. Panic gripped him as he found only empty space; he knew he was lost. Far off, Becky screamed his name in terror.

*****

Nick's eyes snapped open; a gasp escaped him as he sat bolt upright in bed. Bathed in sweat, he fought to slow his breathing. Disoriented, he stared into the darkness for several moments before recognizing where he was. Even after eight months, waking up in the trailer still sometimes confused him. His trembling hands rubbed his face as he groaned under his breath, "Fuck."

The dream was nothing new; it varied sometimes but not much. Sometimes Becky was with more than one person, sometimes it was a woman instead of a man. A few times, the crowd taunted him — called him names like *cuck,* or *bitch.* Sometimes the little girl looked different, sometimes African American, sometimes Latina, but she always died the same way. The dream scared him and it was coming more often. But what really bothered him was that mental flashes of the little girl were now creeping into his head while he was awake.

The bedside clock said 3:50 AM. Experience taught Nick that returning to sleep was off the table, at least for a while. He thought, *It could be worse, I guess, only a few hours to kill.* He slid out of bed, stretched, and shuffled down the narrow hall of the mobile home to the bathroom. After flushing, he ambled into the living room. Turning on the table lamp, he saw Cat sitting on the sofa, staring at him. She looked annoyed at being disturbed.

"What?" He said, "You got something to say?"

Cat looked at him impassively for a few seconds, then closed her eyes and laid her head back down to sleep.

"I didn't think so."

 Cat and Nick were only a few months into cohabitation and still establishing boundaries. He had Jazmine to thank — or blame — for Cat; the jury was still out. After he had left Becky, he crashed at a cheap hotel, then Marcus convinced him to couch surf with him and Jazz until he found something more permanent. Marco or Jazz never said it, but he knew they assumed he would eventually cool off and go home. It took weeks before he found a cheap trailer for rent, complete with ratty furniture. It was perfect, and he moved in immediately. He loved Marco and Jazz like family, but he had to get away—away from the sympathetic looks, away from the unsolicited guidance.

They had unexpectedly dropped in a few months later. Marcus said they just came to "chill and have a few beers." He knew that was bullshit; they were checking up on him. That had pissed him off. He also knew they wanted to talk about *it*—the *big it*—the affair and the aftermath. Worse, they wanted to talk about Becky. The visit was awkward, both of them were reluctant to sit on the couch, afraid of catching something from the furniture -which he considered reasonable under the circumstances- the couch was on the nasty side. In fact, it was Marco who named the place *Casa del Crapo*. Nick knew damn well that Jazz was going to report every miserable fucking detail of his shabby existence to Becky. He didn't much care what Becky thought, but he hated to give her the satisfaction of knowing he was living in a shit hole trailer with nasty furniture.

Jazz showed up a week later with a scruffy cat, a litter box, and a bag of food. She insisted he needed company; he insisted she was out of her mind. They had a brief, tense discussion in which she pointed out everything wrong with his life and personality; he suggested (sort of) she should mind her own business. Finally, she gave him a kiss on the cheek, called him an ungrateful bastard, and left him with the cat and instructions to go fuck himself.

He had every intention of taking the cat to the animal shelter the next day, but somehow never got around to it. Because he didn't intend to keep the cat, he never named it. After a few weeks, a name seemed pointless, and the cat didn't seem to care one way or the other. So, the cat simply became "*Cat.*" The sofa was Cat's private domain; that was fine with Nick. It wasn't like he would ever sit on it; stains from God knows what covered the thing. The two upholstered chairs that came with the place were just as bad, but he'd gotten rid of them. Specifically, he took them to the department's burn tower where they received a *viking funeral* in a live fire training session. He would've taken the sofa too, but that would've required help to move and he wanted no more visitors at Casa Del Crapo. Besides, the ratty sofa fit the décor. The cheap brown paneling, worn shag rug and cracked kitchen linoleum created a perfect mix of nouveau cliché and late century white trash. With some pride, he relished having what was likely America's last functioning avocado colored stove and fridge.

A rumble of thunder vibrated the thin walls of the trailer. He cringed. He liked storms, but lately unexpected loud noises caused a sort of short circuit in his nervous system. It was hard to explain, but it was bothersome and getting worse. He gathered himself before going to the refrigerator for a beer. He stopped himself. *"No, you're on shift in a few hours."* Grabbing a bottle of water instead, he collapsed into one of the two wicker swivel rockers he had bought from a home improvement store. They were actually patio furniture, but they were comfortable and he got them on clearance for half off. Most importantly, they didn't have cooties.

Nick thought about the dream. When he was awake, it wasn't as scary so much as disturbing. He suspected the dream was at the root of whatever was… *What?* he thought. *Pulling me down. Becky, I understand. After all, she is a cheating bitch. But why Lou? Lou had nothing to do with any of it. He had died shortly after I met Becky.*

He avoided thinking about the little girl. She made him uncomfortable — more than uncomfortable- she flat out scared him. She sometimes brought on the panic attacks.

Nick opened his latest paperback. Since moving into Casa Del Crapo, he had become an avid reader. He had a TV, but it was more a nuisance than entertainment. It grated on his nerves, especially the commercials. They were too damn loud; he hated loud. He was currently reading a book by Michael Connelly about a hard-nosed L.A. detective solving the murder of a homeless kid. Nick had little use for cops, but this guy was divorced, lived alone, had bad social skills, and a habit of pissing off his incompetent superiors. Nick liked the guy; they were kindred spirits.

A brilliant white light filled the room, followed immediately by a deafening crash. A second later, the lights went out. Nick's heart leaped into his throat, and he couldn't catch his breath. He sat in the dark shaking when the all too familiar tightening in his chest started, then the tingling in his fingers, followed by the dizziness. The spring in his chest, as he called it, tightened. It was always wound a bit too tight, and he was almost always aware of it, a sort of subtle nervousness keeping him on edge. Like now, it sometimes got worse; the spring would compress to the breaking point, and that scared him. It's when the anxiety attacks came. The last few months the spring was more often strained; he expected it would break sooner rather than later. He wasn't sure what would happen if it did.

He started breathing deeply… slowly. Sometimes it helped, sometimes not; tonight it did.

Cat landed in his lap. That too startled him momentarily. He scratched the animal's back. "Did the lightning scare you, girl? It must've hit really close." Cat purred, it was rare for her to sit on him, and he appreciated it more than he would have expected. "I guess we're the best either of us can hope for."

A moment later, the lights came back on, as a steady rain began drumming on the metal roof of the trailer. He heard a siren in the distance and wondered whether he should just go to the station. Cat jumped to the floor and returned to the couch. "I'll try not to take that personally," he said to the cat. Nick looked at the water bottle. "Fuck this."

He went to the kitchen and put his unopened water bottle back in the refrigerator. He reached in the freezer, grabbed a handful of ice, and threw it into a glass. A generous pour of Dewar's White Label followed.

He studied the amber liquid and wondered what Becky was doing. *It's four in the morning Dumb ass; she's asleep.* Thinking about her sometimes made him angry, it always made him sad. He looked at the laptop on the kitchen table and considered watching the video. He had avoided it for months, but it still taunted him … beckoned him. *No, never again.* He opened the computer to delete the file, but stopped. He closed the lid, and to the empty room he said, "I hope you're as miserable as I am." Then he downed the first drink of the morning.

*****

A rolling thunder rattled the window and woke her. She chastised herself for falling asleep. "*Christ, Becky,*" she thought. "*All you need is to wake up here in the morning. You should've left hours ago.*"

She laid there quietly, not daring to move, hoping he was still asleep. She heard steady breathing and turned her head towards the body next to her. The glow of the streetlight outside cast just enough light in the room to make him out. He was asleep. She slipped out of bed and tiptoed to the bathroom. A wave of modesty washed over her. She felt awkward and vulnerable walking around in a strange apartment without clothes. She knew it was silly considering what they did half the night, but that was in the heat of lust. Now she just felt, well… naked.

She didn't dare turn on a light, but with the door open, there was just enough light to find the toilet. She hoped it was clean. The sound of her peeing somehow seemed incredibly loud. It embarrassed her that he might hear. She whispered to herself, "Get dressed, you idiot, and get out of here before he wakes up." She wondered if she should leave a note, then thought better of it. *What the hell would you write?* she thought. *Thanks for screwing me, best wishes.* She smiled at that, got up, but didn't flush. In the dim light, she checked herself in the mirror; the carnage wasn't as bad as she feared. The eyes were puffy, and the hair was a mess, but the makeup had survived pretty well. She turned the faucet on to a trickle, washed her face, then ran her hands through her hair.

Standing at the bathroom door, she tried to remember where her clothes were. Her dress was in the living room by the couch, her bra and underwear were anyone's guess. She knew they were somewhere in the dark bedroom, but God only knew where. They were new and expensive. Plus, she really didn't like the idea of leaving her panties as some sort of souvenir for him. Even so, she decided it wasn't worth risking waking him up looking for them.

Suddenly, a brilliant flash of white light filled the room, immediately followed by an explosion of thunder. She froze, knowing it would wake him up. To her utter amazement, he didn't even flinch. She took a moment to watch him laying naked in post carnal, alcohol-induced bliss. Even sober, she thought *Trent — no, wait — Travis. Yes, Travis — was gorgeous. What's wrong with you, girl? You just slept with a kid ten years younger than you, and you don't even know his name.* Shame took root in the pit of her stomach.

She and Jazz had gone for supper, then to a blues bar for a couple of Martinis and some dancing. They had hardly touched their first drink when Jazz's babysitter called. She had some sort of problem and Jazz needed to get home. Becky found herself alone in the club. She was just finishing her drink and preparing to leave when Trent—Travis — sat down with a fresh drink. His opening line was, "I have been watching you all night." It was sort of creepy, but he was smiling so innocently. He looked sort of shy, and seemed sweet, but he wasn't much of a conversationalist. Still, he was tall, young, thin, and muscular, so who cared? They talked a little, danced a little, and an hour later, he asked if she wanted to go to his place to "chill." For reasons she didn't want to admit, even to herself, she said yes.

She thought her heart would fly out of her chest when he first touched her. She could feel he wanted her so desperately; it felt so good to be wanted like that. The sex had been fun, not great, but good. Still, she had to give him credit, what he lacked in technique he made up for in endurance and youthful enthusiasm. It had been a long time since she experienced a two-hour marathon session like that.

Unfortunately, he obviously watched too much porn. Every time she had started to really get into it, he wanted to change positions. It sometimes felt like a gymnastics routine. And worse, he *tried* to be dominant. The whole ass slapping and hair pulling thing just didn't work for him. It wasn't like she was opposed to it, but it just came off as contrived. *Travis just didn't have the gravitas to make it work. Not like Dominick... Sly either for that matter.* Reflexively, her hands went to her face at the thought of that awful night. *No! Sly was nothing like Nick. Sly was rough and crude. Sly was selfish in bed.... But it was good, wasn't it?*

She tried to push the thought away. *Being with Sly — with them — had been visceral, but there was no comparison to Dom, to the man I lost.*

Thinking of Dominick always broke her heart. To her, Dom was a natural alpha male, confident and self-assured. He could be forceful without being rough, and could ravish you without being selfish. The man didn't *act* dominant, he just simply was. Surrendering to him felt safe and warm, but there was always the hint of a barely controlled beast just under his surface that thrilled her. Sometimes he growled under his breath when he was close. That, by itself, could almost send her over the edge. She remembered the feel of Nick's powerful body enveloping her, moving in her, controlling her.

Nick was a *man,* in and out of bed. Thinking about him while looking at the boyish stranger on the bed brought on a sudden wave of emptiness. For the hundredth time, she asked herself, *How could I do it? How could I throw it all away?*

As she tiptoed to the living room to get dressed, she muttered to herself, *What the fuck am I doing here*? It took what seemed like ages to gather her dress and shoes, she wanted to leave before he woke up. He'd probably want her to stay, and she had no idea what to say to him.

A heavy downpour began as she stepped into her dress. *Great*, she thought. *I am going to have to stand out in the rain waiting for an Uber wearing nothing but a little cocktail dress. God only knows what the driver is going to think.*

She had just finished ordering her ride when Travis walked naked through the living room to the kitchen. He grabbed a water and asked, "Are you taking off?"

It felt weird, him just standing there naked. "Yeah, I need to go."

He shrugged and said, "So, it was nice meeting you. I had fun. I'll call sometime; we can get together again."

With that, he walked back to the bedroom and closed the door. He had her number, but she knew the call wouldn't come. Truthfully, she didn't want him to call, but being dismissed by a kid stung. Humiliation engulfed her, and she fought back tears. She hated this; it was a pathetic cliché, and it was mortifying. Still, it was better than the months of loneliness that drove her to this. Raining or not, she decided to wait outside and quietly slipped out the apartment door.

# Chapter 2

A warm breeze had pushed the night's storm off, leaving a brilliant spring morning in its wake. As he had done every morning since he had rented Casa Del Crapo, Nick stood in line at the Java Shoppe. Marco took him there once after shift. It stuck; the place was a perfect cliché of every upscale coffee house in America, but it was locally owned and their café mochas were addictive.

The crowd in the small shoppe put him on edge every morning, yet every morning he tolerated it. It made him feel connected to the rest of the world. Fortunately, Haley, the young barista, knew what he would order and had it started as soon as he walked in the door. By the time the line moved him to the counter, his mocha would be waiting for him. A tap of the credit card, a few awkward pleasantries with Haley, and he was out the door. Haley was always friendly, and a little chatty… almost flirty. Most mornings it was pleasant, on mornings following rough nights it could get taxing. He suspected the flirting was an act to bump up the tips; it worked. Act or not, she was cute, and he tipped her well.

This morning, he noticed she seemed nervous… fidgety. "Hi Nick, one large café mocha," she said as she handed him his order.

Nick pulled out his wallet and tapped his card. "Good morning."

As he was punching in the tip, she asked, "So, do you ever drink anything besides coffee?"

Thinking it yet another lame attempt at chit chat, he played along. "Yeah, but not anything you sell here, and not before happy hour."

"Good to know," she said. With a big grin, she slid a napkin across the counter.

Nick absentmindedly stuffed the napkin in his pocket and said, "Thanks, Haley. See you tomorrow morning."

Walking to his truck, he fished his keys out of his pocket and found the napkin. He was about to crumble it up when he saw handwriting; it said: *Shoot me a text if you ever want to grab a drink or hang out.* A smiley face floated above a phone number. As he climbed in his truck, he crumpled the napkin and threw it in an old fast-food bag on the floor.

*Great,* Nick thought. *This will make things awkward next time I'm in there. I guess I need to find a new coffee shop.* As he drove towards the station he thought, *It's weird, why the hell would she ask me out? She's a pretty girl; I doubt she's lonely. Besides, I'm at least ten years older than her.* He didn't want to find a new coffee shop, but he sure as hell wasn't going on any dates. He considered ignoring the note and just pretending he didn't see it but decided it was a bad idea. He wondered how to tell her no without humiliating her. As he turned the corner near the station, He said aloud, "I'll tell her I appreciate the offer, but I am going through a divorce, and I don't think I should date till it's all finalized. That should put her off without embarrassing her." He knew it wasn't the reason he wouldn't ask her out, but it wasn't a lie either.

Nick pulled into the station parking lot and sat for a moment. He thought about Haley and wondered, *Would it really be such a bad idea? It's not like anything would come of having a drink with her.* Then he chastised himself. *No, you're being ridiculous, what the hell would you talk about?* Staring at the bag, and arguing with himself, he finally said, "What the hell, no harm in holding onto the note." He pulled the napkin out of the trash, smoothed it out, and put it in the glove box.

Nick grabbed his bag and headed for the open overhead doors. As he stepped onto the apparatus floor, the unique scent of a fire station greeted him. The mix of smoke, diesel exhaust, and an odd but pleasant musty aroma, always made him feel at home. Every station Nick had ever worked in had that same smell. So did the few stations he visited in other cities. He assumed that the smell of a fire station was universal, something that all firefighters knew and loved. It wasn't only the smell, Nick loved everything about the station; the sounds, the bustle, the routines all grounded him. Like most firefighters, the station was far more than a workplace; it had become deeply ingrained in his identity. Being a firefighter wasn't what he did, it was who he was. By extension, the station became more than a place, it became a part of him.

The station was alive with chatter and activity. The sound of apparatus compartment doors slammed shut, and the shrill alarms of a self-contained breathing apparatus being checked added to the familiar buzz of a station at shift change. "B shift" was being relieved by "C shift"- *his* shift. The voices of officers briefing their replacements, drivers updating each other on inventory, and crews laughing at bad jokes and stories about yesterday's calls echoed off concrete and steel.

The familiar smells, sights and sounds washed over Nick, and he felt the spring in his chest relax a little. This was his home, where he felt most at ease. Like every other third morning for 16 years, he would drop his personal bag in his locker, grab his bunkers from the gear room, stow them on the rig, and join the rest of the crew in starting the shift. The normality brought some comfort; he could lose himself in the routine, at least for a little while.

The sound of a small engine caught his attention. He turned to the squad and saw Charlie performing the daily check on the portable generator. She shut the engine off and lifted it back into the squad's side compartment. Her ability to effortlessly lift the 60+ pound generator impressed him. Charlie was tall for a woman, nearly six feet, with a slight frame. But he knew she worked out religiously and was much stronger than her build would suggest.

He never had a problem with women joining up so long as they could pull their weight. But he had been upset when Captain Janssen had tagged him to be Charlie's departmental godfather. He remembered arguing that he had nothing in common with the 22-year-old woman, and mentoring her would be too awkward. Still, Janssen had insisted.

The role of godfather was an old and honored tradition in the department. As her godfather, he was to be her officially unofficial mentor, guide, and teacher. A department godfather taught the new firefighter about life in the firehouse; its traditions, routines, and culture. The godfather taught all the rules that were not in the manual… the important basics, things like if you use it, put it back- if it's dirty, clean it- if someone's working- pitch in. Godfathers spent a lot of time with probies, guiding their practice sessions, answering questions, offering encouragement when needed, and a kick in the pants when deserved. Old Lou had been Nick's godfather, and he thought the man bigger than life. Nick wondered how Charlie saw him; *was he Old Nick?* The thought made him a little uneasy. He didn't want to get old, and he sure wasn't bigger than life.

At first, Charlie made him uncomfortable. She was young, pretty, single and had a big personality; it seemed like a recipe for trouble. But as they spent more time together, his concerns passed, and he came to genuinely like her. Charlie was good-natured and had a sense of humor, but she was as tough as nails. She could take a ribbing, and in turn, give as good as she got. Importantly, she took her career seriously. Smart and capable, Charlie quickly proved herself a valuable addition to the team. No one on the shift would hesitate *to go in* with her, meaning a fire. There was no higher validation than that.

There was nothing even resembling a romantic connection between him and Charlie, but they became close friends and spent a lot of time together. Even now, he was surprised at how comfortable he felt around her. It wasn't just him either, she had earned the respect of the rest of C shift too. Nick couldn't say the same for several of the guys on the other shifts. Some made it clear she wasn't welcome, others were far more interested in her personal life than her work.

As Nick watched, Charlie slammed the compartment door shut. She next went to the EMS cabinet and tried to remove the medical jump bag. It hung up on something, and the normally calm Charlie responded by calling the bag a name implying maternal incest, and yanked it -and half the equipment in the compartment - to the floor. Cussing again, she violently kicked the unwanted contents aside.

Nick walked over to Gordon Willis. He nodded towards Charlie and asked, "Hey Gordy, what's up with her?"

"Jenkins got on her ass about making him wait to be replaced."

Nick looked at his watch. "It's only 6: 45. What's his problem?"

"You know Jenkins, he's always in a hurry to get out of here. Charlie did her morning run on the way to the station and showered before relieving him. He got his panties in a bunch over it."

"That's bullshit. Regardless of what he wants, she wasn't late. He's got no reason to bitch."

Gordon laughed, "Since when does Jenkins need a reason to bitch? The guy has a constant bug up his ass. Hey, at least he didn't walk in on her in the shower again. Somebody set him straight over that so called little *accident*."

Nick nodded in agreement. "*Somebody* needs to set him straight all right. I gotta tell you, him and his mouth are getting on my last nerve."

"Ah, he's just a dip shit. Ignore him like everyone else does."

Jay from B shift interrupted them. "Hey Nick. Are you my relief?"

"Yeah," Nick said. "Let me grab my gear and you can get out of here."

"No problem. Pretty quiet night last night. A car fire over on Dover, and a couple assist the ambulance calls was all."

"Good, maybe I'll get lucky today, too. Take off, I'll catch you later." Nick made his way to the gear room and grabbed his turnouts. He put them by the rig, then went into the bunk room and stowed his personal stuff in his locker. Deciding to have a cup of coffee while doing inventory, Nick walked into the kitchen. He found Jenkins sitting at the table with his buddy, Sonny Schmidt.

Nick asked, "What are you still doing here?"

"What do you mean?" Jenkins replied.

"I mean, I thought you were in a big ass hurry to get out of here."

Jenkins shrugged. "Nah, I'm just hanging out with Smitty."

"Then why were you giving Charlie shit about not relieving you sooner?"

"What? Are you her daddy? Let me guess, she sent you in here to fight her battles for her."

The spring tightened in Nick's chest; he felt the heat rising in his cheeks. "Tell me, Jenkins, why are you such an asshole?"

Jenkins' face reddened. "Hey, fuck her if she can't take a joke."

"NO, FUCK YOU. You're the joke," Nick shouted.

Jenkins stood up and squared off in front of Nick.

Schmidt said, "Calm down Nick. It was no big deal."

Nick locked eyes with Schmidt, then Jenkins. "Just lay off of her."

Schmidt laughed and said, "Hell Nick, have you got a thing for her? Sorry to break it to you buddy, she's a dyke and unless you got a pussy, you got no chance."

Jenkins said, "I don't know, Smitty. I bet Nick's wife can arrange a porn movie of the three of them together. She's into that… right Nick?"

Something inside of Nick seemed to explode. Without thinking, he grabbed Jenkins by the shirt and was about to throw a punch when two powerful arms wrapped around his chest and spun him away from Jenkins. Schmidt pushed Jenkins back.

Marco snapped, "What the hell is going on here?"

Schmidt answered. "Nothing Lieutenant. Nick and Tommy were just having a little bit of a discussion."

Jenkins added, "Your buddy has an attitude problem. You should keep him on a leash."

Marco growled, "You're both off duty. Get the hell out of here." He waited until the two of them were gone then let go of Nick. "Sit."

Nick was breathing hard as he stared at the door Jenkins had walked out of. "Look, Marco…"

Marco gave Nick a gentle shove towards a chair. "Look nothing. I said sit, goddamn it." Marco watched Nick try to gain control, finally he sat. "Starting a fight in the station — Are you trying to get yourself suspended?"

It took a few seconds for Nick to respond. "Did you hear that remark about Becky? And, they were raking on Charlie pretty hard too."

"Yeah," Marco said. "I heard what they said. It still isn't an excuse. You should know better. Nick, you and I go way back. I love you like a brother, but I'm still your company officer and I am not having this shit. You need to get your act together."

"I am sorry, Marco. But he shouldn't have brought up Becky. That was over the line."

"I get it, and I get splitting with Becky was tough on you, but that was eight months ago. Something's going on with you. You ain't been yourself for a long time, even before that mess with Becky. You're worrying me."

"I am fine," said Nick. "Stop worrying and go do some lieutenant shit."

Marco fixed a hard stare at Nick. "Okay, here's one more piece of lieutenant shit. Go fucking gargle. I got a whiff of booze on your breath. Tell me you didn't drink this morning?"

"Of course not! I had one drink around midnight. I just got up late and didn't brush my teeth,"

Marco fixed a hard, long stare on Nick before speaking. Then said, "Don't do this to me, brother. By rights I should have you take a breathalyzer. Would you pass?" Nick didn't reply. Marco added, "I thought so. Listen close, don't make me choose between you and my duty again. Friend or not, I'll write you up."

"Marco—really, I am fine."

"You're not fine. You haven't been fine for a while. Maybe you should talk to somebody."

Nick scoffed. "I don't need to talk to anybody. Like I said, I'm fine. I just need some time."

Marco patted Nick on the shoulder. "If you say so. But if you ask me, you are one messed up white boy."

A wry smile crossed Nick's face. "That sounds a bit racist, Lieutenant. Don't *make me* have to report you."

Marco laughed, "You can kiss my black ass. How's that for racist?" Marco started towards the door. He stopped and added, "Seriously, Nick, don't make me report you. Get your act together."

"Roger that Lieutenant."

Marco started for the door again and again stopped. "Hey, maybe you need to blow off some steam. Jazz and I are going on a pub crawl this Saturday. Why don't you come with us?"

"I don't think so, but thanks."

"I am serious. You haven't been out since you and Becky split. Get out of that shit hole you call home and come out with us."

"I'm not going to be a third wheel," Nick said.

"Why not ask that little barista at the coffee shop to come too?"

The mention of Haley surprised Nick. "How did you hear about Haley?"

Marco smiled. "She asked me about you the other day— asked if you were single."

"What did you tell her?"

"I said you were."

Nick sighed. "I wish you wouldn't have."

"Why? You should take her out."

"I am married."

"Are you? It doesn't look like it. You haven't spoken to Becky in eight months."

"Not going to happen."

"Why?"

"She's too damn young for me. Besides, think about it, Marco. Just how do you think Jazz will react to me bringing a date? Especially when I tell her it was your idea."

Marco cringed, then laughed. "Yeah, let's forget that I suggested that. Still, come with us."

"Next time."

"Nick, I mean it. Me and Jazz are getting worried about you. You need to get a life."

Nick let out an exasperated sigh. "For the 50th time, I am fine."

Marco nodded and left.

Nick made his way to the apparatus floor and began checking his self-contained breathing apparatus. He just finished up and was stowing it in the jump seat when he felt a kick on his backside. Charlie stood looking at him; arms crossed and smiling. She said, "Hey old man. I hear you and Jenkins got into it."

"The man is a Neanderthal," Nick said.

The smile left Charlie's face. "That's hardly fair to Neanderthals. Hey, I appreciate you sticking up for me and all, but I don't need you handling my battles. If I want help, I'll tell you — Okay?"

Nick replied, "I hear you, but it really wasn't about you. The guy just chaps my ass; has for a long time. He said some shit that just didn't sit with me; that's all."

"Look, Nick, you're a great friend. I love you like a brother, but I don't need a protector. It's hard enough being the only woman on the shift. I can't have the rest of the guys thinking that you're propping me up."

"Yeah, but I get pissed at the crap they throw around." said Nick, "You deserve better…"

"Nick, I've been dealing with idiots like Jenkins since I grew boobs. They either hate me or want to screw me, usually both. I can handle anything he throws at me. You getting all paternal makes me look weak. I don't need that."

Nick put his hands up in a gesture of surrender. "It really wasn't like that, but I understand."

The smile returned to Charlie's face. "With that said, thanks. It's nice to know you got my back if I needed it."

"No problem—and what's with the old man crap? I'm not even forty yet."

Charlie laughed. "Hey, I am not saying you're decrepit or anything, but…"

"I'll have you know I got asked out by a young little hottie today."

Again, Charlie laughed. "I am not surprised. Lots of girls have a daddy kink. It's about time you got out there some."

"Daddy kink? Is that a thing? Sounds kinda sketchy."

"Oh yeah, it's a thing. Hey, not for nothing, you got it going on for a geezer. Maybe she'll put her hair in pigtails and wear a school girl outfit for you, uncle Pervis."

Now Nick laughed, "You watch too much porn—you know that, right?'

"Hey, a girl's gotta do what a girl's gotta do to get by at night."

"Geez, Charlie, I don't need to hear that. Go do some work and leave me alone."

"I think you're blushing! What's the matter Nick, you didn't think that girls…."

Nick threw a glove at her. "I swear, sometimes I think you bumped your head as a kid. Go away before I file sexual harassment charges on you."

 Charlie laughed and walked away, stopped and added, "By the way, will you walk me through some pump ops drills later?"

"Sure." Nick returned to his inventory; another day, another shift had begun.

# Chapter 3

Becky sat with her face turned to the sun. The warmth on her cheeks spread through her entire body, pushing the chill from the surgical suite away. The aroma of lilac and freshly cut grass wafted on the gentle breeze, as did the sound of the fountain's tumbling water. With her eyes closed, she could almost believe she sat beside a brook deep in a forest.

The garden never failed to relax her; it was why the hospital built it. Fortunately, the administrators had realized that the overworked, over stressed staff needed a refuge, a place to decompress if only for a lunch hour, or even a quick break. They had built it just off the employee cafeteria, and the flower beds and the noise of the fountain created privacy; perfect for friends to chat, or for a solitary lunch alone with your thoughts.

Becky had lunch here as often as weather permitted, sometimes with one or two friends from the unit, often alone. She especially appreciated the garden today. This morning's surgery had not gone well. Working with Dr. Gunderson was always unpleasant - the man made condescension an art form- but the morning had gotten plain ugly. He lost a patient and seemed determined to take out his frustration on anyone and everyone within reach. During the following procedure, he had screamed at Becky for not having the tray set up properly – it was. She would never let the jerk see her cry, but it was tough that morning.

*Thank God for Jazmine*, Becky thought. *Somehow, she seems to know when I need her most.*

She and Jazz tried to have lunch together at least once a month, but between Jazz's gallery and her kids, it was getting harder to find time for each other. That's why the girl's night out got started. Becky appreciated that Marco was cool with the two of them blowing off some steam together. Marco trusted Jazz, Becky admired that. Some men might have been insecure at having their wife go out for a night. Considering what she had done to Nick, it wouldn't have been unreasonable for him to object to Jazz going out with her at all. Becky was thankful that her two friends had not abandoned her. She knew staying close to both her and Nick was awkward for them, it would have been easy to choose sides.

The four of them were so close for so long, she knew the breakup was hard on them too. Becky tried not to dwell on what she had ruined. Not only was Dominick gone, so was the life they had. Gone were the vacations, the couple's dates, the dinners, and the backyard barbecues. She missed her old life and treasured her friendship with Jazz and Marco more now than ever. They connected her to what had been, and the fading hope of what she could regain. But it wasn't the same anymore. Lately, there were fewer calls and fewer invitations; they were moving on with their lives.

Becky guessed Jazz's lunch offer was making up for bailing on her last weekend. It wasn't necessary, but Becky was thankful for the text nonetheless. The garden reminded her of a café the four of them found outside of Savannah. *What was it called? Frankie's — Something like that,* she thought. *Had it only been 4 years ago?*

Jazz interrupted her reverie. "Are you meditating or napping?"

"Neither. I was thinking about that day we all spent at Tybee Island."

"Yeah," Jazz said, "that was a good day."

"What was the name of that place where we ate? It had that big polar bear by the door."

"Fannies by the Beach, Marco still wears the hat he bought there."

Becky opened her eyes and saw her friend hovering over her. As usual, Jazmine was dressed impeccably… stylishly… with a hint of sexy. Her raven hair and ebony skin were striking against the white sleeveless sundress she wore. Becky suddenly felt frumpy in her surgical scrubs. She said, "Not fair, you're all dressed up and I look like something the dog found in the yard."

"Nonsense," Jazz said. "You look fabulous, as always. Although you're getting too damn skinny."

Becky shrugged and smiled. "No such thing as too skinny."

"Yes, there is, and you're getting there. You're a nurse; you know you need to take better care of yourself."

"Yes mother. It's pasta buffet day in the cafeteria. That'll fatten me up some. Happy?"

A brilliant smile broke across Jazmine's face. "Ooh, Italian cuisine. Let's hope they have a good wine pairing."

"God, I could use some wine, but no such luck, I'm afraid."

"Tough morning?" Jazz asked.

"Bad week," Becky said. "Today is just another in a continuing saga."

Jazmine frowned as she studied her friend. "You look tired and miserable. You need a vacation or something." It reminded her of why she arranged lunch, and added, "Hey, I'm sorry about last weekend. My babysitter's mom got food poisoning and had to go to the hospital. That's why I had to get back home. I hated leaving you like that. I was really looking forward to cutting loose. Marco hasn't taken me dancing forever."

"How is Marco?"

"Same as always." Jazmine waited for the inevitable question. It came.

"And, Nick? How is he doing?"

"Not great. He's still holed up in that ratty trailer. We're worried about him. He needs to get out more."

"So, he's not dating?"

Jazz sighed. "He's barely breathing, much less dating. A a a n d — it wouldn't hurt you to get out some too."

"As a matter of fact, after you bailed on me, I met a guy." Becky watched a look of surprise cross her friend's face. *Why did I say that?* She thought.

"Do tell?" Jazz teased. "This sounds interesting."

A wave of heat bloomed in Becky's cheeks. "Never mind, forget I said anything."

"Oh, no you don't." Jazz said. "You don't get to drop a bomb like that and brush it off. We're going to get our food, and then you're going to tell me all the juicy details."

Jazz wasted no time grilling her friend. They had no sooner sat with their food when she asked, "So tell me about this guy."

Becky thought to herself, *Me and my big mouth!* She said, "It wasn't a big deal. After you left, he sat down and started talking to me."

"What did he say?"

"I don't know — something lame, like he had been noticing me all evening. So, we just started talking. He was sweet."

Jazmine was practically beaming. "Just like that. You're sitting there and he comes over and tries to pick you up? That's gotta feel good."

"I'll admit it was an ego boost. A guy hasn't hit on me in a bar since college."

"So, what was he like? Was he hot?"

Becky could not help but grin. Jazz's enthusiasm was infectious, and the conversation took her back to their late night wine and gossip sessions in the dorms. "Yeah, he was cute, blonde, kind of tall and a pretty nice body." She paused, then added, "But he was pretty young."

"How young?" Jazz asked.

Embarrassed, Becky hid her face in her hands. "Young — I don't know for sure — Maybe 25?"

"Holy shit, girl. You had a 25-year-old hitting on you. Good for you. What's his name?"

"Travis."

"Does Travis have a last name?"

"Honestly, I don't know."

"Okay, what does he do?"

"I don't know for sure, something with graphic design, I think."

Jazmine grinned. "It doesn't sound like you talked much. So, did he ask you out?"

"Sort of — Not really."

Jazz shrugged and took her first bite of her lasagna. "Probably just as well. Guys that age are still wet behind the ears anyway. I bet he still lives in his parent's basement."

"He actually has his act together. And, for your information, he has a pretty decent apartment."

Jazmine put her fork down and rested her chin on her folded hands. "Oh? Just how did you discover this?"

Becky realized she had said too much. "He told me."

"Uh huh, why are you blushing then?"

For reasons that Becky didn't fully understand, she suddenly felt a desire to share what happened with Jazmine. It was a big deal, and she wanted to talk about it. She trusted her friend. She said, "Jazz, can you keep a secret?"

"Of course. Honey, I've been keeping your secrets since we were 19."

"I'm serious. You can't tell anybody. Especially Marcus. I don't want him thinking any worse of me than he already does."

"Becky, Marcus loves you like a sister, you know that. We both do."

"Still, he might tell Dominick. Nick can't know about this."

A look of shock crossed Jazmine's face. "Holy shit! You slept with that kid, didn't you?"

Becky nodded sheepishly.

"Oh, my God. Spill it, how was it?"

"Christ," Becky said, "I don't want to go into details. It was okay."

Jazmine took a bite of lasagna, then pointed her fork at Becky. "Bullshit. I am a bored married woman with two rotten kids and a couch potato for a husband, and I just found out my best friend did the nasty with some young stud. Girl, don't tell me you don't want to give details."

Becky sighed. "It was good, I guess."

"Just good? That sounds like disappointment." With a devilish grin, she held her thumb and index finger an inch apart, and added, "Was he packin' a little smokey instead of a salami?"

"Jesus Jazz, I swear you need therapy." Becky then laughed and added, "For your information, he brought plenty to the picnic, and it was better than just good. You know how young guys are."

Jazz took a drink then said. "I've been married since the dark ages, remind me."

Becky grinned shyly. "Honestly, he was like the energizer bunny. It seemed like he could go forever, take a 10-minute break, and go again. He could've gone at it all night if I would have let him. I'm not gonna lie. I was a little sore the next morning."

Jazz laughed, then said, "Mmm, I gotta get *me* a young little energizer bunny to hop around with. Marco's batteries go dead after one session."

"Don't even joke about that," Becky said. "When it was all done, I felt horrible, like I did something stupid — again."

Jazz reached across the table and took Becky's hand. "Sweetie, you and Nick separated almost a year…"

"… eight months."

"Okay, eight months, you got no reason to feel guilty."

Becky felt tears welling in her eyes. "Don't I? I thought I was coming to terms with the separation, but when I looked at that guy and thought about what I had just done with him; it all came back. I was right back where I was when we separated. All I could think about was Nick. I just started really missing him again. I can't shake it; I've been down a hole ever since that night. It felt like I did it again, you know — like that night with *them*. I felt sick inside."

Jazmine gave her hand a squeeze. "I am so sorry, Becky. I know this has been hard on you, but it will get better."

Wiping away a tear, Becky said, "No, it won't. I had the perfect man—the perfect life — and I fucked it up."

"It wasn't all that perfect. For more than a year, you cried on my shoulder about how Nick was pulling away from you, about how lonely you were, how he didn't find you attractive anymore. You even thought he was cheating. I think you're forgetting how miserable you were before the breakup."

"He was just going through something; I don't know what…"

Jazz interrupted her, "He still is. Marco and I are worried about him. Something is going on with him, he his messed up over you splitting, but there's more to it."

Near sobbing, Becky said, "I could have helped him. We could have fixed it, but I ruined everything."

Jazmine took a deep breath, sighed and asked the question that she had waited months to bring up. "Look, you never wanted to talk about it, and I didn't pry, but I have to ask, why *did* you do it?"

For months, embarrassment had compelled Becky to avoid talking about what happened, even to Jazz. She thought reliving it all would be too painful, but somehow, sitting in the bright sun, among the flowers, the dirty truth felt less awful. She took a deep breath, dabbed at a tear, and started. "Honestly, I am still not sure how or why I let it happen, it just did. We were short staffed on the unit, and Racheal rotated up from ICU. We kind of hit it off and got together a few times after work, when Nick was on shift. At first, it was just hanging out — nothing special."

Jazz sat quietly. Becky took a sip of water and went on. "After a while, I started going over to Racheal and Sly's house some evenings; Sly was her husband. The three of us would just hang out, you know, sip some wine and chat; maybe watch a movie. They were cool, and you know how things were with Nick then. I really needed the company. They both started flirting with me, nothing over the top, just some suggestive remarks. It was a little weird, but honestly, I sort of enjoyed the attention. I guessed they were swingers or something like that, but it seemed harmless, so I let it slide."

Becky could not help but notice as Jazmine rolled her eyes. It stung a little. Jazz said, "Harmless? Really? Come on Beck, you're not that naïve. You had to know what they wanted."

"Jazz, things were getting bad with Nick. We hadn't been — you know — intimate, for like three months. You don't know what it's like when you're forced to admit to yourself that your husband doesn't want you anymore. It was foolish, but the attention felt good — more than that, even. How do I describe this? It was like I felt alive again. Anyway, one night we were drinking wine and Sly pulled out some edibles. They suggested the hot tub, and it sounded fun. So, we all ended up skinny dipping. We were just splashing around like teenagers when suddenly Racheal kissed me. Something in me clicked, and I kissed her back. Next thing I know, we're all in bed together."

Jazmine slowly shook her head. "So, the three of you are just chilling, then y'all decide to get naked. Then it's what the hell, let's all just fuck. Oh, and hey, let's make a porn video while we're at it. Come on, Beck. Do you hear yourself?"

"Don't be that way. Yes, it was impetuous and stupid, but I sure as hell didn't agree to any video. Those perverts filmed me without me knowing. I didn't learn about that until they sent it to Nick. I knew I screwed up bad as soon as it was over. I was — I was just stupid."

"So," said Jazz, "why *did* you let it happen then? I'm not judging, honey. I mean, we all get tempted sometime, but you knew better."

"It was Racheal. I felt being there with her was somehow okay. It never occurred to me she was seducing me. With a guy, I never would have let myself get into that situation. I never would have let my guard down. I mean, I let it happen, but it was like we already started before I realized what I was doing."

Jazz shook her head. "Honey, I'm on your side. Really, I am, but don't kid yourself. You had to see it coming; you put yourself in that spot. People don't get naked with people and then wonder how it turned sexual. You'll be happier if you come to terms with it."

"You're right, I know. What I can't forgive myself for is that I wanted to do it. I enjoyed it. I guess I'm the disgusting whore everybody thinks I am. But Jazz, I swear I regretted it the second it was done."

"Stop that!" Snapped Jazmine. "I don't want to hear that or any of that other sexist bullshit that gets dumped on us women. Were you desperate? … maybe. Foolish? … for sure. But I don't want to hear any of that slut shaming. You are a woman who had an affair, end of story. If Nick had done it instead of you, would he be wringing his hands and calling himself a whore? Ask yourself, did you regret doing it, or just getting caught? That will tell you all you need to know about yourself."

"Jesus Jaz, you have no idea how horrible I felt. In the moment, the excitement of it was like a drug, but when it was over, it hit me… what I had done. I practically ran out of their house as soon as I could. I was a wreck… the guilt, it was… I threw up on the way home; I cried the whole night. The next day, I texted Racheal and told her we couldn't see each other anymore, not to call, and to not tell anyone about what happened. Of course, she didn't listen, she kept wanting to talk. She said she was worried about me — yeah, right. I should have told Nick, but I convinced myself that it would just hurt him; I was so stupid."

Becky choked back the lump in her throat and again wiped her eyes. It felt good to finally talk to someone. "I guess they got pissed at me for ghosting them and got even. A month later, I came home from work and Nick was gone, so was all his stuff.

No big fight, no goodbye, just a note on the kitchen counter saying he never wanted to see me again. He left a copy of the video on my laptop. Jazz it was dreadful. It looked like a porno — a really hard-core horrible porno. I felt so gross. I almost threw up when I saw it; no wonder Nick can't stand the sight of me."

Jazmine took both of her friend's hands and tried to comfort her. "It's okay sweetie, it wasn't that awful. You just have to give him time. He's hurting pretty bad but he will come around."

"No, he meant it when he said he never wants to see me again. You know how hard I tried to reach out. Those first few months, I called and texted him so many times; begging him to just talk to me, to let me explain, to just say I'm sorry. Nothing — he has me blocked on his phone. I even got desperate enough to show up at the station. He wouldn't talk to me, even look at me. He had the Captain tell me to leave. Jazz, I knew he was mad, but I never thought he would ever be indifferent about me. I mean nothing to him now, I know it."

Jazz said, "If you really didn't matter, he wouldn't be so hurt. Give him time, seeing that video really messed with him, it was a shock. You really didn't know they filmed you?

"No, of course not. You know me, I wouldn't even let Nick take a naked picture of me. I didn't know a film existed until Nick left me that damn video."

"Nick thinks you made the film on purpose," Jazz said.

"That's crazy. Why would I?"

"I don't know. Why would you have a threesome with some strange couple? And, I'm sorry, but it kind of looked like you were an enthusiastic participant."

"Oh god, Nick thinks—wait—what, you saw the video? Nick showed it to you? I can't believe Nick would do that. Even as mad as he is, that's just not right."

Jazz took a deep breath and said, "Nick didn't show it to me. Nick won't even talk about it. Marco showed it to me. You were so distraught right after Nick left you, I tried to talk to you about what happened and you wouldn't say anything. I assumed Nick fooled around on you. I got pissed and was going to go over and tear him a new one. Marco told me to stay out of it, and we had a big fight. Finally, Marco told me what you had done. I didn't believe him, so he showed me the video."

Becky felt like she had been gut punched. "Nick gave the video to Marco? It's bad enough you saw it but, Marco too? He saw me doing — oh god." The lump in Becky's throat threatened her breathing, and she was getting light-headed. "You both have been with me dozens of times and you said nothing? You kept a straight face, after watching that awful sex tape, and acted like nothing happened? Tell me, did you talk about what a disgusting whore I was, or did you have a good laugh? Oh my God, I will never be able to look Marco in the eye again. How could you not tell me?"

"Calm down," Jazz said. "What were we supposed to do? We thought you knew about it. We didn't understand why you did it, but how the hell do you ask about it? I mean, were we supposed to just come out and say, Hey Becky, we saw your sex tape, what's up with that?"

"Yes," Becky gasped. "Jeez, Jasmine, I trusted you, how could you not tell me?"

"If you came across a sex tape of me and Marco on the Internet, what would *you* do? And we didn't laugh at you, and no one thinks you're a whore. Marco and I both love you. We were shocked, and mad at you for doing that to Nick, but we know marriages get complicated. We've always had your back, and we always will. As far as Marco goes, it's been months since he saw it, and he's over it. I know you're embarrassed, but it's not that big a deal. He's a big boy; he knows people have sex, and for what it's worth, he and I can get a little kinky sometimes too. You don't wanna see what's on his phone."

Becky could feel her pulse pounding and was still having a hard time catching her breath. "Congratulations, until this afternoon I didn't think I could ever feel any worse than I have the last eight months, but you managed. I don't care what you say, it was petty and wrong for Nick to share that video with Marco."

Jazz let out a sigh. "Becky, I told you Nick did not share the video. Marco pulled it off the website."

"What are you talking about? What website?"

"You didn't know?"

Frustrated, Becky said, "No, what are you talking about?"

Becky noticed a look of trepidation pass over her friend's face. Cautiously, Jazmine said, "Look, your so-called friends didn't send the video to Nick. A guy at the station left an anonymous note in Nick's locker telling him it was important for him to check out a website. When Nick got home the next morning, he logged on to some amateur porn site and saw your video, along with a bunch of other videos and pictures. I guess one of the guys stumbled on it and recognized you. I'm sorry Becky, but it got passed around the station for a while. Eventually, somebody felt bad about it and tipped Nick off. When all hell broke loose, Marco asked around and found out about it too."

"Jesus Jazz," Becky said, "you mean to tell me that there has been a porn video of me on the Internet for all these months and you never told me?"

"No, no. Marco convinced Nick to get a hold of a lawyer who contacted the website and threatened to sue them if they didn't pull it down. He told them that it was posted without consent. At the time Nick thought you had consented, but he wanted it deleted, so he lied. As far as anybody knows, it's gone, although you know how things go on the net. I'm sorry, sweetie, we really kind of thought that you knew."

Becky said, "Nick actually thinks I made a porn video — that's just crazy. No wonder he went off the deep end."

"You have no idea. We have had to talk him down from all kinds of crazy shit. At one point, he thought you had some sort of whole other secret life. He still sorta believes that the video wasn't a onetime thing. He even thought you had a site of your own somewhere."

"Jazz, you have to set him straight, tell him what really happened. He needs to know the truth."

"We will. Marco will make him listen, but Beck, don't get your hopes up. Nick is in a bad place; I don't think it will change much between you."

"No, maybe not—probably not. But it's important he knows the truth."

Jazmine nodded. "I am so sorry for not talking to you sooner. It's just that you were so closed off about it all. I'm—just—sorry for this whole shit show, and what you're going through."

A half-hearted smile forced itself on Becky's lips. "It's okay."

"So, we're good?"

"I'm still pissed at you, but I'll get over it. Just make sure and talk to Nick—soon."

"I'll confess, I am still having a hard time getting my head around the whole mess. Maybe you should come over and explain it all to Marco."

"Fuck that! It will be a long time before I can face Marco again."

Jazz grinned. "Stop worrying about Marco. He's fine, truth be told, I think the video turned him on a little — me too."

"Christ Jazz, shut up. That's worse. What's wrong with you?"

Laughing, Jazz said, "Hey, I'm just saying. You were pretty hot. You couldn't blame the guy. They love that lezi stuff."

Becky threw a napkin in Jazz's direction. "Enough already, it's not funny."

"Okay, okay," Jazz said. "But seriously, we've known each other since college. We even lived together. How come you never told me you liked girls?"

"I don't — not really. Well, maybe — some; I don't know. Sometimes I got a little curious is all; that night I just sort of went with it. It was naughty and exciting—you know, all of it— with both of them. But it wasn't worth it and I felt all kinds of shitty after. I don't have any desire to repeat the experience."

Jazz said, "Really, I get it. I love my big, dumb husband, but sometimes I wish I had been a little more adventurous before we got together. Sometimes I think I missed out."

"Trust me, Jazz, you didn't miss out on anything."

Jazz chuckled and said, "So, no plans to look up your girlfriend again, huh?"

"You're wrong there. I most definitely will be paying that little bitch a visit. She and that idiot she married ruined my life, this ain't over."

"Becky, don't do something stupid."

Becky twirled her fork in her mostly ignored salad. "A little late for that, don't you think? One more thing, tell Marco to send me that link."

"Why?" Jazz asked.

"I want to make sure I'm not still on that website."

# Chapter 4

He studied her as he waited in line; she was pretty. He knew that already, but had really never given it much thought before. Haley had pulled her reddish-brown hair into a ponytail. If she used makeup, he couldn't tell it. She wore a retro-looking Beatles t-shirt, very short shorts and the ever-present smile. The look screamed young — too young. Her asking him out was an ego boost, but Nick knew it was silly.

Haley beamed as he stepped to the counter. She slid the waiting cup to him and said, "Hi Nick. Cafe Mocha, right?"

"Yeah, thanks Haley."

"You haven't been in for a while. I began thinking I ran you off. Sorry if I came off thirsty."

She wasn't wrong; he had avoided the place for a week, and still wasn't completely sure if coming back was a good idea. He hoped they would both just ignore her invitation and move on. Her bluntness made that impossible. Reflexively, he tried lying as a next best option. "Thirsty? No, not at all." he said, "I just had some stuff come up."

She said nothing, just nodded. The smile remained, but the look on her face made it clear that she wasn't buying his explanation. He reluctantly added, "Look, here's the thing. My life is pretty complicated right now. My wife and I separated, but I am still married. And — well — I am just not in a place where I can handle complications. I'm sorry."

He had expected disappointment, or embarrassment, even anger. He didn't expect a grin and a dismissive wave of the hand. She said, "Hey, it's fine. No big deal. I get it, but for the record, I was only suggesting getting a drink and hanging out. Trust me, I don't do complicated. It's just that I don't really know many people around here, and I was looking to get out."

*Dumb Ass!* Nick thought. Then said, "Well, I feel foolish. Sorry if I read too much into it. I haven't been single in a long while, and I don't know how dating stuff works anymore. But I get it. I spend almost every night at home too. You go stir crazy after a while."

"Yeah," she said. "It sounds like we both could use some time out and about. No pressure, but if you change your mind, let me know. I promise it will be no big deal, only hanging out. Heck, we don't even need to call it a date."

Her comment brought relief. Nick relaxed and thought, *maybe—someday*. He said, "Sounds good."

She broke into a smile. "Cool, how about Saturday? We can meet at Rizzi's over on Dunbar."

Somehow, he heard himself saying, "Ah, yeah, sure." To himself he said, *What the hell...*

"Nice! I'll see you at seven. First round is on me."

As Nicked walked out the door, he muttered to himself, "What the hell did I just do?" He wondered if he could go back in and make some excuse about forgetting he had something going on Saturday. He knew he couldn't. It would hurt her feelings. *Like it or not, you're going on a date,* he thought, *or a quasi-date, or something—I'm not sure what.*

As Nick was finishing up the morning inventory on the rig, Sonny Schmidt leaned against the rig next to him and said, "Hey Nick. I wanted to say that I am sorry about what went down the other day. Look, I was being a jerk, and that remark about Charlie was out of line."

Nick nodded. "Yeah, okay. Thanks, Smitty."

"So, are we good?"

"Sure, no worries." Nick replied.

"For what it's worth, that whole deal with your wife… anyway, you deserved better. Oh, and I'll talk to Jenks about cutting Charlie some slack."

Nick didn't look up from his work. "Like I said, thanks."

Schmidt had no sooner walked off when Marco took his place. "What did he want?"

"Nothing much. He wanted to smooth things over from the other day. We're fine."

Marco said, "Good. What about Jenkins? Have you heard from him?"

"Nope, and I'd be surprised if I did. Schmidt has a big mouth sometimes, but he's not a bad guy. Jenkins — is another story."

Marco chuckled. "Yeah, he is a piece of work. Hey, have you thought more about Saturday night? Jazz is bugging me; she misses you."

"Sorry, no can do."

"Look," Marco said, "I am not trying to mother you, but you need to crawl out of your hole. It won't kill you to hang out with us."

Nick shook his head and leaned back against the apparatus. "Yeah, crashing your date would be big fun, but the thing is, Haley, from the coffee shop, asked me out again. For some stupid reason, I said yes. We are meeting for drinks on Saturday."

Marco gave Nick a playful punch on the shoulder. "Good for you. I am glad you are getting out, but it seems weird. I'm still trying to get my head around the fact that you and Becky are done."

Nick nodded, and said, "Yeah, whatever. Still, do me a favor. Don't tell Jazz about Haley. It's only a buddy date; nothing is going on there. Jazz will get pissy about it. Plus, she will blab it to Becky, and she doesn't need to know about it."

Marco nodded. "Yeah, no problem — but why do you care?"

Nick shrugged. "I just do. Don't tell Jazz." Nick noted the pensive look on his friend's face. "What? Hey, I am not asking you to lie to your wife. Just keep your mouth shut."

Marco sighed. "It's not that. Look, the reason Jazz wants to see you is that she needs to talk to you — about Becky. They had lunch the other day and got into a pretty heavy conversation about what happened. There's some stuff you need to know."

"No thanks. I know what I need to know."

Marco pulled Nick into his office. "No, you don't. A lot of what you think Becky did, ain't what really happened."

"Let me guess, she claims it was her long lost identical twin." Nick replied.
"No, smart ass. That stuff about Becky leading some kinda secret life, you know, running around behind your back, and even doing porn, it turns out it wasn't like that at all. From what Becky told

Jazz, the three of them had only got together the one time. Becky had been hanging out with them. They got drunk and high one night and things just got out of hand. Becky felt horrible about what happened."

Nicked scoffed, "Bullshit. you saw the video same as I did. She knew what she was doing, and she sure didn't look upset to me." He paused, then added, "Another thing, it couldn't happen like she says — you know, just a spur-of-the-moment mistake — that doesn't work; you don't *just* make an impromptu sex tape. That just doesn't happen, it gets discussed. I know Becky, she wouldn't agree to be filmed, unless she was into it; really, really into it. No way it was their first time together."

"She didn't know they had filmed it. I guess she was so messed up she didn't notice the cameras, or maybe they hid them. And she didn't know about the whole website thing until Jazz told her this week. They set her up, Nick. They got her drunk and high and seduced her. It really messed her up. You need to talk to her."

"And you believe her?"

Marco nodded. "Yeah, we believe her. Why would she lie? And, even if she tried, Jazz would know. She's like a human polygraph. Trust me, I know."

Nick thought about what Marco had said. As he did, graphic images of Becky having sex with the woman, then with the man, then both at the same time raged in his head. As it had a hundred times before, the memories brought on anger, despair, and confusion. Also, like so many times before, the light-headedness began, as did the tightness in his chest. Just as the fireflies crept into the periphery of his vision, Nick pushed the images away, took in a slow, deep breath, and tried to clear his head. He looked at Marco and saw concern. He said, "Don't worry, I'm okay."

"Are you sure?"

Still angry, he growled. "Even if she is telling the truth, it doesn't make a difference."

Marco's eyes locked on Nick's. "Of course, it makes a difference. All this time you've been thinking that she was playing you for a fool. You thought she had a history with these two, and maybe others. You even accused her of being a porn actress. None of that's true. Nick, she just did something stupid one night with the wrong people, and they took advantage of her. She's a victim too, and like I said, Becky's pretty torn up about it."

"A victim? Bullshit. She cheated on me, pardon me for finding it hard to feel sorry for her. If she wasn't running around on me, she wouldn't have been partying with them behind my back. She got burned — it's her fault."

Marco shook his head. "I am not excusing her. She cheated, and you have every right to be pissed, but you gotta admit that what really happened is better than what you thought happened. She screwed up — bad. Still, at least she's not the monster you thought she was. She made a mistake, people do. Forgive her or don't, that's your thing, but talk to her man. You two owe it to each other."

Nick said, "I don't care what she intended or what she didn't. The fact is that she ruined our lives and I don't owe her shit."
"Nick, buddy, you're hurting yourself as much as her."
Nick walked out of the room. He stopped and turned. Looking at Marco, he said, "I know you got my best at heart — I do. I...

This…it's just this is all so raw; I need time to think. Tell Jazz whatever you want about how I took all this, and she can tell Becky what she wants, I don't care. But it changes nothing, Marco. Becky cheated, she screwed other people, how or why doesn't matter. One more thing, remember, don't say anything to Jazz about Haley. I don't need the hassle."

*****

Rose frowned as she looked at the yellow stain on the carpet in front of the patio door. This was Walter's third accident this week. She turned to confront him and found that he already looked remorseful- head down, tail between his legs. Her mood softened, she couldn't really blame him, he was going on 12 now, old for a pug. He just couldn't hold it through the night anymore. Still, she wished he wouldn't sneak downstairs to pee, it would be too easy to miss. She might have not noticed this latest accident if it wasn't for the stench of urine filling the room. She looked at the little dog and grumbled, "Are you sure you're worth the trouble?" The dog whimpered in reply. Rose sighed and said, "Oh, don't worry, mommy still loves you." He was a good dog, and after her husband had passed, he was her constant, and nearly only companion. She could forgive him for almost anything.

Deciding to first deal with the smell, she pulled a long butane lighter out of a drawer. Moving around the room, she lit several sandalwood scented candles. After retrieving a bucket, carpet cleaner, and a brush from the hallway closet, she set to work on the carpet. She hoped it wouldn't stain, but suspected it probably would; the others did. She looked at Walter again and said, "You know I am going to have to call the cleaning service eventually, thanks to you."

Seeing the evidence of his crime being removed, Walter felt better about himself and replied with a wag of his tail and an enthusiastic, "Woof."

She couldn't help but smile, and with a tinge of sarcasm said, "Well, I'm glad you're not beating yourself up over this."

Walter's tail went into overdrive at the sound of her voice. The natural enthusiasm inherent to pugs made it difficult for him to stand still. He trotted up to the wet spot and sniffed.

With effort, Rose got off of her hands and knees to inspect her work. Walter took his place next to her. He gazed at her expectantly. "What?" she said. "No, no treats now." At the magic word -treats- Walter put both paws on her shin, and whimpered. "If you behave long enough for me to get some work done, we'll see."

"Rrr woof." Was the reply.

Rose returned the cleaning supplies to the closet, and made her way to the back room she had converted to her studio. She shut the door to bar Walter. The next two hours were hers. Her kids had given her some sort of fancy radio that streamed music off the internet. It took a while to figure the thing out, she mostly avoided technology, but it was worth the trouble. The gizmo, as she called it, had several excellent classical stations. Turning it on, the beautiful and mournful *Adagio in G minor by Albinoni* greeted her. "Perfect," she said, as she pulled a fresh smock over her clothing and sat at her easel.

She studied her latest effort, an almost cartoonish rendering of Walter nose to nose with an elf. She dismissed her as work simple even a bit juvenile. People's reaction to it still surprised her; she especially marveled at the ridiculous prices Jazmine got for it in her gallery.

As happened so often, she got lost in her work and time slipped away. She was nearly done shading in the background when Walter's barking interrupted her. She yelled through the door, "Walter hush, or no treats." His barking only became more insistent, and it sounded like he had moved upstairs. She wondered if someone was at the door; putting down her brush, she opened the studio door. Dense black smoke and searing heat immediately enveloped her. Half blind and barely able to breathe, she desperately stumbled down the hall to find Walter.

*****

Nick was having a hard time concentrating. He tried to focus his attention toward the front of the training room, where Captain Janssen was reviewing the pre-fire plan for the S&K manufacturing plant. The place was full of nasty chemicals and was one of the prime target hazards for the district. The training was important, and he knew he should pay attention; but the stuff Marco had said about Becky was still running through his head. He didn't want to, but he believed the story. The truth was, it sounded more like the Becky he knew than the whole porn movie thing. He just wasn't sure how he felt about it, or if it even really mattered after all this time.

The 3-tone alert snapped him out of his reverie. "This is a general alarm for Station 8, Engine 6 and Truck 3. Structure fire reported at 3718 Deer Creek Lane. Repeat, this is a…"

Nick and the rest of the station were moving before the dispatcher could finish. As they hustled to the apparatus floor, the house radio speaker relayed Engine 6 and Truck 3's acknowledgment of the call.

In moments, Nick was in the jump seat, weaving his arms through the straps of his self-contained breathing apparatus. As they pulled out of the station, he looked across the cabin at Charlie. He smiled to himself; her expression was a perfect mixture of determination, excitement and eagerness. If she was nervous, it didn't show.

A few minutes later, the engine came to a quick stop, and he, Charlie, and Marco were on the move. As he moved to the back of the rig, he noticed heavy smoke pouring out from under the eaves. *It's cooking*, he thought. The next few moments were like a well-practiced ballet. Marco helped the squad crew deploy the RIT kit- the tools designated for the Rapid Intervention Team. They were to stand by in case interior crews got in trouble. Capt. Janssen dismounted Truck 3 and began a 360-degree assessment of the fire scene. Nick met Charlie in the back of the apparatus and assisted her with deploying an inch and three-quarter pre-connected hose line. Simultaneously, Engine 6 pulled up alongside their rig and their crew began connecting a 5-inch supply line.

Over his radio, Nick heard Capt. Janssen give the situation report. It was a one-story ranch with a walkout basement. Heavy smoke was showing on all sides, and flames were showing at the back of the house on the main floor.

A woman, probably the neighbor who called in the fire, was screaming at Marco that a lady named Rose was probably inside. Nick followed Charlie as she advanced the uncharged line towards the house. Marco and Chris from Truck 3 joined them at the door. Marco called for water, then said, "me and Chris will start the primary search. You and Charlie hit it." They all went on air while they waited the few seconds for water. A call came in over the radio. "Battalion is on the scene and is in command. E6, move an exposure line to the back."

Another member of the Truck 3's crew forced the front door open. Nick took the nozzle and started to move forward. Marco grabbed his coat and held him back. "Give it to Charlie," he yelled through the face mask. Nick nodded and waved Charlie forward. Together, the four of them moved in. Inside, Charlie and Nick pushed forward, Chris and Marco peeled off to the left, towards a hallway.

This was a perfect fire for Charlie to gain more nozzle experience. The fire was in the back of the house, probably in the kitchen. Open a window or door behind it, and attack from the opposite direction. They would have it down before the truck crew even grabbed the roof. It was a *"walk in the park,"* as old Lou would say.

At the door, they found a small dog. It looked alive, but barely. Nick handed the dog to the truckman from 3's. Charlie and Nick crawled into the house. He'd only gotten a few feet into the room when he saw flames rolling out of what looked like the kitchen. Charlie opened up the nozzle and trained a tight water stream in a Z pattern across the ceiling, then brought it down to the visible flame. The fire immediately darkened and Charlie shut down the stream. Nick smiled inwardly; *she had jumped the gun a little, maybe should have got closer; but all in all, not bad.* With the fire down, they paused to see if it would rekindle. With more than a little satisfaction, he thought, *This — this is what it's about.*

Firefighter Ivan Garcia had moved around to the back of the building. Active flames were visible in what he assumed was the kitchen. The sliding door on the deck was unlocked, so he opened it up to evacuate smoke. Within seconds, the hose line from inside had done the job; the flames went down, and steam pushed out the door. He reported on the radio that fire at the back of the house appeared out, then swept his leg into the door, checking for a body. Suddenly, black heavy smoke pushed out of the open door. It wasn't the lazy, lighter, steam infused smoke he expected. Pulling back, he noticed growing flames through the patio door at the basement level. He keyed his mike and said, "Command, this is Garcia on 'C' side. We have fire in the basement."

"Roger that, fire showing in the lower level," came the reply.

Nick heard, but could not see Marco in the hall. The smoke had thickened, obscuring all visibility. Still, he could tell he and Chris were close. Marco called out, "Fire in the basement — the stairs are over here. Charlie — Nick — get over here." Charlie and Nick wrestled the hose line toward the stairs and started down. Heavy smoke rose from the basement, but a faint orange glow was still visible.

As they began their descent, Dawson and Moore, from Engine 6's crew, arrived at the basement door with a hose line intended for exposure protection. Garcia used his pocket spanner to pry the patio door open, thinking they intended the line for entry. When the door opened, things turned bad.

In the academy, Charlie had learned about a thing called flow-path. It essentially meant that a fire needed a fresh air intake and exhaust to burn efficiently. Close off either and there is a dampering effect, sort of like a fireplace needed an open chimney. Basic tactics said you always worked from the intake side of the fire, not from the exhaust, and never, never get stuck in the middle of the flow path - the chimney. By opening the door, Garcia created an intake of fresh air for the fire, and the open door above became the exhaust. With fresh air, the fire exploded in the basement and Charlie learned firsthand what it felt like to be stuck in a fire's chimney. Worse, on seeing the rapid growth of flames, Moore opened his nozzle and directed a fog stream into the basement. Dawson yelled, "No!" and quickly grabbed the nozzle's bail, shutting off the water.

On the stairs, Nick was about to tell Charlie to throw some water at the basement ceiling to cool it before descending when an inferno engulfed them. Just behind and above him, Nick heard Marco yell, "Out! Everyone out." To her credit, Charlie didn't panic. Her training kicked in, and she immediately turned the nozzle to a wide fog mode. It created scalding steam, but afforded just enough protection from the flames for them to crawl up the steps and out the door. Nick, Charlie, Marco, and Chris laid in the yard for several seconds before moving. Nick eventually pulled off his mask and looked up. He saw the house was now fully involved.

Nick heard Marco say, "It got a little warm in there. Is everybody okay?"

Charlie replied, "I'm fine. What happened?"

Nick looked over at Charlie. She was sitting up, sweaty, and red faced, but no worse for the wear. Her gear was another story; steam was rising off her coat, and the shield on her helmet had melted. Worse, the face piece on her breathing mask cracked and distorted from the heat. It had been a close call. He said, "Congratulations, you've been baptized. You just survived your first shit show."

Charlie looked at her face mask and groaned. "That got nasty quick. It was like the whole place went up at once. I've never seen anything like it."

Marco patted her shoulder. "The place *did* go up all at once. You did good in there, Charlie. You saved our ass — no kidding."

"So, was it a flashover or a backdraft or something?" she asked.

Marco stood up. "Nah, it was more like a rollover. We'd be dead if it flashed over. My guess is the fire in the basement somehow got air. Come on, let's get clear of the door."

Moments later, Battalion Chief Hicks and Captain Jansson walked up to them. Both looked surprised and concerned. Noting their scorched gear, Hicks said, "Jesus, that was a close call. Are you all okay?"

Marco answered for the group. "We're good Chief — it got a little toasty is all. It lit up on us."

Hicks shook his head. "Yeah, when 6's crew tried to move a hose line in through the basement, the fire got air."

Without thinking, Nick blurted out. "Whose stupid ass idea was that? That would have set up opposing hose lines, and how come the truckies didn't ventilate. We nearly got cooked in this circle jerk."

The captain snapped. "Stow it Nick. Marco, get your crew into rehab. Get hydrated and replace your breathing apparatus. Hold there till you're called."

Nick noticed Chief Hicks glaring at him and knew he stepped in it. It was a cardinal rule; when things go bad, don't poke the brass. The only thing a chief hates more than a screw up is having a firefighter call him on it.

Charlie spoke up. "Hey Chief, how's the little dog?"

The Chief shook his head. "What dog?" He turned and walked away.

As they walked back toward the rig, Marco said, "Smooth move there, Nick."

"Sorry Marco. It's just that stupid crap drives me crazy."

The members of Engine 8 and Squad 8 spent the next 30 minutes silently sitting on the ground drinking water and watching the house burn down. The chief had called in an additional engine company, and switched into what is called a defensive posture. This meant protective lines got placed around the building, and no one could go inside. It was a waiting game. Eventually, the fire would consume enough of the structure and start to dwindle, then crews would drown the remaining fire. It wasn't a big house, and the fire was down in about 20 minutes. Next would come the gruesome job of sorting through the debris for the missing occupant. Once crews located a victim, the coroner and cause and origin team would spend a few hours investigating, documenting, and photographing. Then overhaul would start. They would sift the debris, put out spot fires, and secure the building. This was the reality of firefighting, minutes of adrenalin followed by hours of hot, hard, dirty work. The work wasn't glamorous, but it needed to be done.

Nick's crew did a few minor tasks in the ensuing hours, but mostly, they sat and waited. Finally, Captain Jansson walked up and said, "Marco, take your crew down to the basement. They are ready to remove the victim, but she's buried under some unstable debris, and it's not safe for the coroner's crew to bag her."

Instantly, Nick felt his stomach sink and his throat tighten. Every fiber in his being screamed for him to avoid seeing or touching that body. Abruptly, the little girl from his nightmare stood in front of him. He pushed the image aside and choked out, "This ain't right, Cap. We shouldn't have to do that. We made the hit, give it to somebody else."

The captain fixed a hard glare at Nick. "What's wrong with you, Adler? You've been a pain in the ass all day. Knock off the moaning and do your job." He stormed off, obviously angry.

Marco studied his friend; he looked off, a little pale. "That's a good question, Nick. What is going on with you today?"

"This is crap, is all," Nick said. "Why is he giving this to us?"

Marco crossed his arms and stared at his friend. "Gee, I don't know Nick. Maybe it has something to do with you shooting your mouth off to Chief Hicks. Now, get off your ass and let's get this done."

Nick remained silent while they gathered some medical gloves, flashlights, and a body bag. The dread continued to build as they walked down the hill to the back of the house at the basement level. Investigators had set up floodlights in the basement, illuminating the devastation that was once the family room. The fire gutted the room, leaving a bluish smoke hanging in the air. The walls were stained black, and most of the ceiling had collapsed. As they approached, Nick saw the woman's partially buried body. Although not badly burned, the intense heat left her severely bloated and discolored. Thankfully, he smelled nothing but the smoke. Nick stood nearly transfixed at the sight of her. He had seen this before- too many times- but this was different. His chest tightened, almost unbearably, and suddenly he couldn't breathe. His head began to swim, and a strange metallic taste formed in his mouth.

Marco noticed Nick hanging back, and that his hands were shaking. He asked, "Nick, are you okay?"

Nick said nothing. He simply stood staring at the body.

"Come on Nick, get over here," Marco snapped.

Charlie reached out and grabbed Nick's arm. He jumped as if shocked and pulled away. "I… I Ccan't do this. I just can't — I'm sorry." He half ran, half stumbled out the door.

Marco and Charlie watched Nick flee the room and then exchanged a meaningful glance. He said to Charlie, "Are you okay with doing this?"

She nodded. Marco then keyed his radio and requested command for another two firefighters in the basement. While he and Charlie waited for help, they cleared the debris and wrestled the woman's body into the bag. When reinforcements arrived, Marco helped Charlie and the two new guys carry the body to the gurney waiting outside. He then told the three of them to wheel it up to the coroner's van.

Once the area was clear, and they were alone, Marco walked up to Nick, who was sitting on a bench at the end of the patio; his head hung between his knees. Marco asked, "You doing okay?"

Nick replied, "I think so."

"Do you want to explain what the hell that was all about?"

Nick shook his head. "I am not sure I can. I suddenly felt lightheaded is all. Honestly, I think I'm just hungry and dehydrated."

Marco knew better, but said, "Sure, do you want a medic to look at you?"

Nick nodded no.

"Maybe you should go home."

Nick was about to say he was fine, but thought better of it. He really wanted to get the hell out of there. "I don't need a medic, but it could be I am fighting off a bug or something. Maybe I should take the rest of the day off, if that's okay."

Nick's agreeing to go home worried Marco as much as anything else that happened. It just wasn't like him. Especially leaving a fire scene. "Yeah, okay Nick. The squad is heading back pretty quick. I'll have them drop you off at the station and you take the rest of the day off. I'll clear it with Jansson."

Nick sat alone on the rear bumper of the squad, waiting for them to collect their gear. He knew he should help; he simply couldn't will himself to do it. So, he sat staring at his coat and helmet laying between his feet. He wanted to scream; he wanted to hit something; mostly, he wanted to cry.

He felt someone sit next to him; it was Charlie. "Not a good time, Charlie," he said.

"Yeah, I suppose not—Wanna talk."

Her voice was gentle and soothing. He had heard her like this before, when she consoled the badly injured, or calmed terrified children. It exuded empathy and compassion. Nick's sense of fair play had always made him support the right of qualified women to pursue a career in the fire service. But, it was watching Charlie interact with people that convinced him that women brought an attitude and mindset to the job that was pretty valuable. He always admired the way she handled the emotionally wounded, but hearing her talking to him in that voice brought on a wave of humiliation. *She pities me*, he thought.

"No, I don't want to talk." he said.

"Okay then, listen. I don't know what's pulling you down. Maybe it's your marriage, maybe something else, but don't give up. You can beat it."

"Charlie, you don't get it — Let it go."

Charlie hooked her arm through his and took his hand. "Nick, you're as good a man as I know. And you're a great firefighter. You got this. It will be okay."

The physical contact shocked Nick. He and Charlie had gotten close, but this was the most intimate moment they had ever shared. He was about to reply, when the squad's compartment door slammed shut. Charlie quickly got up and said, "See you next shift."

The guys on the squad called, "Time to go."

Charlie stopped and added. "Hey, the little dog made it okay. That's something, right?"

# Chapter 5

He felt her breath on his chest, slow, deep, and even. She was awake but completely relaxed, content in her post orgasmic bliss. *Good*, he thought, *she's getting past the nerves and guilt*. He ran his fingers lightly down her bare back, and she snuggled into his arm.

She let out a sigh and whispered, "Mmmm, that was incredible — *you're* incredible."

He kissed the top of her head. "We are good together. I needed you so bad."

Her eyes found his. "Do you think about me — you know — when we are not together?"

"I think about you all the time. I think I am getting addicted to you."

A look of concern clouded her face. "Sylvester, I love our time together, but understand — I have kids and a life. I can't risk that. This is just a fling."

*Christ, dumbass*, he thought. *You spent months getting her in bed, don't fuck it up now*. He said, "I know, I'm not asking for more. Besides, I am not ready to leave Racheal yet either." In truth, he had no plans to leave Racheal at all. Not that he would particularly miss her, he just didn't make enough money at the spa to support himself. He had high hopes for the website, but it wasn't making nearly what he needed.

He had no illusions about what would happen with Carol. Eventually, the thrill of an illicit affair, of the secret rendezvous and seedy hotel rooms, would wane. Then guilt would set in, and she'd end it. That was fine by him. He only needed a few more sessions to have enough video. Carol was okay in bed, eager but vanilla. Lately though, she was getting on his nerves, she was developing an independent streak that annoyed him. It was getting time to move on to the next conquest. *Maybe Pam Whitford,* he thought. She was getting friendly.

He hated working at the spa. Rubbing down fat old men was gross, but it was great for meeting women, especially neglected and bored wives. Carol had been easier than most, the perfect combination of insecurity and frustration. After a few massage sessions, she got comfortable, then chatty. A sympathetic ear and a few delicate compliments were all it took. Soon came subtle, then not-so-subtle flirting. Finally, after months, he made his move. He confessed how much he looked forward to talking to her, and would she like to grab an innocent cup of coffee when they were done? Coffee dates turned to lunch dates and soon they were making out in her car, then hotel rooms. He said to himself, *Bing-bang-boom. Stroke their body, then their ego's egos and you own them — works every time. Well, sometimes anyway.*

He loved seducing lonely women, especially married ones. The idea of taking another man's wife was oh so empowering. The sex was satisfying — sometimes. It was often just okay. It was the secretly filming them that really turned him on. The voyeur kink blossomed when he was still a boy. He spied on his mom and sister growing up, he even tried window peeping. That was a thrill until he got caught. Luckily, he was just a kid, and nothing really became of it. But it taught him a lesson; caution and patience were key. *I am a hunter*, he liked to tell himself. *And my prey is the sweetest of feasts.*

The development of miniature cameras was a game changer for him. Now he could own his *prey* forever. Nothing got him off, like touching himself while watching the videos of the stupid women he filmed. Possessing them, then using them at his leisure, he often liked it better than the actual sex. Even filming Racheal was thrilling for a while. At first, he let his buddy Jimmy see her videos. That little wimp had a thing for Racheal, which was funny because she hated him. Thinking about him getting worked up over her, and her being disgusted by him, was too sweet. *Giving* her to him was even sweeter. She was his- to share as he saw fit.

The whole website idea came to him while surfing the net. He found a subscription site for amateur porn; The idea of guys getting off watching him and Racheal turned him on. At first he intended to just post videos of him and Racheal, but seducing unknowing women became addictive. That's what pushed him to set up the site… that and the money.

Sly reveled in the humiliation his *prey* would feel if they knew strange men had watched them get screwed. Better yet, he loved thinking about what he was doing to their husbands. *Cuckold* was one of his favorite words; he liked the way it sounded; he *loved* the implication.

He used to worry that his wife would find out about the website. But he knew how to keep her in line. She'd have a hissy fit, but she wouldn't do anything about it; she wouldn't dare.

Carol said, "Sylvester? What are you smiling about?"

He playfully slapped her ass. "I told you, call me Sly. I hate being called Sylvester."

"Why?"

"It sounds old fashioned. Plus, I got the name because my mom had a huge thing for Stallone. It's kinda creepy that she named me after her fantasy guy."

Carol giggled. "It could have been worse. She could have named you Rambo. Then your name would have been Rambo Roberts; or better yet, Rocky Roberts."

"Funny," he said.

"Hey, maybe she really named you after Sylvester the Cat, you know, the silly cat in the cartoon. *I tawt I saw a poodie cat!'*

"I'll stick with Rambo," he said in reply. In his head, it was, *Yeah, yeah, laugh it up. How about I send a copy of our video to your husband, so he can see you acting like a little whore… How's that for funny?*

She got off the bed. "The kids will be home soon. I need to go.".

*It's about time. I got stuff to do later;* he thought. He said, "Sure you can't stay a while longer?"

She dressed, gave him a peck on the lips and said, "See you next Thursday, Rambo."

As she walked out, he flashed the one-finger salute to her back. "Bye sexy, till next time."

*I'll fucking show you Rambo, bitch.*

Confusion gripped Carol when she glimpsed Sylvester flipping her off in the mirror. More alarming was the look of utter contempt on his face. It sent a chill down her back. By the time she reached the car, she knew there would be no next time. By the time she got home she wondered if she should tell her husband about Sly. She couldn't get past that look on his face as she left, something deep in her lizard brain told her that he might be trouble, bad trouble.

# Chapter 6

Nick sat at a corner table in Rizzi's bar and grill. He liked the place; it looked and smelled like a bar. He disliked the so-called sports bars the gentry loved so much, they seemed like amusement parks masquerading as bars. He hated their cheesy memorabilia, and all the damn big screen TV's screaming at you. Yeah, he liked Rizzi's; it was a dump but an honest one, and a quiet one. He just wished he wasn't here to meet Haley.

Bailing sounded appealing, but he knew it wasn't an option. Even on a good day, the date would be a bad idea; this was not a good day. Sleep mostly eluded him in the two days since the fire. He obsessed over his behavior, and it humiliated him. Worse, his reaction to the woman's body scared him. He was running out of excuses about what was wrong with him. He was losing it, and for the first time, he wondered if he could still handle the job.

Then there was the stuff Marco said about Becky getting played. He knew that if what he said was true, she'd be devastated. Somehow, he had come to worry about her, and he didn't want to. For months, anger was all he had to sustain him. Anger at her kept the grief at bay, and it helped him ignore the growing crisis within him. As long as he could blame her, he could avoid dealing with whatever else was going on inside. He wasn't ready to let go of the anger, but it was fading, and he suspected nothing but sadness and fear waited to take its place. Sadness, he knew, fear was something alien to him.

And so, he sat, strung out and on edge; waiting like a damn fool for a date with a kid he barely knew. He took a sip of his scotch; shut his eyes and cradled his face in his hands. *I need to get out of here and get some sleep;* he thought.

Her voice startled him. "You made it. I was half afraid you'd stand me up."

Nick opened his eyes and saw her standing by the table. Gone was the cute kid in the ponytail and baggy T-shirt. Her long brown hair cascaded onto her bare shoulders. She wore a clingy excuse of a dress that left little to the imagination. The only thing that remained of the coffee shop girl was the brilliant smile.

*Good Lord, I'm in trouble,* he thought. Unable to think of anything better, he said, "Yep, I made it."

She extended both arms and struck a pose. "I don't get many excuses to get dressed up. It's not too much, is it?"

"No, you look nice."

She put on a theatrical frown. "I bought a new dress and spent an hour getting ready, and all I get is a 'you look nice' — you're killing me."

Half amused and half chastised, Nick said, "Sorry, how about you look lovely?"

"Better, but you kind of sound like my dad on my prom night."

Despite himself, Nick had to chuckle. "Okay, how about you're a total smoke show?"

The electric smile returned. "There you go." She sat down. "What are we drinking?"

"Dewar's on the rocks."

"Cool," she said. "Hard-core, I like it." She motioned to the waitress for two more.

Amused, he said, "You sure? I don't take you for a whiskey kinda girl."

"Oh, and what type of girl do you take me for?"

"I don't know, white wine maybe, or one of those fruity seltzer mixes."

The waitress set the 2 drinks down. She also brought 2 glasses of water as well. Nick reached for his wallet, but Haley grabbed his arm. "Uh, uh. I said I'd by the first round."

As the server bent forward to take Nick's empty glass, she turned and gave him a wink and a sly smile. A wave of guilty embarrassment rose in him. He thought, *I shouldn't be here. She thinks I'm an old fool chasing young women.* At his best, he was uncomfortable in social situations, and he was a long way from his best. And this was his first -first date- in a long, long time.

Haley hoisted her drink. "Here's to new friends!" She took a generous sip of the whiskey and spit most of it back out. She coughed and hoarsely said, "Holy hell, how do you drink that stuff? It tastes like lighter fluid."

Nick laughed and pushed the glass of water to her. "It's an acquired taste, but I applaud the effort. How about that white wine now?" She nodded, and blushing, pushed the scotch over to him. He found her awkward moment and her obvious embarrassment altogether charming.

Apparently watching, the waitress magically materialized and asked if they needed anything. Guessing she liked her wine sweet; he ordered a glass of Moscato.

"So," Haley said, "Tell me about Nick."

"Not much to tell."

"How about you start with your last name and work from there?"

"Adler, my last name is Adler. I'm 37 years old, married but separated, and I am a firefighter. That's about it, pretty boring stuff."

Haley sipped her wine. "This is excellent—well done. And how is being a fireman boring?"

"Firefighter, not fireman. There are women firefighters too."

"I don't see how they do it," Haley said. "Lord knows I couldn't."

"You might be surprised. I work with a firefighter named Charlie — well, Charlotte, actually. Anyhow, she's about your age and no bigger than you. She's still kinda new, and still has stuff to learn, but she is already damn good. The woman has a helluva career ahead of her."

"That's so cool! So, what's it like — you know, fighting fires? It must be so exciting."

He thought, *there it is, the question everybody asks.* People's curiosity was part of the job. As soon as people found out what he did for a living, the questions would start. Like most firefighters, Nick enjoyed the apparent respect, especially from women; but he thought it a mixed blessing. The whole hero thing could get a little embarrassing sometimes, and the questions got tiresome; especially for someone who didn't like talking about themselves. He answered, "Well, it's nothing like you see on TV. There's a lot of smoke, most of the time you never even see the fire. You just see an orange glow. It's hot and dark and you crawl in blind. You're wearing really heavy clothes and sucking air through a tube. Mostly you just try not to fall down steps, or get lost. I'll tell you this much, it's hot, and it's exhausting. You sweat like a pig."

"It sounds awful, and so dangerous."

He shrugged. "Not as much as you might think. If everybody does what they're supposed to, we all go home in one piece."

"Have you ever — you know — gotten burned?"

"Burned? No, not really." Nick flashed back to his most recent fire, and how close it got. He never tried to explain the really dangerous stuff to civilians, not even to Becky. All firefighters knew that only other firefighters could really understand. How do you calmly tell an outsider that you almost got killed twice- three times now- and not have it sound like you're bragging? He knew some guys, like Jenkins, would lay the whole *bravery in the face of death* crap on pretty thick, especially for a pretty girl on a first date, but that always struck Nick as cheesy. He said, "I've made a few trips to the ER, gotten a few stitches here and there, and a bunch of bumps and bruises; but nothing too bad."

Haley shook her head. "Just a few trips to the hospital, huh? No big deal? You're pretty modest, mister."

Nick said, "Really, we never give getting hurt a lot of thought. I will let you in on a little secret. It's not getting hurt that scares us, it's getting sick. Smoke is a toxic soup of nasty chemicals. Way more firefighters die of cancer, and heart disease than accidents. I read somewhere that firefighters get cancer and have heart attacks more than twice as much as the rest of the population."

Haley took a sip of wine and studied Nick closely. "Then why do it? I expect it pays good, but still…"

"Because it's the greatest job in the world. Every 3$^{rd}$ day I go in and work alongside the best people I know. They're like my brothers and sisters, even the ones that piss me off. I tell you the truth, I've never had a morning when I didn't want to go to work. Every day is different, you just never know what can happen. I see people at their worst, and their best, it's an incredible thing."

"Still," she said, "you see so much tragedy. That has to take a toll."

Nick saw Haley hanging on to every word. Usually, he didn't enjoy talking about the job, but he found her enthusiasm contagious. "Sure, some of it's tragic, but not all. Mostly it all turns out okay, sometimes calls even get funny. Even the bad stuff is sort of fulfilling — sort of. I get paid to help people in trouble; sometimes it's the worst day of their life. It's a privilege, really. I never go home thinking I wasted my time, or that my job was meaningless. In a tangible way, I make a difference. How many can say that? I'm lucky, I guess."

Haley reached across the table and took Nick's hand. "You're a good soul, Nicholas Adler."

"Not Nicholas, it's Dominick."

"Ooh, I like that better. It's kind of sexy?"

"Very Funny. I never really liked my name. Dominick always sounded sort of fancy, like I am trying to be cool or something."

"Nonsense," Haley said. "Dominick is an awesome name, and it suits you. You *are* cool — *very* cool."

Her subtle flirting caused a stir in him. It was unexpected and something he hadn't felt in a long while. Flustered and wanting to change the subject, he said, "Okay, enough about me. Tell me about you."

Haley gave Nick's hand a gentle squeeze and let go of it. "Compared to you, I *am* boring. Let's see, Haley Stewart, 26 years old, born and raised in Cedar Rapids Iowa and graduated from Northern Illinois University. I'm single, no boyfriend, and live with a cat named Chet."

Nick said, "I have a cat too."

"Really? You strike me as a dog guy, maybe a Lab or German Shepard. What's your cat's name?"

"I'm kinda embarrassed to admit it but, I never named her. I just call her Cat."

Halley laughed. "Yeah, you *should be* embarrassed. You know, something's not really yours till you name it."

"Not sure she really is mine. It's more like we put up with each other, a sort of mutually beneficial arranged marriage."

"Oh-oh, I smell commitment issues," she teased.

Nick ignored the jab. "So, you're a long way from Cedar Rapids. How did you end up here?"

Haley shrugged and started folding her napkin. "I guess I am a bit of a cliché. My boyfriend got a job here. We were already living together, so I quit my job and I tagged along. 6 months later he accepted a transfer to Denver, and that was that. So, here I am."

"I'm afraid to ask, but why didn't you go with him?" Nick asked.

"Funny thing, his girlfriend from work had a problem with me coming along."

Nick said, "Ouch. He cheated on you? That sucks."

"Yeah, they started up right after we moved. I didn't even see it coming."

"What a tool. I am sorry you had to go through that. It's rough, I know from experience."

Haley had stopped folding her napkin and started tearing it into little pieces. "That's the thing though. He really isn't a tool. He just fell in love with someone else. Heck, they're even engaged now. I can't blame him for being in love."

"You're excusing him," Nick growled. "He cheated, and you can damn well blame him for it."

"Oh, hell yeah, I was furious that he lied to me and strung me along. But I could get past that. What broke my heart was that he fell in love with someone else."

"So, what if he came crawling back saying he made a mistake? Would you take him back?"

Haley cocked her head and rested her chin in her hand. "Wow, good question; I never really thought about it. No, I suppose not. Whatever he didn't find in me then is still probably missing. Plus, I had invested too much of myself in him, it was unhealthy. No, going back with him would be a step back, not forward."

"So, you're saying you moved on? You're good with how it worked out?"

Haley said, "A part of me still loves him, and that stings. But going back with him wouldn't be what's best for me."

"But you're not furious over the way it ended? I don't get that. My wife cheated on me too, and I can't get past the anger. I guess you're a better person than me."

"What's the point of hanging onto it? It just eats at you like a cancer."

Nick sighed and said, "I can't believe I'm telling you this; I barely know you. Sometimes, I feel like anger is all I've got. I'd rather be angry than depressed."

"Can I ask, did your wife leave you for another guy? Did she fall in love with someone else?"

Nick shook his head. "No, she had a one-night stand. At least she says it was one night."

"You seem like a great guy. Why do you think she did it?"

"That's what gets to me. I don't understand it, I can't get my head around it. I guess sometimes life just decides to kick you in the balls."

Haley reached across the table again and took his hand. "In college I studied Carl Jung; his stuff really had an effect on me. He wrote about something called *locus of control*. Each of us has a certain orientation; some people believe events control their life; other people believe their choices shape events. I decided it was better to accept responsibility for my life."

Nick scoffed. "I hate to tell you this, but awful crap happens to people every day, and there is no controlling it. Drunks fall asleep at the wheel and kill innocent people. Drug addicts murder people for pocket change, and wives and boyfriends you trust lie and cheat."

Haley squeezed his hand. "You're missing the point. Of course, bad things happen to good people and we have no control over some things. But we *do* have control over how we feel about them and how we respond. I really believe this; happiness is a choice. We choose what we build our life around. Yes, there's a lot of ugliness in the world, but there's a lot of beauty too. Tragedy could be around the corner, but so is joy if you embrace it. Sure, I could wallow in self-pity and anger over what Jeremy did to me, but what does that do for me? I'd rather accept what happened as part of life, learn from it and then go look for something better. I want to embrace life, not hide from it."

Her simple philosophy startled Nick. It was as if someone or something had read his life story and sent her to deliver a message. It reminded him of who he had been once. He shook his head and chuckled. "Semper prorsum."

"Excuse me?" Haley said.

"Semper prorsum," Nick replied. "It's Latin; it means *ever forward.*"

"Don't tell me you speak Latin."

"No, I picked it up somewhere, and it stuck with me. I even have a tattoo of it."

Haley's face lit up. "Nice! Show me."

"No can do, I'd have to take off my shirt. This place is a dive, but I bet they would still frown on it."

"Modest? How sweet," she teased.

"How about you — any ink?"

She blushed, "Yes, but not anywhere you're going to see, so don't ask."

"Yeah, we better change the subject. Tell me about growing up in Cedar Rapids."

"Okay, but I'm getting hungry. Let's split some chili cheese fries."

An hour passed quickly. They talked, ate, laughed, and had 2 more rounds. Nick found Haley utterly remarkable. She was funny and bright, and wise beyond her years. He was at ease with her, and he found himself opening up to her. They talked about growing up, about movies, and books. He told her funny stories from the firehouse. She talked about wanting to be a journalist, and how she was applying for jobs around the country, and even oversees.

After a while, Nick said, "Haley, I have a confession to make. I was pretty nervous about going out with you. The truth is, I almost canceled. I wasn't sure we would have anything to talk about — you know, with the age difference. But I have to tell you, I've had a really great time. I'm glad I came."

Haley smiled and said, "Well, if we're being honest, I was nervous too. I wasn't sure what to expect."

"Then why did you ask me out?"

"Like I told you the other morning, I don't have any friends in town and I wanted to get out of the house. You seemed like a nice guy, and probably not a serial killer. So, I took a shot." Smiling broadly, she leaned forward and rested her chin on her palm. "Plus, you got that whole sexy fireman thing going for you."

He chuckled. "Yeah, I think I heard somewhere that chicks dig firefighters."

"I know you're kidding, but there's something to it. I can't speak for all women," she said, "but I like my men masculine. There is something about being a firefighter that seems bigger than life — sort of an alpha male thing, you know?"

"Shit, I must be doing something wrong, or else you watch too much TV."

"There you go, being modest again," she said. "I bet women come on to you all the time."

The compliment felt good; it also made him nervous. "You would lose that bet. And, while we're at it; I find it hard to believe that you don't get asked out on dates all the time. You're kind of the total package, smart, funny, gorgeous…"

She wrinkled her nose and teased, "I know, right?" Then, in a more serious tone, she added, "I don't want a boyfriend right now because I have plans and I don't want the complications of having another person in my life. I told you before, I have a history of losing myself when I get into serious relationships. But I do get lonely sometimes. I'm glad we did this. You have turned out to be way more than I hoped for — thanks." She then finished her wine and added, "As great as this has been, I need to get going. I work tomorrow."

Nick threw a couple $20 bills on the table and said, "Let's go." When they got outside, he asked, "Are you okay to drive?"

"No problem, I walked. I only live about six blocks away."

"Just to be safe, I will walk you home."

"That's sweet, but you don't have to," she said.

He took her hand. "No, I want to."

"Look, Nick," she said, "I am attracted to you — a lot. But I don't do first date hookups, or one-night stands. Sorry."

Nick's reaction surprised him. He really hadn't intended to spend the night with her and was relieved that it wouldn't be an issue; still there was still a pang of disappointment. "I hear you, and that's okay. But if it's all the same to you, I'd still like to walk you home."

She took his arm. "Such a gentleman." As they walked, Nick marveled at the evening. He debated whether to ask her out again. He wanted to, but getting rejected would ruin the night. There was also the question of a good night kiss. He wanted to, but he still wasn't sure if he was on a date, or if they were just hanging out.

When they got to her townhouse, she stopped and gave him a chaste kiss on the lips, then said, "This is it. Thank you again for a great night. It was just what I needed." She then moved towards her door.

"Haley, I had fun too. Any chance you'd like to do it again sometime?"

She turned and said, "I don't think we should. I asked you out because I figured it would be casual — no big deal. The thing is, I really like you. If we go out again, we're probably going to end up in bed. Heck, I almost talked myself into asking you to spend the night tonight; and like I said, I don't do that. I think you and I could turn into something, and that won't end well. You're married and not over your wife, and I'm going to move away." She moved close and kissed him again; it was a lingering kiss. After several seconds, she pulled back and said, "Too bad though, I wish things were different." Then she smiled and said, "See you tomorrow, your café mocha will be waiting."

He kissed her on her forehead and said, "Thanks. See you tomorrow."

# Chapter 7

Racheal waited in the garden food court, struggling to calm her nerves. After their night together, she had reached out to Becky dozens of times; only one terse text response ever came; "What we did was a mistake, we can't see each other anymore. Please don't contact me again."

Becky was right, letting Sly talk her into initiating a threesome with Becky had been a mistake. The night had been great, but she lost a good friend. Then there was Sly; he was being an ass about the whole thing. Since that night, he talked about little else but doing it again with Becky, or somebody - anybody - else. She missed Becky but was glad that a repeat of that night was impossible. For her, it was a shared experience with a good friend and her husband — *just innocent fun;* she had told herself. She knew that for him; it wasn't a fun fling they had together. Nope, for him it was just wanting to screw other women — any women; he didn't care who.

*I married an asshole*, she thought

A few months after that night, she had heard Becky and Nick had split up. She felt guilty about that, even though she knew it wasn't her fault. Becky had been as enthusiastic about it as she and Sly were. She guessed Becky's conscience had got the better of her afterwards and she told her husband. Becky ghosting her hurt, but she understood it. That's why the message to meet for lunch surprised her. She hoped that maybe, since

Becky was single now, they might be friends again. *Maybe even more than friends*, she thought.

Racheal never considered herself bisexual. She had experimented some in college and thought it fun, but she really liked men better. Still, that night with Becky had been different, even extraordinary. Sex with Sly was rough and demanding; it was different with Becky, it was tender, somehow moving. She would be open to exploring some kind of relationship with Becky — without Sly knowing, of course. She often fantasized about leaving Sly; gay or not, being with Becky would probably be better than being with him. *Maybe, just maybe*, she thought.

And so, she sat waiting and hoping. Hoping that Becky missed her, hoping that they would smile, and hug, and talk, and plan to meet after work. Hoping it was Sly and not her that Becky felt guilty over. Racheal's anxiety grew when she saw Becky approaching; there was no smile.

Racheal stood to embrace her friend. "Becky, I'm so glad you texted me. I missed you."

Becky pushed her back into the chair; then loomed over her former friend. "Fuck you. How the hell do you live with yourself?"

"What? What do you mean?"

Becky practically snarled, "I mean, what the hell did I ever do to you? What kind of monster are you? You ruined my marriage and destroyed my life."

"No — no, I didn't. You can't blame me for that. That night just sort of happened, we were just having some fun. You wanted it too. You shouldn't have told your husband. That's on you."

"I didn't tell him. He saw that fucking video. Somebody sent it to him; probably you and your asshole husband."

"What video?" Racheal asked. "What are you talking about?"

Becky pointed an accusing finger at Racheal. "Don't give me that shit, you had to know. Look, if you and your pervert husband want to make porno videos, that's your business. But you had no right to film me and not tell me. That shit is against the law, you're damn lucky that video isn't on the website anymore or I would call the cops."

"Becky, you're talking crazy. What video are you talking about?"

"Don't play innocent with me. I'm talking about the video from the night you, me, and Sly got drunk and messed around. There's no way you didn't know."

"I swear — I don't know what you're talking about."

Becky sat down and studied Racheal for several seconds. "Come on, you really want me to believe that you're that stupid. That your husband had cameras in your bedroom and you didn't know it. I don't buy it."

"I honestly don't know what you're talking about." Racheal said.

"Okay, I'll play along. Your pervert husband filmed our night together and put it up on the Internet."

"No way," Racheal said. "Sly can be a jerk, but he wouldn't do that."

"He would, and he did. But you know that, don't you?" Becky said.

"I don't believe it. Maybe somebody's just fucking with you — lying about it."

"Stop the act, Racheal. Somebody sent the video to my husband. He thinks one of his firefighter buddies found it online. I think you and your husband sent it."

Stunned, Racheal stuttered, "No, this must be some sort of mistake. Sly wouldn't — he wouldn't do that — especially to me."

"Oh, there's no mistake. I've seen the video. It's disgusting. And, for good measure, he blurred out his face, but not ours. I — we — looked like a couple of stupid bitches in heat. It was the most humiliating thing I've ever seen."

"Becky, I swear I had nothing to do with it. I'm so sorry. If there is a video, I promise you I had nothing to do with sending it to your husband, and I don't believe Sly did either. Why would he?"

"Why? Why would you two make the damn video to begin with? Because you're fucking predators, that's why. This whole mess has ruined me. My husband saw that disgusting video, so did my friends and the guys he works with. God only knows who else may have seen it. I will never get over it. You and your husband are evil creeps and deserve to die a slow and miserable death."

Racheal felt tears welling in her eyes. "Oh Becky, I'm so sorry. You know me, I would never be part of that."

Becky snapped. "I thought I knew you. You're either a monster or the dumbest bitch on the planet. My money is on monster, and that would make *me* the dumbest bitch on the planet because I went along with everything that happened.

Filming us and posting it on the Internet is beyond skeezy. I feel so damn violated. For one woman to do that to another is pretty fucked up. I thought only men could be that callous."

"Becky, there is some mistake, I can't believe Sly did what you say."

"There is no mistake. And don't tell me it was just Sly. You had to be in on it."

Racheal tentatively reached across the table and took Becky's hand. She was thankful Becky didn't pull away. "I swear I knew nothing about a video; I wouldn't do that, not to you, and I would never be in one either. If it's true, it's awful. But you said the videos aren't there anymore. So that's something — I guess."

Becky shook her head and laughed. "You really are stupid. Do you think that shit ever really disappears from the net? No, we're going to be porn stars forever. And by the way, the video of the three of us is gone. The videos of you and the others are still there."

Panic crept into Racheal's expression. "What? Videos of me? Of other women too? What women?"

"Surprise, Honey! You're a star." Becky said. She then pulled her phone out of her pocket. She tapped a few buttons, then handed the phone to Racheal. Becky sat quietly while Racheal watched the videos.

Racheal could hardly believe what she was seeing. First shock, then anger welled up within her. Tears flooded her eyes as she watched her husband commit every imaginable act of adultery possible with several women. Then, humiliation replaced anger. There were two raunchy videos of her and Sly having sex. Worse, he had somehow captured a video of her alone, touching herself. She realized there must've been at least three cameras in the room because there was more than one angle, even revolting close ups. *How — how is this possible? Becky was right. I am stupid;* she thought.

It was bad enough that he cheated, but to violate her privacy, to post humiliating pictures and video's of her for a bunch of strangers on the web to see … it was an inexcusable betrayal. And it was a pay site, he was making money off her. The complete and total disrespect he had for her was stunning.

Through her tears, Racheal looked at Becky and asked. "How long have you known about this?"

"Nick got the video about a month after — *that night*. I just now found out about the website. I always thought you were in on it; your betrayal made me angrier than Sly's. I trusted you; we were friends; was I wrong about that?"

Racheal hid her face in her hands. "All these months, men have been looking at me — watching me get…   and the whole time my husband has been making money off of me. My own husband turned me into a – what - prostitute? And I didn't even know it."

Becky saw the total despair in the woman across from her. She realized that, as unbelievable as it was, Racheal really hadn't known. "You're not a prostitute, you're a victim, we both are."

"What about those other women? Do you think they know?"

Becky shrugged and said, "I didn't; you say you didn't. I expect they don't either."

"I am married to a monster."

"Yes, you are. What are you going to do about it?"

Racheal choked back a sob. "I'm going to leave him, I'm going to take everything from him, and maybe castrate him. And then I'm going to kill him, then divorce him, then maybe kill him again."

Becky nodded in agreement. "Somebody should. He deserves it, he deserves it all." She stood to leave.

"Becky, I am so, so sorry this all happened."

"Yeah, I imagine you are." she replied coolly.

"Is there any chance we can get past this and be friends again? I miss you, and I am going to need…"

Becky cut her off. "Absolutely not. I may never get over this, but I sure can't do it by being around you and the train wreck you call a life." Becky took two steps away, then stopped, took a deep breath, and said, "I guess I don't blame you. I just feel — I don't know — dirty, I guess. You remind me of something I am ashamed of, and I suppose that's not fair. Maybe I will check in on you — maybe. Give me some time to process all this."

Racheal said nothing. She only wiped away a tear and nodded.

# Chapter 8

He came home and found her crying in the bedroom. Immediately annoyed, he thought, *Now what?* He quickly realized that whatever it was, it was bad – very bad. Sounding as caring as he could muster, he said, "What's the matter, sweetheart?"

She answered with an unintelligible muffled scream into her pillow.

"Is everything okay?"

Another scream into the pillow, this one quite clear, "Fuck you."

"Whoa," he said, "calm down — what happened?"

She sat up, the fury that contorted her face nearly made her unrecognizable. There were tears, but not of sadness; he saw nothing but rage. She practically growled, "What happened? How about *you* tell *me* what happened?"

"I don't know what you mean?"

"Bullshit," she spat. "You know exactly what I mean. Let me help you, you cheated on me, you son of a bitch."

"Look honey, I don't know what someone told you…"

"Don't look honey me. How could you do it to me? I have always known that you're a jerk, but I thought you at least cared about me. I never dreamed that you would betray me like you have."

"Sweetheart, I love you. You know that. You know that you're the only woman I care about, the only woman I love."

"Love me? You cheated on me, with God only knows how many women. And that's not even the worst of it. No — You filmed yourself with them; and, like some sick pervert, you did it behind their backs. Then you put us on the Internet for your creepy friends to enjoy."

The word *-us-* didn't escape his attention. "What are you talking…."

"… Stop the crap Sly." She pointed at the pile of cameras on the floor.

His stomach tightened. "Honey, I can explain…"

"No! You can't explain it. There is no explaining it, and there sure as fuck is no excuse for it. You're a disgusting pervert."

Anger rose in him, mixed with equal parts of fear. He knew she would get suspicious of the other women eventually, but always assumed that he could handle her. She had always been weak and pliable. He knew he could talk her into forgiving anything if he had to. If not, he could just scare her. *Keep it up bitch, and I'll slap the sass out of you for mouthing off like this. What right do you have to judge me, to call me a pervert?* Still, he had never seen Racheal like this before, and she could cause him trouble. Calmly, he said, "Racheal, I'm not a pervert, it's not like that. I just do it because…"

"I don't care why you screw other women, or why your twisted mind gets off on humiliating them. You're a jackass; I've known that for years. What I want to know is how you could do it to your own wife. How could you make disgusting sex tapes with your wife without her knowing it, and then sell them to a bunch of horny men for money? Tell me Sly, why would you turn your own wife into a prostitute? When did I start meaning so little to you that you would sell my dignity for $13 a month? Tell me that. Tell me how in your twisted fucking mind, that it's worth $13 for men to leer at your wife naked? Explain to me how you thought it was Ok to rent me out as jack off bate? When did I become something to sell? Explain that to me."

Her outrage was pushing him to the edge. *The bitch always blew shit out of proportion. Women take nude shots all the time,* he thought. "Racheal honey, calm down. Let's talk about this. I was going to tell…"

"… Hey," she interrupted, "were you going to just stop with videos? Maybe you were thinking about just selling me outright. What do you think sweetheart, how much do you think I'm worth? Maybe your dirt bag buddy, Jimmy, would give you fifty to fuck me for a while. He's always liked me, right? I know that sounds pretty cheap, but then again, I guess I'm not worth very much, am I?"

Inwardly he cringed. *Had Jimmy told her?* Sly forced a laughed. "Come on, you know I wouldn't do that, and even if I did, you would be worth way more than $50. He'd go as high as $500."

"You think this is funny?" Racheal screamed. "You're a fucking pig. We're done. Pack your shit and get out!"

*I've had about enough of this,* he thought. He stepped closer, looming over her. He kicked the bed frame and said, "I am not going anywhere, you little bitch. Settle down or I'll give you something to really be upset about."

She got off the bed and moved close, putting her face near his, invading his space. "Oh, are you going to slap me around again, tough guy? Fuck you. How about I give *you* something to be upset about?"

"Yeah, and what's that?"

A menacing smile curled her lips. "I did some research. Turns out that website of yours is illegal. In this state, you go to jail for posting explicit material without consent. You're looking at 1 to 5 years for each offence, dumb ass. If you don't leave right now, and take all that crap off the net, I am calling the cops. Your ass will be in jail, that is, if some pissed off husband doesn't find you first."

A rage boiled in him. He thought, *who did she think she was, talking back, even threatening him? It was disrespectful.* He struck her reflexively, and harder than he intended. The blow lifted her off the ground; he heard a loud thud when her head hit the bedpost. Standing over her, he felt more than a little satisfaction at how she now lay docile at his feet. He took a breath and composed himself, pushing down the urge to hit her again. He knew his wife; one good shot was all it took to settle her down. *At least now, I can talk some sense into her.* Trying to sound a little contrite, he said, "I am sorry I had to do that, Racheal. Now get up, and we will get this worked out. It's not such a big deal. A lot of women have sites like that; we can make some real money, and have some fun doing it."

She laid on the floor, not moving, refusing to answer. "Racheal, don't make me angry again. Stop acting like a child and get up. We'll talk." Again, she ignored him. "Fine, have it your way." Angry, he kicked her hard in the hip. No reaction. A pang of worry edged into his chest. "Racheal?" he asked. He knelt beside her and rolled her over on her back. Shaking her failed to rouse her. Her chest didn't move like she was breathing. He put his hand in front of her nose… nothing. Grabbing her wrist, he tried to feel a pulse. He had never checked a pulse before, but was sure he would feel it if she had one. He felt nothing. It was only then he noticed the growing halo of blood spreading on the carpet by her head.

Now fully panicked, he said, "Oh no, no, no." He thought, *the little bitch died on me. They will burn me for this! Think Sly, what do you do now? Run? No, that never works.* He got up and sat on the bed for several minutes, muttering. Finally, he reached for his phone. "Hello, I need an ambulance… I think my wife fell… I don't know what happened, I just found her on the floor… No, I don't think she is breathing, she won't wake up… Sly, I mean Sylvester Roberts… 2929 Cyprus Court… Yes, I will stay on the line…"

While he waited, he looked at his dead wife on the floor. "This is your fault, not mine."

*****

The boys in the park were playing some sort of concocted wiffle ball game. Nick always enjoyed sitting on the tailboard of the rig and watching people in the park across the street, especially the kids. It was bittersweet sometimes; he often wondered what it would be like to be a dad. Becky had miscarried twice; it devastated her. Him too, but he had done his best to hide that from her. He struggled with watching her suffer; they had decided it would be best for him to get snipped. With how things stood with Becky now, he wondered if that had been a mistake. He thought, *Maybe, someday…*

"You look deep in thought." It was Marco.

"Nah, not so much. Just sitting really."

Marco playfully poked Nick in the ribs. "So, how did it go with that hottie from the coffee shop?"

"Better than expected. Turns out she is pretty fantastic."

"Is that right? So, there's a little something going on there. When are you going to see her again?"

Nick said, "Probably won't. Not going to lie, there was some chemistry, but she is going to be moving soon, and — I am still married."

Marco's voice sounded light, but Nick saw a hint of seriousness in his friend's face. Marco said, "I was wondering if you remembered that little detail."

"Yeah, I was just thinking about Becky when you showed up. How is she doing?" Nick saw a sly smile cross Marco's face. "What?"

"Nothing," Marco said. Then added. "It's just the first time you have asked about her since you two split."

"No, it's not."

"Yes, I am pretty sure it is. And, for what it's worth, she's not doing very well. She's struggling, Jazz and I are worried about her. Finding out about what that couple did to her has her twisted up."

Nick gazed toward the park as he spoke. "I can only imagine how she feels. She has always been pretty modest. I hate she got treated that way. I'd like to catch that guy in an alley some time. Tell her I said it will get better."

"*You* tell her. You talking to her would do her more good than anything."

"I don't see how."

"She thinks she disgusts you — her words, not mine."

"That's crazy. I just can't…"

Marco cut him off. "Look Nick, since she found out that I saw the video, she won't even be around me. She barely even talks to Jazz. I know you're still pissed, and I am not saying you need to reconcile or anything, but this is Becky we're talking about, and she's in trouble. Swallow your pride and talk to her. Like I told you the other day, it will do you both good."

"There is nothing to say, nothing that would fix anything, anyway. I'll be honest, after all this time, the idea of seeing her terrifies me. I can't go through all that crap again."

"Nick, you don't have to fix anything. Just let her know you don't hate her."

"How do you know I don't? Lord knows I am not sure."

Marco shook his head. "Because I know both of you. You can't hate each other; neither of you have it in you."

"Maybe, maybe not. Let's drop it, okay?"

"Alright," Marco said. "So, do you wanna talk about what happened at the fire the other night?"

Nick said, "There is nothing to talk about. I just wasn't feeling great."

"Bullshit. Something is going on with you, and it's been going on for a while."

"Stop. You're making too big a deal of the other night. Let it go, Marco."

"No," said Marco. "I have been letting this go too long already. We are going to talk."

"Look, Marco…"

The tone alert stopped the conversation. *"Squad 8, assist Medic 3. Woman down, 2929 Cyprus Court. Possible domestic disturbance. Be advised PD on scene…. Repeat. Squad 8, assist Medic 3. Woman down, 2929 Cyprus Court."*

Seconds later, Nick heard Captain Janssen yell from the office doorway, "Adler, jump on with squad 8; give a hand."

*****

The blue, red and white oscillating lights of the ambulance and squad cars bathed the small yard and house. The emergency vehicles drew the predictable crowd, all gathered in their yards or on the sidewalk. Nick met Ronnie Baker at the door, a cop Nick knew from his softball league. "Hey Ronnie, what's the story?"

"Not much to tell. Same crap, new night." the cop replied. "Looks like the husband slapped the wife around and got carried away; he knocked her out, got scared and called an ambulance. A neighbor heard them going at it and called us. We found her unconscious, but she's awake now and seems okay. The asshole claims he found her on the floor. Surprise, surprise, she's not willing to say he did it. You'll find the party is in the back bedroom."

"Yeah, okay."

Nick walked into what old Lou would call a dollhouse- a basic starter home; one story, under a thousand sq feet, with 2 bedrooms. *At least it's clean*, Nick thought. He moved down a narrow hall to the bedroom. He found Kelly and Jason from Medic 1 tending to a woman on the floor. She was lying flat with a cervical collar around her neck. Kelly was applying a bandage to the back of the woman's head while Jason was taking her blood pressure. Nick noticed the angry-looking bruise around her left eye and cheek. Standing a few feet away stood the scared-looking asshole who used her for a punching bag. A cop Nick didn't know hovered near the guy, and from the look on his face, Nick guessed he was hoping for an excuse to *subdue* the asshole.

"What've you got?" Nick asked Kelly.

"Hi Nick. This is Racheal. she took a pretty good shot to the head and was out for a while. She has a decent sized scalp laceration and hematoma on the occipital. They want us to run her in for a 24-hour concussion protocol; probably a CT scan too. Can you guys package her on a long board for us?"

"No problem." Nick knelt to position himself to *log roll* the woman when, out of the corner of his eye, he noticed the picture above the bed - dozens of butterflies hovering above a single flower. He knew that picture, it was from the video. At first, he doubted himself, but his blood turned cold when he looked closely at the woman's bruised face. *It was her!* The woman in the video - Becky's video. His eyes sought the man standing a few feet away. A horrible image from the video flashed in his mind- Becky on her knees in front of a faceless man, him yanking her head back by her hair, pushing himself into her; making her gag.

His face was blurred in the video, but Nick recognized his tattoo - two snakes wrapped around his forearm. *The scared little wife beater was him* - the man who seduced his wife, who used her, who filmed her, who humiliated her. He was the man who destroyed his marriage and ruined his life. Nick looked away, trying to control the rage that enveloped him. His fury wasn't just an emotion, it was palpable; it had dimension and mass within his core. White specs floated in his vision; he felt blood rushing to his face and his mouth went dry.

Sly saw that the firefighter seemed to know him and looked pissed. He looked at the name on the coat and saw it was Adler. *Small world,* he chuckled to himself. He had never met one of the dip shits whose wife he had borrowed, and couldn't resist the chance to fuck with him a bit. *After all,* he thought, *what's he gonna do in a room full of cops?* He said, "Adler? Are you Becky's husband? How is *our* little hottie doing? Tell her Sly said…"

Something inside Nick snapped. He wasn't even aware he was moving. From his kneeling position, he exploded upward, driven by every muscle in him. His fist connected with Sly's upper jaw and nose before he finished his sentence. Nick didn't feel the contact but heard the near sickening thud of bone cracking, and saw in slow motion the disintegration of the man's face into a haze of blood.

# Chapter 9

He fidgeted with the coffee cup. The mocha tasted bitter.  He had both looked forward to and dreaded seeing Haley at the shoppe; but it hadn't turned awkward. She gave him the usual smile and had his order waiting as usual. He got her usual chirpy greeting; it was all so normal, as if nothing had changed at all between them. *Our date was no big deal after all,* he thought. That was good, that was what he wanted, but it stung a little. Deep down, he hoped she would be excited to see him.

It had been 4 days since the altercation with Sylvester Roberts; he stayed more or less drunk for three of them. Now with a head throbbing and acid reflux, he sat waiting in the reception area of the Chief's office. Nick looked at Larry Stafford, the union president. That he showed up and not a rep told Nick just how bad a mess he was in. Stafford was a short, pudgy guy - a bit of a loudmouth - but smart. Nick had known Larry for years and although he never really liked the guy, he was glad he was there. Not that he thought the Union could help him much, he just didn't want to sit alone.

The door opened and Chief Walsh walked in, followed by Deputy Chief Stevens, Battalion Chief Hicks, Captain Janssen and Marco. The procession didn't pause or speak to either of them as they filed into an adjoining conference room. Nick took it as an ominous sign that no one but Marco even made eye contact.

"Holy shit," said Stafford. "There's more brass in there than a marching band."

"Is that unusual?" asked Nick.

"Yeah, it is. I expected we would just sit with Stevens, and he'd formally notify you that you were the subject of an internal affairs investigation. Then put you on paid leave while they do their thing."

"So, what do you suppose is going on?"

Stafford sat quietly for a moment and pondered the question. He then said, "I think it means that the chief is satisfied with the information contained within the reports, and whatever interviews Stevens has already done."

"I guess I am screwed, huh?"

Larry patted Nick on the shoulder. "Don't get ahead of yourself. If the chief wants to act, he has two choices. One is that he will just suspend you; he can give you up to a month off without pay."

Nick groaned and asked, "Ouch, What's the good option?"

"Shit Nick, that *is* the good option. The bad option would be that he leaves you on administrative leave and then refers you to the board of commissioners for a formal hearing. They can suspend you for up to three months without pay, or demote you to a lower pay grade, or terminate you."

Nick had spent the last three days trying unsuccessfully to convince himself that they wouldn't fire him. His stomach rolled over when Larry said the word *termination*. "I was afraid you were going to say that," said Nick. "What's my chances?"

Larry's eyes met Nicks. "Not good; here's the down and dirty. You hit a civilian without provocation, and you put him in the hospital. One way or the other, they are going to put a big hurt on you. If he believes there were extenuating circumstances, he might only give you time off. If the chief sends it to the commission, it's because he wants you gone, and his recommendation carries a lot of weight with them. Here's the deal Nick, if they try to fire you, I promise that the union will do everything it can to fight it. But Nick, if they give you a suspension, any suspension, consider yourself lucky and accept it."

"You didn't answer the question. What do you expect?"

Stafford sighed. "A rush to judgement like this would be a mistake if he intended to suspend you. He would have had Stevens interview you at the very least. My guess is he is referring you to the commission for a full hearing."

Nick buried his face in his hands. "So, I am screwed."

Larry put a hand on Nick's shoulder. "Who knows, maybe you'll get lucky, and the Chief has an ex who cheated on him."

Nick said, "At least I won't have to wait long for the axe to fall."

*****

Chief Walsh settled into the chair at the head of the table. The other men sat and waited silently while he reviewed some documentation. After a couple of minutes, he broke the silence. "So, what are we doing here?"

Deputy Chief Stevens spoke up. "It's pretty straightforward, Chief. At around 1830 hours on Friday, Firefighter Dominick Adler was on a domestic disturbance call, and with no significant provocation, struck a bystander–one Sylvester Roberts. The attack on Roberts put him in the emergency room. Mr. Roberts got treated for facial trauma and released. PD transported Adler to the station. However, they did not book him, instead they released him into Battalion Chief Hicks's custody. Per department policy, Chief Hicks placed Adler on administrative leave pending the investigation of possible charges — and here we are. I will note that the altercation occurred in front of six witnesses, including a police officer and members of Squad Eight and Medic One. I've spoken with them, and there is no disagreement about what happened."

The Chief asked, "They didn't charge him? That's surprising."

Hicks added, "From what I gather, the cops on the scene didn't arrest Adler as a matter of professional courtesy. Plus, the so-called victim had beaten his wife up pretty bad. I guess they considered his getting punched as some street justice. For whatever reason, Roberts didn't press charges. So as far as legal implications, it looks like Adler got lucky."

Stevens said, "There may not be any criminal charges, but you can bank on the department getting sued. And it will cost us an arm and a leg."

Walsh pondered this for a moment. Then said, "The press will have a field day with this. They've already pestered the mayor for a comment. I'm sure he's worried about another fiasco like PD had last summer. He will want the guy's head on a stick." Walsh leaned back in his chair and tapped the file on his desk. "No provocation? He just up and hit the guy? Look, I reviewed this guy's records. He's as clean as a whistle. Something doesn't add up, did they have words? Does Adler and this Roberts guy have a history?"

Marco cleared his throat. "Chief, if I may?" Marco noticed a sharp look from Battalion Chief Hicks, he ignored it.

Walsh turned to Marco. "What is it, Marcus?"

"Chief, Nick…I mean, Firefighter Adler's wife and this Roberts guy had an affair. It turns out he's a real piece of work. He made a really compromising video of her without her knowledge and posted it on the internet."

Walsh winced and shook his head. He looked at Stevens and said, "Make sure that ends up in the commission report — word it delicately." Turning to Marco, he added, "So, Roberts deserved a punch in the nose, I get that. Still, it doesn't excuse his actions. Our people have to have some self-control."

Battalion Chief Hicks said, "Chief, this isn't an isolated incident. Recently, Adler had an altercation with another firefighter in the station. He also mouthed off to me at a fire. There is a pattern of inappropriate behavior here."

Captain Janssen rolled his eyes at Hicks's comment. Hicks didn't notice… the Chief did.

Marco said, "Chief Hicks is right sir, there is an escalating pattern over the last year or so. Even before he found out about his wife. I'll add that at that same fire, he had a sort of breakdown when I asked him to help me bag a burn fatality. Chief, I've known Nick Adler for a very long time. He is a good guy and a rock-solid firefighter — one of our best. All of what happened in the last few weeks was out of character for him. I am convinced there is something going on with him — something serious. I think running into this Roberts guy was the straw that broke the camel's back."

Captain Janssen noticed Hicks eyeing Marco, he didn't look happy. Sensing trouble, Janssen spoke up. "Marco is right, sir. Nick is one of our best. Marco and I have both noticed him struggling for a while. We sort of chalked it up to him being separated from his wife. But lately we got to thinking it was something else, and maybe he needed some help. We had been looking into referring him to the chaplain." This last statement wasn't true, but Janssen wanted to get in between Marco and any repercussions coming from defending Nick, especially from Hicks. He was also pissed that Hicks wasn't defending his man.

Walsh said, "What are you suggesting, Cap, PTSD? Or are you thinking psych issues, or maybe substance abuse?"

Janssen replied, "I'm not sure, but I'd be shocked if it was booze or drugs. If there is a problem there, I'd guess it's something else."

Hicks said, "Regardless of why, if Adler is acting out, he needs to be dealt with."

Marco thought, *What a dick.*

The Chief fixed his gaze on Hicks but said nothing, he only nodded. Turning to Deputy Chief Stevens, he asked, "What do you think?"

Stevens sat quietly for several moments. Walsh appreciated that Stevens never jumped to conclusions. He was always analytical and methodical. Stevens finally said, "Adler's emotional state has to be considered. If you suspend him and nothing else, and he has a problem, it will get worse, not better with time. If you send this to the commission, the union will probably make an issue of his mental and emotional state, anyway. They may force an evaluation, and the hearing will drag out for months. The press will be all over it, things could get really messy."

Walsh nodded. "The press will feast on this, regardless. We should be glad it wasn't on the street or we would be watching bystander video on CNN."

Stevens continued. "There is the probable civil suit to deal with as well. If we have some sort of documentation that Adler was suffering from a stress disorder; that coupled with his and Robert's history may limit our exposure to only actual damages and not a punitive settlement." Stevens shot a glance at Hicks, then added. "And Chief, most importantly, Adler is one of ours. If he has some sort of problem, we owe him help."

Walsh nodded, obviously pleased with Stevens' analysis. "Chris, are you suggesting Father Tom?"

Stevens nodded. "If Father Tom reports the guy just has anger issues, you can suspend him or send him downtown. Plus, if the union makes an issue of his emotional state at the hearing, we have documented that we looked into extenuating circumstances. If, on the other hand, Adler does have some sort of problem, we can deal with it. We have nothing to lose but a couple of weeks, and there is no rush."

The chief tapped his fingers on the desk. Stevens knew him well enough to know that meant he was close to a decision. "No rush? Tell that to the mayor. Still, you're right, if we fire him, we need to get our ducks in a row. And if he has some issue, I want to know what it is."

Stevens replied, "The mayor won't be happy, but it's the smart move. Like you say, it covers all the bases. I'll add, I trust Father Tom, he'll sort it out."

Walsh turned to Marco and Janssen. "Okay, Marcus and Cap, I want the two of you to write up a narrative report detailing the incidents and circumstances leading to your concerns regarding Dominick's emotional state." Turning to Hicks, he said, "Bob, work up a memo reviewing his work history, personal evaluations and any disciplinary actions. This will be an addendum to my report to the commission. Keep it strictly factual. I don't want any opinion or editorial comments. Chris, work up a report on today's meeting."

Hicks asked, "Chief, should I have Adler report for light duty while he is being evaluated? No use in giving him a free vacation."

Stevens answered for the Chief. "Keep him on administrative leave. We can always dock his pay for the time later if we suspend him. If he gets into another altercation on duty and we suspected he had issues, we are open to liability. I think it's best if he sits at home."

Walsh added, "I agree, Chris. Oh, you and I should visit the city attorney today or tomorrow and make sure we have our T's crossed and I's dotted. Tell Claire to make us an appointment." Walsh then turned to the group. "Anyone got anything to add?"

The room was silent. Walsh nodded, suggesting the meeting was over. As the men stood, he said, "Chris, stay here. Bob, tell Dominick and Larry to hang on. I'll talk to them in a minute."

Marco breathed a sigh of relief. He expected the Chief to suspend Nick; he thought sending him to the commission with a recommendation of termination wasn't likely, but who knew? The commission scared him; even if the chief didn't recommend termination, they might still make an example out of Nick. His friend wasn't out of the woods, but he at least survived today.

That the Chief ended the meeting using everyone's first name - including Nick- encouraged Marco.

*****

Nick sat listening to the hum of the fluorescent light above and muffled discussion emanating from the staff room. With each passing moment, his headache intensified, as did the nausea and acid reflux. He would have given anything for a bottle of water. After several minutes, he whispered to Stafford, "What do you think is going on in there?"

"Beats me," said Larry. "I expected their meeting to be a quick formality."

Several minutes later, Janssen, Hicks, and Marco filed out of the staff room. Hicks looked annoyed. Nick took that as a good sign. Hicks said, "The Chief wants the two of you to wait. He'll get to you in a few minutes." Janssen and Hicks moved towards the door; Marco stood looking at Nick, apparently about to say something. Hicks said, "Marco, I need to talk to you and Janssen, come with me."

When they left the room, Larry Stafford said, "Hmm, I wonder what that was about."

"Who knows?" Nick said. "Hicks is alright, but it doesn't take much to piss him off."

"If you say so, personally I never trusted Hicks; he's pulled off some petty stuff over the years."

They sat quietly for several more minutes before Deputy Chief Stevens appeared at the door. "Gentlemen, you can come in now."

"Here we go," whispered Stafford. "When we are in there, let me do the talking. Don't speak unless you're asked a question. Even then, keep it short and simple — yes and no."

Nick and Larry followed Chief Stevens into the conference room. Chief Walsh was sitting at the head of the table, he motioned them to sit close by. He nodded at Stevens, who produced a voice recorder, which he plugged into an omnidirectional mic setting on the table. Walsh nodded again and Stevens turned on the recording device and said, "This is an auditory record of a disciplinary meeting. I am Deputy Chief Christopher Stevens. I am joined by Fire Chief James Walsh, Firefighter Dominick Adler, and Union President Larry Stafford." Stevens then directly addressed Nick. He said, "Firefighter Adler, it is my duty to inform you that you are under investigation for violation of one or more department policies stemming from your alleged actions on or before the evening of March 24 of this year. You are advised that anything you say during this meeting may be used as evidence supporting possible charges of misconduct. You are obligated by department policy to cooperate with this investigation. Your failure to cooperate, or providing false statements, will be grounds for further charges. As a firefighter, you have the right to refuse answering any question which may put you in jeopardy of disciplinary action. You also have the right to union representation, or legal counsel present during this meeting. Do you understand what I have just told you?"

The weight of Stevens words, and the cold formality of how he said them, left a hollow feeling in Nick's gut. He cleared his throat and said, "Yes — Yes, I understand."

Stevens added, "For the record, Union President Stafford is present and represents Firefighter Adler at this meeting."

Chief Walsh said, "Firefighter Adler, I have read the preliminary internal investigation report written by Deputy Chief Stevens. According to his report, while on a medical assistance call, you struck and injured a civilian by the name of Sylvester Roberts. Is that factually accurate?"

Nick leaned forward in his chair. "Yes, Chief. But you need to understand that…"

Larry reached over and squeezed Nick's forearm. "Chief, Dominick does not dispute that statement."

The chief continued, "As I am sure you are aware, striking civilians is a serious violation of department regulations. I assume you also understand that the district attorney may file assault charges. Frankly, there is little excuse for such behavior, and I won't tolerate it. If found culpable, suspension and or termination are possible."

Nick's heart sank. He was sure that the next words out of his mouth would be that he was being referred to the board of police and fire commissioners for a termination hearing. He had spent 3 days preparing himself for that outcome, the reality of it still struck him hard.

The chief paused. Hearing no comment, he continued. "However, it has come to my attention that there may be possible extenuating circumstances which might have affected your behavior. As a result, I am leaving you on administrative duty and referring you to the department's counselor. He will evaluate your mental and emotional wellness and report on your fitness for duty. I order you to meet with him at his discretion and fully cooperate with his assessment. Do you understand?"

Nick said, "Chief, I don't think you…"

Again, Stafford squeezed Nick's arm. He said, "Yes Chief, he understands and will fully cooperate."

"Good," Walsh said. "This meeting is concluded. You will be notified when the counselor's assessment has been reviewed and a course of action has been determined." Walsh nodded at Stevens, who turned off the audio recorder. Walsh leaned back in his chair in a more casual posture. He said, "Okay, we are now off the record. Nothing said from here on out leaves this room. Are we okay with that?"

Nick nodded, Stafford said, "Fine."

Walsh's eyes fixed on Nick. "What the hell were you thinking? I understand why you wanted to punch the guy. Hell, I would too, but you know better. Both you and the department are going to get our asses sued off. Let me tell you, my friend, I had every intention of tossing this to the commission for a termination hearing. I still probably will, but your lieutenant and captain seem convinced your sorry ass is worth saving. They tell me you have some sort of personal problem that is messing with you. We'll see about that. To be clear, this evaluation is a formality, your ass may still be on the line."

Stafford said, "Chief, thanks for looking into it. Your restraint is appreciated."

"Larry," the chief said. "Against my better judgment, I'm throwing Nick a bone here. So, hear me, I don't want the union using this as some sort of new precedent; no demanding a psychological profile on every guy who screws up — don't screw me on this."

Larry stood up and shook the chief's hand. "We'll play nice. You have my word. Oh, and tell Donna I said hi."

"Will do, now get out. I have to explain this mess to the mayor."

When Nick and Larry made it into the waiting room, Nick whispered, "What the fuck was that?"

Larry smiled, "That was a miracle, that's what that was."

"Bullshit. The chief thinks I'm a basket case. He's evaluating me to see if I am fit to be a firefighter."

Larry shook his head. "I don't think you get what's going on. When we walked in there, you had one foot in the grave, my friend. If you convince Father Tom that you're having some sort of emotional crisis, you might just keep your job."

"I am not having an emotional crisis. I just punched out the guy who screwed my wife; even the chief said he understood. I'll take my chances with the commission giving me a few days off."

"That's not an option," Larry said. "The chief ordered you to see Father Tom, that's a done deal. Besides, if the chief thought that a few days off was appropriate, he would've done it. And if he expected the commission to go easy on you, he'd have suspended you today and saved them the trouble. No, buddy, your neck was -is - on the chopping block. The suits downtown have a lawsuit to worry about, and a bloodthirsty press. Barring special circumstances, somebody is going down, and that's you."

"This is crazy. There's nothing wrong with me."

"Okay Nick, there's nothing wrong with you. Just meet with Father Tom and convince him you were just a little freaked out. Do a couple of counseling sessions, maybe take a few weeks off, then go back to work."

"Right Larry, no problem. Just how am I supposed to convince Father Tom that I am only temporarily nuts?"

"Not nuts Nick. Just stressed out."

"Over what?" Asked Nick.

"Oh, I don't know. Maybe tell him you found out your wife was making porn movies behind your back."

"Fuck you," Nick growled.

"Look, everybody's heard the stories, probably even Father Tom. It sucks that you had to go through that, but at least you can use it to save your ass."

Nick got in Larry's face. "Yeah, I got upset about it. But I am not crazy. Me and Father Tom go way back. He's a good friend, and I respect this department. I will not run some kind of con on him or the department to cover my butt. I'm not a liar."

Larry folded his arms, obviously annoyed with the conversation. "Okay Nick, do it your way. Go to the counseling sessions and convince Father Tom that you're absolutely fine, but you just enjoy punching people in the face once in a while. When you're done with that, I suggest a visit to the unemployment office."

Nick glared at Larry, considering what he just said. "Last I heard, they don't allow crazy fuckers to be firefighters."

Larry Stafford let out a long breath. "Again, no one is saying you're crazy. The suggestion is that you are stressed out. They won't let you go for that. Even if they did, it would be an off-duty disability, or if you're lucky, even an on-duty disability. Either will provide you with a partial pension and a path to come back later. If you don't cooperate, you may well get fired, and you will lose your pension and benefits. You are hanging from a cliff, and you have just been tossed a rope. My advice to you, Nick, is to grab it."

"Okay, I will meet with Father Tom, but like I said, I won't run some kind of con. I will be honest with the guy. What happens, happens."

Larry walked away saying, "Suit yourself."

Nick walked outside and groaned. He saw Marco leaning against his car, arms folded, face grim. *Great*, he thought, *just what I need, another lecture*. When Nick got close, he said, "You fucked me."

"You're welcome." Marco replied.

"You told them I was unfit. The chief sent me to be evaluated for fitness for duty. You had no right."

"I am not so sure you *are* fit. Nick, I've been trying to get through to you for the last month. I don't recognize you anymore. You don't go anywhere, you don't do anything, and you're pissed off at the world."

"Gosh Marco, I can't imagine why. Becky…"

Marco shook his head dismissively. "Stow it. This has been going on long before you and Becky split. In fact, from what Becky says, whatever the fuck is going on with you caused your marriage problems."

"Look Marco, you're like family, so don't take this wrong. You- and Jazz too- are cordially invited to stay the hell out of my marriage. This is my life and I'm dealing with it the best I can."

"Is that right, Nick? You're dealing with it? You pushed everybody away. You don't answer phone calls, you barely talk to me or Jazz. Your marriage is on the rocks, and you haven't spoken one word to your wife in eight or nine months. You can barely control your temper, and you're one hot second away from losing your job. Yeah buddy, you're doing just great."

"You don't know what you're talking about."

Nick tried to walk away; Marco grabbed him, spun him around, and pinned him against the car. Nick felt the adrenaline surge, his body became tense as his fists clenched.

Marco said, "Yeah, that's right, Nick. Hit me, do it."

"Leave me alone, Marco. I'm tired of hearing this crap from you."

Nick relaxed so Marco released his grip. "Maybe I don't know what I'm talking about, but you're going to fucking hear me anyway. You are heading for a meltdown, and if you don't pull your head out of your ass soon, it may be too late to put your life back together. You're driving your friends away, and you're going to lose your job. If not now, it will happen eventually. And listen closely — the woman you love is going to eventually move on. You're going to end up a broken, angry shell of a man. The clock is ticking, dumb ass. So yeah, I told the chief that you needed to see a counselor. If you're pissed off about that, too fucking bad."

Marco shoved Nick back against the car and walked away.

Nick yelled after him. "If you had any idea what's it's like to lose it all you would have stood up for me. But you don't know… nobody does. I need time and space."

Marco turned back to Nick. "We all gave you that. What good has it done?"

"You couldn't leave it alone; you gave up on me man - just like Becky did. You should have had my back, instead you fucked me – just like she did. Just leave me be damn it.

"I should bail on your dumb ass. Your so messed up you don't know what is and isn't. You want space? Go fucking sink in whatever hole your digging."

# Chapter 10

Friday night promised the same routine as all the others: shower, wine, and TV. Becky tried hard to distract herself from obsessing over the pathetic mess her life became. With wine in one hand and a bagel in the other, she nestled into the couch. Well into the frustrating task of finding something - anything - she hadn't seen on Netflix, her phone dinged. The all too familiar rush of excitement surged in her… *Nick*! Her all but expired hope had rekindled when Jazz told her Marco and Nick had talked about her. Nick had even seemed a little sympathetic about what happened. *Maybe*, she thought, *maybe it's enough.*

The message came from Travis; he sent a cheesy one-word text: "Hey," accompanied by an eggplant and water splash emoji. As lame as it was, she considered taking him up on the not-so-subtle invitation. Anything other than another lonely evening of self-loathing sounded tempting; instead, she sent a thumbs down emoji and blocked his number.

An hour later, her bagel sat mostly ignored, although she was well into her third glass of wine. Julia Roberts had just told Hugh Grant that "she was just a girl," when Julia got interrupted by the doorbell. A flash of panic seized her — Travis? *No, he doesn't know where I live, and coming over would be too much effort. It's probably Jazz.* As she moved to the door, an awful notion occurred to her. *Shit, what if Marco is with her? I'm not ready to face him, not after what he saw.*

With some trepidation, she opened the door. It took her a moment to recognize the woman on her porch. Her face looked swollen and bruised. Not the usual purple bruise; it was the sickening yellow of a healing injury. The left eye's sclera was blood red. Becky said, "What the hell are you doing here?"

Racheal replied, "I need your help."

"What happened to you? Did you get hit by a bus?"

"Something like that. Can I come in?"

"Why? What do you want?"

"I need to ask a favor," Racheal said softly.

"Are you kidding me? You have some nerve asking me for anything."

"Becky, we need to talk. It's important."

Becky moved aside and pulled the door open. Racheal walked in and looked around; her eyes found the sofa in the living room, then went back to Becky. Becky made no move from the door, nor did she gesture for her guest to sit. "Okay, talk. Make it quick," she said.

Racheal sighed. "Can we sit down?"

Becky acquiesced and nodded toward the couch. Racheal sat pensively on the edge of the cushion, obviously uneasy. Becky sat in an overstuffed chair facing the sofa. She saw that the normally bubbly Racheal was near exhausted, scared, and beaten down. She also noticed her hair needed washing and her clothes looked worn and ill fitting. For several seconds, Racheal sat quietly, her tired eyes remained glued to the hands she had folded on her lap.

Becky waited, then became impatient and said, "Look, let me make this easy and quick. After what happened, we can't be friends. There is just too much… if that's why you're here."

Racheal still refrained from looking up. In a timid voice, she replied, "I know. I understand."

Unbidden, a wave of sympathy washed over Becky. The bruised face and trembling hands drained the anger from her. With a softened voice, she asked, "Would you like a glass of wine to calm you down?"

Barely above a whisper, Racheal replied, "Yes, please."

Becky went to the bar for a glass. Pouring, she asked. "He beat you up, didn't he?" Racheal emptied half the glass in a single swallow, then stared into the burgundy liquid remaining. Without looking up, she nodded agreement. Becky growled, "Someone should pound that motherfucker's face in. Give him a taste of his own medicine."

Racheal looked up with a hint of a smile, it made her wince a little. "Someone did."

"Really?" Becky said. "Good. He deserves whatever he gets. Did a pissed off husband do it?"

"Yeah, sort of. I confronted him about what he did. The cheating, the website — all of it. He tried to deny it at first, but finally admitted to it. We argued, and I told him to get out, and that I wanted a divorce. As you can see, he didn't take it very well."

Becky shook her head in disbelief. "What a prick. You should have called the police on his ass."

"Yeah, it was a mess. When he hit me, I fell and cracked my head — I was out for a while. I guess he panicked and called an ambulance. A neighbor heard the commotion and called the cops. It's all kind of fuzzy, but when I woke up, cops and firefighters were there. They took me to the hospital; they kept me overnight and most of the next day. I got a couple of stitches in my scalp."

"Did the cops arrest him?"

"No, they asked me if I wanted to press charges. I don't know why I said no, scared — I guess."

"You should have," Becky said. "He shouldn't get away with hitting you."

"That's what I want to talk to you about. I want to report the website to the police. Sly needs to pay for what he did to those women — and to us."

"You should. What's that got to do with me?"

Racheal finished her wine and said, "Sly isn't what you would call smart, but he has the survival instincts of a sewer rat. I am sure he has taken down the site and gotten rid of all the videos and cameras. I - I -was hoping that you would go with me to the police and testify, or make a statement, or whatever they call it. If we both go, they might believe us, even if the evidence is gone."

Becky shook her head. "I'm sorry, but I can't deal with that crap anymore. I just want to forget and move on. Besides, with the evidence gone, I doubt they will do much with it."

"You're probably right, but I want to try. Besides, a criminal investigation might help me in the divorce. He doesn't earn much, and I'm sure he is going to bleed me dry just for spite."

"I would think him putting you in the hospital would be enough."

Racheal met Becky's eyes. "I want him to burn, Becky. I want him to pay for what he did. Suppose you and the other women could sue him — you know, for damages."

Becky shook her head. "Racheal, I hate the bastard. I want him dead. But I won't go through that. I doubt the other women will either. And if you're going to fuck with him, you better be careful. He may hurt you."

"Yeah, my counselor at the shelter helped me get a restraining order against him. But, she said I should watch my back. A lot of husbands don't pay attention to them."

"What?" Becky said. "Why are you in a shelter?"

"They took me there from the hospital. I got nowhere else to go. He's still in the house and I won't go there while he's there. Getting a lawyer and getting him removed will take time. Even then, I won't feel safe. That's one reason I want him arrested."

"What about a hotel?"

Racheal shook her head. "The bastard emptied out our accounts and killed my credit card while I was in the hospital."

Becky suddenly understood the old clothes and unkempt hair. On an impulse she said, "I can't believe I am saying this. Do you want to stay here for a few days?"

"Thanks, that's sweet, but no. It's better I stay in the shelter for now."

A little relieved, Becky said, "Yeah, that makes sense." A thought occurred to her, and she added, "Do you need cash, maybe some clothes?"

Racheal hesitated. Her uninjured cheek turned bright red. Looking at the floor, she said, "That would be really helpful. I could actually use something to wear to the lawyers and the police station. The Shelters' emergency stuff is kinda limited. And, if you got some spares, I could use some scrubs for work, if you don't mind. I promise I will return everything."

"What about money?"

Tears were streaming down Racheal's face. She sniffed and whispered. "God, this is humiliating."

Becky stood. "Stay here; I'll get some things."

Racheal sniffed again and wiped away a tear. "Becky, wait. There is something else. That night — that Sly hit me and the cops and firefighters showed up; it was your husband who punched him."

"What? What do you mean, my husband punched him?"

"Your husband, Nick, was one of the firefighters who came to help me. I guess Sly made some smart-ass comment about you, and your husband hit him. He hurt Sly pretty bad; they took him to the hospital."

All at once, Becky felt a rush of emotion. There was a glowing sense of satisfaction that Sly got punched. Mixed with that was gratitude that Nick had stood up for her; that he cared enough to defend her.

Racheal continued, "I am not sure what all went on, but I think Nick got arrested. If I know my husband, he's going to get even. He's spiteful, he'll do everything he can to fuck over your husband — like press charges, or try to get him fired. I suppose he'll sue him too."

Panic swept over Becky. "Wait here. I have to make a phone call."

Snatching her phone off the coffee table, Becky called Marco.

He answered on the third ring. "Becky? This is a surprise."

"Why the hell didn't you tell me Nick was in jail?"

"Wait, what? Nick is in jail?"

"I just heard," Becky said. "He got arrested for punching out that creep. Has he made bail?"

"No — no. The cops took him to the station, but they let him go the same evening. He wasn't arrested, they just wanted to get him out of there."

Breathing a sigh of relief, Becky said, "So, he's okay?"

Marco paused before answering. "Well, he's in a lot of trouble at work. He may get fired."

Becky began to cry, "They can't do that. He was just defending me."

"Take it easy. He may come out of this okay. They are sending him to Father Tom for some counseling. If he cooperates, and Father Tom says that something is going on with him, they may put him in some sort of counseling program instead of firing him."

Becky sniffed. "What do you mean? What's going on with him?"

"Becky, I'm not sure what to think exactly, but Nick hasn't been right for a while. You've had to notice it too. It's like he's going through some sort of crisis or something; he's just not himself. I believe he *needs* counseling. This could be a good thing."

Becky was trying hard not to sob. "You're saying I did this? This is my fault. What I did… it messed him up."

"No, honey, not at all. It's been going on for a while. Even before — ah, you know — you and Nick split."

*My selfish crap didn't help. That's for sure,* she thought. "Marco, what can I do to help?"

"Nothing really. It's up to Nick. You know how he can be; he's stubborn and won't admit anything is wrong. I'm afraid he'd rather get fired than ask for help. He's always been one of those guys that keeps things bottled up, but lately he has really been closed off, more than usual even. If this thing with Father Tom doesn't go well, I am not sure what will happen."

"Marco, do what you can — promise me. And tell him I am praying for him, that I am here if he needs me."

"Not much I can do now. I wish you two were talking, might be you could get through to him. The damn fool needs you. He's just too proud to admit it. He's hurting; you both are, I guess."

"No chance of that," Becky said. "He hates me."

"No, he doesn't. Don't give up just yet. At least now he understands what really happened. He feels bad about what those two did to you."

"Yeah, it was him, not both of them."

"What does that mean?" Marco asked.

"It was all that son of a bitch's doing; the guy Nick punched. I wish he would've killed him." Becky looked at Racheal sitting on the couch. An idea occurred to her; she took a deep breath and asked. "Marco, do you have a copy of the video?"

"NO! Of course not. Jesus, Becky, you're sort of like my sister. I regretted seeing it the first time; I sure wouldn't keep a copy. Becky, Jazz told me you're upset about — you know — me seeing it. I put it behind me. Please don't feel uncomfortable around me."

"Yeah, that's going to take some time. But that's not why I brought it up. Does Nick still have a copy?"

Marco paused before answering. "I really don't know. It's not something we really ever talked about."

*Men,* Becky thought. *I swear they don't talk to each other about anything.* "Ask him for me."

"Ah, we should just leave that alone, don't you think? Really, it's not something I feel comfortable getting into with him. If he kept the video, he has his reasons. I'm not sure that telling him you want him to get rid of it is something he wants to hear from me, or you either, for that matter."

"No," Becky said, looking at Racheal. "I want a copy."

"Why the hell would you want that?"

"Because, one way or the other, that guy needs to pay for what he did."

"I don't follow," Marco said.

"His wife wants to have him arrested for illegally posting explicit material without consent. I want to help her lock him up."

"You should reconsider that. It probably won't work and it could get messy for you."

"Marco, that guy is going to try and hurt Nick. He's probably going to sue him and pressure the city to fire him. I can't stand by and let that happen."

# Chapter 11

Cat sat on the sofa watching Nick. A light, intermittent tap-tap of raindrops on the roof was the only disruption to the silence. A single small lamp bathed them in a dreary light. An open book lay on his lap, a glass of scotch sat on top of it. He stared blankly at the darkness outside the window, lost in thought. He wondered about Becky, why she did it, and if she really had gotten duped. Mostly, he worried about meeting with Father Tom, and what he would do if he got fired. Marco's warning repeatedly echoed in his head; "You'll end up a lonely, bitter shell of a man." The idea of losing everything, his job, his friends - Becky - it all terrified him.

Could I live like that? Would I want to?

An unwelcome memory intruded; the morning he first learned about what she had done, sitting on the bed, broken and desperate, gun in hand. He had sat staring at it all morning. When he packed to leave, a voice deep within insisted he leave it. His head told him he never intended to hurt himself. The hollow of his gut said otherwise, as did his lingering fear of seeing Becky again. She could easily crush what remained of me — then what?

If Cat knew, or cared, what Nick was thinking, she didn't let on. Nick didn't call the cat to him, even though he wanted comfort from his feline roommate. It wasn't their deal, and he assumed she wouldn't want any part of it. So, they sat, each kept to themselves.

A knock on the door startled him. It wasn't loud, but it made him jump all the same. He grunted and thought, *Marco - probably came to give more advice.* He was tired of talking, and was sure he didn't need advice, not from Marco, or Father Tom, for that matter. He wanted to be alone. *My life is fucked, and there is nothing, or no one, that can change that.* He would have ignored the door, but another thing Marco said stuck with him too. "You're driving away all your friends."

The knock came again. Nick sighed and put the book and drink aside. *Maybe I could use some company.* He looked around Casa Del Crapo, *this place is getting to me.* As he moved to the door, he decided that he and Marco, Jazz too, if she was with him, should go to Rizzi's. At least there, the conversation wouldn't get too deep. Plus, he could have Marco buy. *God knows I won't be able to afford it soon enough.* He opened the door, it took a few seconds to comprehend what, or who, he was seeing.

"Is this a good time?"

"Haley? What are you doing here?"

"I'm sorry. I shouldn't have come."

Nick gathered himself. "No, it's fine. I'm just surprised."

"It's okay I came? I should have called first."

"No, it's good to see you. Come in." *How the hell does she know where I live?*

As if reading his mind, she said, "I stopped by one of the fire stations. One of the guys told me where you live." She grinned and added, "He was very helpful. I think he thought he was doing you a favor. Don't be mad."

"He shouldn't give out home addresses or phone numbers, but it's fine I guess."

As she looked around the trailer, he noticed her nose wrinkle slightly. Her reaction embarrassed him a little. "I know. It doesn't look like much. I gave the staff the day off." She smiled; it faded when Cat walked up to sniff her. He noticed tears gather in the corner of her eyes. "Haley? What's wrong?"

"Chet died yesterday," she sobbed.

"Chet?"

"Chet is — was — my cat. Oh god, you must think I am a whack job, showing up at your door crying about my cat."

*Yeah, kind of,* he thought, but said, "No, not at all. What happened?"

"It's my fault. I took him outside to — you know, play in the grass. We've done it a lot; it's always been okay. He spotted a bird and took off. He — he got hit by a car." She was sobbing and fell into his arms. "He screamed and tried to drag himself away — his back legs wouldn't work. It was awful; he was in pain, I could tell. I wanted to pick him up, but I was afraid I'd hurt him. So, I just laid next to him until — until he passed. What else could I do? I'll never forget the way he looked at me. I felt so helpless."

Nick wrapped his arms around her. "He was glad you were there, Haley."

She sniffed. "I know it sounds silly to you, but I never saw anything die before. I loved him so much. He was all I had; you know?"

Nick looked at Cat who had returned to the couch. He thought, *Yeah, Haley, I do.* Not knowing anything else to do, he just held her and whispered, "I am so- so sorry."

She pulled away from him and used the back of her hand to wipe away the tears. "I'm really sorry for showing up like this. I know we hardly know each other. But I've spent all day feeling lost, and I don't have anybody else. Pathetic, huh? A full grown woman with a crappy job, no boyfriend, no friends and a dead cat. And I show up at your door and dump on you. I'm sorry, this was stupid. I should go."

"You're not pathetic. Trust me, I know what lonely is. I am glad you came."

Haley looked at him, grabbed his shirt, and brought her lips to his. Her kiss was tentative, and Nick resisted the urge to pull her to him. She leaned back and her eyes found his; he saw an incredible softness in her gaze. She kissed him again, fully this time. Her hand caressed his cheek, and he felt her tongue tease across his lips as if seeking access. He opened his mouth slightly, and she entered him. One of his hands gently stroked her hair, the other found the small of her back and drew her close. He felt her melt against him.

There was no clumsiness between them, no awkward false moves; Their kiss possessed the gentle passion of familiar lovers. It seemed to last minutes, although he knew it to be less. With each second, her urgency grew, and with it, his concern. She stepped back and took his hand, leading him toward the narrow hall — to the bedroom.

Nick hesitated. "Haley, this is a bad idea. You're upset — emotionally vulnerable. You'll regret this tomorrow. I don't want to take advantage of you."

She still held his hand. "You're not taking advantage. I want this. I came here knowing I wanted this."

"You were right the other night. We won't work as a relationship. Like you said, I am married, and you're looking to move on."

"I *am* moving on — sort of," she said. "I called my parents, and I am moving back home in a few days. It's time I got my life together. I am not doing any good here. I want to start over."

"You said you don't do one-night stands."

Softly, she said, "I usually don't. Nick, I'm a grown woman. I know what I am doing, and why. We both want this; why are you making this hard?"

Confusion and trepidation seized him. The young, cute, flirty girl was gone; a beautiful woman stood in her place, vulnerable, but seductive. He couldn't deny the attraction, or that he had fantasized about her after their date. Still, uncertainty and nerves competed with his growing desire. It had been a long time since he had been with a woman, and what seemed a lifetime since he had been with anyone but Becky.

"Please, Nick. I don't want to be alone anymore. I know we are practically strangers, but can you pretend you care for me? I need to be touched, to connect and feel loved. Can you do that for me?"

"I — don't have any condoms." Nick said.

She blushed, then said, "I brought some. Like I said, I came here for this, for you."

Nick nodded and led her to the bedroom. Standing by the bed, she kissed him again. Her fingers found *him* and squeezed; her other hand fumbled with the zipper of his jeans. Her eager aggressiveness surprised him; he expected her to be timid. He broke the kiss and pulled his t-shirt over his head and pulled off his pants. While he did, she slipped out of her shorts and top. Her arms went around his neck and her lips found his. He unclasped her bra, and he caressed her back. Her hand found his now naked manhood.

She broke off the kiss, sat on the edge of the bed, took him in her mouth for a moment, then laid back, her hair spilling out around her shoulders. Nick slid off her tiny black thong and lightly traced his fingers across her thighs. *My God*, he thought, *she is beautiful*. Her eyes fixed on his - he saw no hesitation in them. Haley reached up and pulled him down to her; they shared a long, gentle kiss. Nick's lips found her neck, then her breasts. Pausing there only briefly, he slowly kissed and nibbled ever lower until he reached her sex. When his mouth found her, she let out a soft moan as her hips rose to meet his tongue. He was slow, deliberate, relishing her scent, her taste, her wetness. She gasped and gripped his hair as his tongue found her most sensitive flesh. Too soon, he felt her pull him up and away. She whispered, "Later. I need a connection, not an orgasm."

Nick stood and reached for one of the condoms she tossed on the bed. Haley sat up; her mouth went to his erection as she took the small package from his hand. She opened it, rolled it on him, then laid back. She wrapped her legs around his back, pulling him toward her. Nick pushed gently into her, waiting for her body to accommodate him. They groaned in unison at their coupling. His arms went under her knee's and he lifted her legs and hips. He pushed into her again, more forcefully.

She reached for him and pulled his face to hers. "Don't fuck me — love me, I need tenderness."

Nick understood. He bent down and kissed her lightly, his hands stroked her face and hair. The position was awkward for him, so a few moments later, he slipped his hands under her back and lifted her. As if they had been together many times before, she instinctively wrapped her arms and legs around him as he picked her up. Still joined with her, he turned and sat on the bed. She sat in his lap, and for a while she barely moved. They simply held each other, kissed and stroked each other's skin. Soon, she started to undulate on him, slowly at first. As she moved, they never broke eye contact. Eventually, her pace quickened, and she ground down on him. The growing passion in her mesmerized him, he watched as she embraced pleasure. After several minutes, she pushed him onto his back and rode him in earnest. It didn't take long until her breathing became labored, her eyes closed, and her head fell forward. She stopped moving, a loud moan, and the familiar rhythmic contractions in her core told him she was slipping over the edge. The sheer beauty and eroticism of her release pushed Nick to the brink. He grabbed her face with both hands and whispered, "You are so beautiful."

She replied, "Finish."

He pushed up into her a few times and let himself go.

Haley collapsed down on him. Her tangled hair covered his face, and he felt her hot breath on his neck and cheek. He wrapped his arms around her and pulled her close. He relished the softness of her dewy skin on his, and the sweet scent of her hair.

She whispered in his ear, "Thank you. You were wonderful."

Eventually, she rolled off of him and laid her head on his chest. His breathing fell in sync with hers, slow and lazy. For the first time in months, he felt peace.

They lay together for a long while and Nick was about to doze off when he felt her fingers exploring his chest and abdomen. He enjoyed the caress.

"Nick?" she whispered.

"Hmmm."

"Remember what you were doing before, and I said later?"

It took a second, but he soon realized what she meant. "Again?"

"I've had, you know, fantasies about us together, but this is real. I don't want to waste it. Have you thought about me — us, like this?"

He said, "Yeah, a few times. So, our date wasn't just hanging out, huh?"

"I didn't lie. It was what I said it was. Girls have thoughts like guys do. It doesn't mean they intend anything. But yeah, I thought you were hot." She took his hand and placed it on her breast. "What was it like when you thought about us?"

He replied, "Pretty much like what just happened. You?"

"That night after our date, I dreamed about us together. You wanted me. I invited you in, and we ripped each other's clothes off and went at it like animals. You took me, like you were possessed, like you *had* to have me."

"Hmm," said Nick. "I had you pegged for innocent and timid. You're a naughty one."

"Believe me, this is out of the norm for me. I can't believe I am about to say this but, the last time was sweet and wonderful; It's what I needed. Now I want the fantasy, fuck me like you mean it."

He found it hard to wrap his head around sweet young Haley being so raw, but it sent a thrill through him. 45 minutes later, they lay in the tangled bed sheets, spent, sweaty and out of breath. Panting, Haley gasped, "Holy hell — you — you're a freaking beast. I've never had it like that before. I think I have a new kink."

Nick was too winded to talk, so he just said, "Thanks."

"I need some water."

"Me too," said Nick. "Stay here, I'll get us some."

Haley sighed. "I couldn't move if I wanted to."

Nick walked through the living room to the kitchen. Cat sat on the couch appraising him. He swore she looked disappointed in him. "Mind your own business," he said.

He pulled two water bottles out of the refrigerator, opened one, and drank half in two large gulps. As he put the cap back on the bottle, he heard a knock at the door. *Are you fucking kidding me? Now Marco? Now you show up?* Annoyed, he was about to open the door when he realized that Jazz might be with Marco- and he was naked. *Fuck it*, he thought, *serves them right.*

Positioning himself behind the door, he opened it a crack. He was stunned to see his wife standing on the porch.

"Can I come in?" said Becky.

"What? Why are you…"

"Please Nick."

"Um, give me just a second. Let me grab some pants."

Becky smiled as she watched her husband's bare ass cheeks retreat down the hall. She had all but forgotten what a cute butt he had.

Nick grabbed some shorts that laid on top of the washer in the hall, he heard Haley in the bathroom. A small panic set in as he returned to the door. "Becky, what are you doing here?"

"I know you don't want to, but we need to talk. I just found out about what's going on with you. There are some things you need to know."

"Look," said Nick. "This isn't a good time."

Becky pushed the door open. "I know I should've called first, but I didn't think you would answer. It won't take…"

Becky's face froze, and her eyes went wide. Nick followed her gaze; he saw Haley walking naked out of the hall. When Haley saw the two of them, she shrieked, tried to cover herself, and dashed back towards the bedroom.

Becky stammered, "Oh shit. I — I'm sorry. I didn't know — I didn't realize you had company." Before Nick could reply, Becky ran down the steps to her car. She was gone in an instant.

Nick watched her drive away and said, "Damn it. What the hell?"

He closed the door, retrieved the two water bottles, and walked back to the bedroom. Haley had put on her panties and was hooking her bra. She said, "I should go."

Nick thought a moment, then said, "No, don't."

"Are you sure? I think I better," said Haley.

"Yeah, I'm sure." Nick slipped off his shorts and laid back down on the bed.

"I guess that was your wife. I told you, I don't do complicated, if you and her are…"

"Really Haley, it's okay. I am as surprised as you are."

What do you think she wanted?" Haley asked.

"No idea. It's the first time I've seen her since we split."

Haley teased. "Maybe it was a booty call?"

Nick chuckled and said, "That's unlikely."

Haley dropped her bra on the floor and climbed onto the bed next to him.  "She's pretty."

"Yeah, I suppose so."

They lay quiet for a minute before Haley asked, "What happened with you two?"

"I told you, she cheated on me."

"You told me it was a one-time thing, right?"

"That's what she claims. "

"Do you think she still loves you?"

A lump suddenly grew in Nick's throat. It always did when he tried to talk about Becky. "She says she still loves me. That it was just a big mistake. It's all such bullshit. You don't cheat on people you love."

Haley sat up and looked at him. "It happens more often than you would think. Sometimes, love and sex have nothing to do with each other."

Nick shook his head. "You've been cheated on; you know what that betrayal feels like. How can someone do that to somebody they love?"

Haley shook her head. "I get what you're saying, and sometimes people are just selfish. They want something new, or something exciting. But sometimes, people *need* something, they get confused and lost. Sometimes, you need to look past the pain they cause. Like I did with my ex."

"No offense, Haley, that's bullshit. You're giving people too much credit. I'm glad you made peace with what he did, but it was different with him."

Haley took Nick's hand. "Yeah, it was different. He fell in love with someone else, and that's worse. At least your wife still says she loves you."

"Okay Haley, you got it figured out. You tell me, why does a woman in love cheat?"

"Don't get mad. I'm just saying that even good people can stumble."

Nick sighed. "You say that, but why cheat?"

"Different reasons for different women, I guess. You're going to think I'm awful, but I cheated on a boyfriend once."

"I find that hard to believe. You don't seem the type."

Haley said softly, "That's the thing. Given the right circumstances, anybody's the type. For me, I needed validation, I guess. I loved the guy I was with, but he got distant. I found myself competing for his attention. He kept me at arm's length for weeks at a time, would barely talk to me, and sometimes I felt like I annoyed him when I tried to talk to him. He shut me out, I was with him, but I really wasn't part of his life. I just felt worthless."

Nick shook his head in disbelief. "He sounds toxic. Why didn't you just break up with him?"

"That's the thing. I loved him; or at least who I thought he was, sometimes it was great between us — sometimes. Anyway, one night I was feeling so sorry for myself, and desperate, and I hooked up with a guy I knew from school. He was there for me, sort of like you tonight. It was a stupid, one night thing and I felt horrible about it when it was done. I guess that's why I don't do one night stands."

"No offense but I think you believed you loved him, but you really didn't."

"No, you're wrong. I did, still kinda do. I left him because I needed more than he could give."

"Maybe,' Nick said, "but that still isn't Becky and me."

"Nick, I don't know what your deal with your wife was. I'm just saying that it's possible that she could love you and still have been with someone else. It's shitty, but it happens."

Nick sighed. "Marriage means putting all that aside."

"I guess," said Haley. "Did she say why she did it?"

"No. we never talked about it. When I found out, I packed my stuff and left. She sent some texts and tried to call, but we haven't spoken since."

"How long were you married?" she asked.

"Twelve years."

"Shit, you walked out on a twelve-year marriage without saying a word to her? You just left? That's cold."

"Well," Nick said, "this conversation is a real mood killer."

Haley patted his thigh. "I'm sorry. You sure you don't want me to get out of here?"

Nick stroked her arm. "Actually, I was hoping you would spend the night."

Haley smiled. "I'd like that. But I have to warn you, I get kinda frisky in the morning."

Nick chuckled. "You're going to kill me."

"I hope not, we have three more condoms left."

They got under the covers, he wrapped her in his arms and kissed the top of her head. "Goodnight," he whispered.

"Nick?"

"Yeah?"

"This night has been special. I mean it, really special, but we won't see each other again. I am leaving soon; you get that right?"

"I know."

She wiggled closer, and he felt her body relax against his. As he waited for sleep, he thought about Becky, about her seeing him and Haley together. For a moment, he felt a little satisfaction at getting even, it didn't last. A nagging worry replaced it; even after all that had happened, he couldn't bring himself to want to hurt her. Laying in the dark, pressed against another woman, he wondered what she was feeling, if she was okay. To himself he said, *I am sorry, Becky. You shouldn't have seen that.*

A surprising thing happened just before he drifted off. He felt Cat jump on the bed and lie next to Haley. He sensed she stroked her. Haley sighed and heard Cat purr.

# Chapter 12

The aging priest studied the papers in front of him. Shaking his head, he said softly, "Dominick, my boy, what's going on with you?" The report was surprising. Dominick had struck a citizen while on a call and had one or more near altercations with other firefighters. The priest found it difficult to believe. He had known Nick for years, and violence seemed so unlike him. Now, the chief was asking for an assessment of Dominick's emotional fitness, and if substance abuse was indicated.

The chief's report and request were straightforward enough, but this was the first time the department had ordered this type of assessment. He felt conflicted about the mandate. Of course, it was important for firefighters to be diagnosed and treated, but reporting a problem to the department felt duplicitous. It felt especially uncomfortable because he and Dominick were friends.

He considered the ethics involved. As a priest and a counselor, he had an absolute obligation to maintain confidentiality. However, his contract with the department required reporting any condition that could pose a threat to a firefighter patient or to others. The priest understood he had to walk a very fine line. He sighed, "Dom, my boy, I wish you had come to me earlier, and of your own volition. It would have been better for both of us."

Nancy cracked the door open and, leaning in, said, "Father, Dominick Adler is here."

"Thank you, Nancy. Put him in the study, please. I'll be along in a minute."

She scolded, "I don't *put* people in places like knick knacks, but I will *show* him to the study."

"Well, you're in a mood. Fine, and while you are *escorting* him, would you be so kind as to get him some water or coffee?"

"I offered. He said he was fine."

"Good, Thank you." As she closed the door, he added, "Now that I think about it, I'd like a cup."

A frown crossed the dour woman's face. "You've had two cups this morning already. That's enough."

"Good grief woman, another cup won't hurt anything."

"Your blood pressure was high yesterday. You're lucky I gave you a second one."

"You're a coffee miser, Mrs. Holthouse."

"There is decaf," she replied.

"Lord have mercy, and may the saints save us from decaf coffee."

Nancy waved off his objection. "*Somebody* needs to look after you, that's for sure. You'll be asking for mercy when you're on the floor with a stroke."

"As the bible says, 'The quality of mercy is not strained. It is twice blessed: It blesses him that gives and him that takes.' There is a message there you should heed."

She shook her head. "That's Shakespeare, not the bible."

He laughed. "Are you sure? Oh, well no matter, I'm sure the bible says something useful about mercy too."

She exhaled in mock exasperation. "I'm sure it does. You might try reading it sometime. I hear tell some priests find it quite instructive. Do you want the decaf or not?"

Father Tom laughed. "No. Be gone, and torment me no more."

As she closed the door, she said, "Gladly, and don't keep Mr. Adler waiting. You know how easily you get distracted."

He smiled at the door for several seconds after she closed it. Nadine -Nancy for short- Holthouse had been there when he arrived 20 years ago and had started with the parish almost 20 years before that. They had grown close over the years; he had helped her cope with the loss of a son and husband, she with the loss of his mother. Nancy was as close to family as anyone he had left.

*She seems snippier than usual*, he thought. *I wonder if she is down in the back again.*

He returned his attention to the papers. Marco's report concerned him. Marco believed that Nick was struggling with his separation from Becky, and maybe something else. Tom frowned at this; he had married Rebecca and Dominick. Their separation was so very disappointing; they were both such lovely people. *I thought they would be together for the long haul. Why didn't they reach out if they were struggling?* He read with interest Marco's observations about Dom's behavior- withdrawn, irritable, restless. Setting the papers down, he stood, and he said, "Well, Dominick, let's see what's what."

Father Tom found Nick in the study; his back was to the door, scrutinizing the picture wall. The priest appraised his friend for a few seconds before speaking. He looked thinner, and he lacked his normal deep summer tan. The priest also noted Nick's bearing, standing instead of sitting, arms crossed, feet set apart. *He's uncomfortable*, he thought. "Dominick, it's good to see you!" He noted Dom had noticeably flinched. *Hmm,* he thought, *obviously on guard, but still startled by unexpected noise.*

Nick spoke without turning his attention from the wall. He tapped a framed diploma. "A Master's degree from Notre Dame, pretty impressive. I didn't know you were a shrink."

Father Tom replied, "I'm not. When people say 'shrink', they mean a psychiatrist. I studied behavioral therapy."

"What's the difference?"

"A medical degree, and about $40 an hour in fees," the priest quipped. "I haven't seen you in a while — more than a year, I believe. I wish you and Becky had come to the Christmas party."

Nick finally turned to face the priest. "Yeah, sorry about that. Life just gets away from you, you know."

"How is Becky?" He watched closely for Nick's reaction, looking for micro-expressions that might indicate stress. Nick's reaction was far from micro- the jaw had set, and the brow furrowed. Most telling was a loss of eye contact.

"You would have to ask her," said Nick. "We split up eight — no, nine months ago."

"I am truly sorry to hear it. How are you handling it?"

"I think *you're* supposed to be the one telling *me* how I'm doing. That's what I'm here for, right?

"Oh?"

Nick fixed a hard stare at his old friend. "Look, Father, let's not dance around. I know you're supposed to evaluate whether I'm losing it and report to the chief."

"You always were one to get to the point, Nick, so I'll put my cards on the table. Yes, I will send a general report to the chief about your fitness for duty. But understand this — people who know and care about you believe you're struggling. My first priority is to make sure you're doing okay, and help if I can."

Nick inhaled deeply, finally he said, "If you want to help, write a note to the chief, telling him I am fine. That I just lost my temper for a moment, and I'm good to go back to work. This is all foolish."

"Well, that's blunt," said the priest. "But I am afraid we are going to have to give the chief his money's worth. Speaking of the chief, I want you to know that I will report on your fitness for duty, but nothing you say here will leave this room. You can speak freely, it's important we are honest with each other."

Nick shook his head in disappointment. "Okay, Padre, it's your party. Let's find out if I am off my rocker."

"Do you think you're Napoleon? Or do you believe that a cabal of alien mutants are stealing your thoughts?"

"What? No, of course not," replied Nick.

"Well then, let's assume your rocker is still firmly planted beneath you — at least for the moment." Father Tom noted a hint of a smile, and some, not all, the tension eased from Nick's shoulders.

Nick shrugged and said, "Okay, let's get this over with. How do we start? Am I supposed to lie on the couch and tell you all about how my mother didn't love me?"

"I've met your mother several times; she's a lovely woman. And I'll thank you to keep your feet off my furniture. That couch is expensive. How about you park your rump in that chair, and we'll just talk?"

Nick sat and said, "Look, Father, I appreciate your taking time for me, and it's always good to see you, but this is a waste. I don't need counseling."

"Perhaps, but you're here, so why not make use of it? Let's talk."

"Sure, what do you have in mind?"

Father Tom leaned forward in his chair. Placing his elbows on his knees, he rested his chin on his folded hands. "That was quite a bombshell you dropped on me about Becky and you splitting. What happened there?"

"I imagine you heard the stories," said Nick.

"One of the many blessings of the priesthood is that I am spared from the constant prattle of gossip. It seems most folks are hesitant to share salacious stories with the clergy."

"Well, there's not much to tell. She cheated on me."

"Oh no," said the priest. "I'm so sorry. That must've been very painful."

"Yes, it was. But I'm adjusting."

"Had the two of you been having problems for a while?"

"I didn't think so," said Nick.

Father Tom leaned back in his chair. He noticed the building strain on Nick's face. "So, it took you by surprise?"

"Yeah, you could say that."

"Has she taken up with this man? Are they still together?"

Nick's chin fell close to his chest as he slowly shook his head. He took a deep breath, then answered, "No, it was a one-night stand. At least, that's what she says. She also says he was the only one. Like I said, that's what she says."

"You don't believe her?"

"Honestly, Father, I don't know what to believe. But — I suppose I do."

"I have to tell you, Dom, I'm shocked. It seems so out of character for Becky."

Nick ran his hand through his hair. "I guess you never know about people; they lie and cheat all the time. In the end, we're all sinners and psychos. I guess that's what keeps priests and therapists in business."

"That's a bit cynical, don't you think?"

"Maybe," Nick said, "but I haven't seen much evidence to the contrary."

"Why do you think she did it?"

"Who knows? She did it; does it really matter why?"

"It should matter — at least to you."

Nick looked uncomfortable now. "If you say so, but I honestly don't know."

"Okay, what did she say when you confronted her?"

"I don't want to talk about this. Let's get to why I am here."

"Your marriage is important, don't you think? What did she say?

"She didn't say anything. When I found out, I left a note and took off. We haven't spoken since."

"Why?"

"Because I was—I - I just did, okay?" stammered Nick.

Nick looked beyond uncomfortable now; he was close to unloading but resisting. Father Tom suspected that whatever was going on with Nick was being fueled by his feelings about Becky. The split probably wasn't the cause, but it *was* gas on the fire. He said, "A few seconds ago, you said that she claimed that her infidelity was a onetime thing. So, I guess you have talked, at least some."

Nick shifted in his seat. "No, we haven't talked. She sent me a bunch of texts and voice mails. We haven't spoken since I found out about what she did. She wants to talk, I don't. It's messed up, everybody says so, I get it."

"So, tell me, do you think Becky is a dishonest, cruel woman who didn't care about hurting you? Or — do you think something pushed her to it?"

Nick barked, "Pushed her to it? What the hell does that even mean? I don't know what she was thinking — she did it; enough said. This is not why I am here. Now, can we change the subject?'

Father Tom realized he had pushed too hard. He could see the tension building. Nick's posture was rigid, his face was flush and his breathing shallow and rapid. He realized then that Nick was closer to losing control than he had realized. De-escalating the moment, he said, "Okay, Dom, what do you think we *should* talk about?"

"How about the reason they sent me here? It's about punching that guy out, right?"

"Okay, let's talk about that. Why did you punch him?"

"Because," Nick said, "He was a piece of shit, and he deserved it."

"Why? Why did he deserve it?"

Through a clenched jaw, Nick snapped, "You know damn well why."

"Nick, let's stop focusing on what I do or don't know, or what I do or don't think. What's important is what *you* think. Why did you punch him out?"

Nick let out an insincere chuckle. "That's just it. That's why this whole mess is so stupid. I hit the guy because he was the one who slept with Becky. The department is making a big deal out of all of this, and it's bullshit. What is so unreasonable about a guy punching out the guy who screwed his wife?"

"Because you were on duty, and it was eight months after the fact. Do you think that kind of rage is normal months later? It sounds like you were out of control."

Nick sighed and said, "Okay, I admit it was stupid. I made a mistake, but it's not like it wasn't a fairly reasonable one. The guy made a remark about Becky. He was fucking taunting me about screwing my wife… pardon my language. He deserved it."

The priest paused for a moment, letting Nick settle. "And what about the altercation you had with Firefighter Jenkins? Did he say something about Becky too? Why did you try to punch him out?"

Nick began fidgeting with one of the buttons on his shirt. With his eyes focused on a nearby picture, he said, "That's an exaggeration of what happened. We just had words. I didn't really try to punch him, and for the record, he *did* make a comment about Becky."

"Nick, be honest. Do you think your response to those situations was appropriate?"

"I already said they were a mistake. Yes, I lost my temper, and I shouldn't have. But I *was* provoked, and under the circumstances my behavior was kind of understandable, don't you think?"

Father Tom sat back in his chair. "I'll tell you what I *do* think. I have known you since you were barely more than a kid. In all that time, I've never seen or heard of you being inclined towards violence. In fact, you are usually one of the most even-tempered and self-controlled people I know. You *tell* me — and be honest, do you think that the way you handled those situations is consistent with who you are as a person?"

Nick practically growled. "That's one of those loaded questions psychiatrists ask. I am not even sure what that means."

The priest ignored the jab. "Let me rephrase then. Would the Dominick of 2 years ago be surprised by the behavior of the Dominick of today?"

"I don't know — maybe — maybe not. But I'll tell you this; the guy deserved what he got, and Becky too, for that matter. Everybody seems worried about why I hit him, and why I don't talk to Becky, and why poor Becky cheated on me with that piece of human waste. Yes, I messed up, but what's getting lost in all this nonsense is that I'm the victim here. Fuck this whole thing. I am tired of it. MAYBE I SHOULD KILL HIM AND THEN THEY COULD JUST LOCK ME UP AND BE DONE WITH IT. I'd be better off."

"Dominick! Take a breath and calm down."

Nick rubbed his face with both hands for several seconds. "Sorry Father. Look, I admit I kind of lost it there for a few seconds. I also admit that I've been under some stress lately. But I swear to you, I'm okay. There's nothing going on with me that a little time won't cure. I am okay to be at work."

Father Tom nodded and leaned forward toward Nick. "Some stress? Eight months after your separation, and you lose control at the mention of your wife's name? Talking about her, you were on the edge of a meltdown. My boy, you're twisted up so tight you're about to explode."

Nick seemed to deflate in his chair. "Is that what you are going to tell the chief; that I'm about to explode?"

"I am not going to tell the chief anything just yet. We should meet again. I will tell you this much; you need to resolve your issues with Becky. I strongly advise you to sit down with her and talk."

"You think so? Everybody tells me that I owe it to her, but I have to tell you I don't think I owe her anything."

"As a priest and a marriage counselor, I would argue that you are wrong. You do owe it to her — and your marriage to at least try to be civil. But that's not why I'm telling you to meet her. As your therapist, I'm telling you that you haven't had closure. The way things got left is like an open wound inside you. It's been several months, and you haven't even begun to adapt. For your own sake, and for your own emotional well-being, you need to talk to her. You need to hear why she did what she did, and most importantly, you need to tell her how she hurt you. I also think you need to be honest with yourself about what you really want."

"What I want? What's that supposed to mean?" asked Nick.

"It's been nearly a year; you haven't filed for divorce, nor have you tried to reconcile. You obviously still have a strong emotional connection to her, hence the frustration and anger. My boy, you are stuck in purgatory. And until you make peace with your feelings about your marriage, one way or the other, nothing else is going to get better."

Nick nodded in resignation. "So, you're saying that if I work things out with Becky, everything gets better? That's your solution, forgive and forget?"

"No," said the priest. "As your friend and spiritual advisor, I hope you and Becky can work things out. And I would love to sit down with the two of you in couples' counseling. But my point is this; whether you and Becky make it or not, whatever is going on with you won't get any better until you get closure with her. It's a start, not an end."

"I have to tell you, the thought of confronting her, and hashing all of that out scares the bejesus out of me."

"Why? What scares you about confronting her?"

"I am afraid I'll say some things I shouldn't, that she will too — things I don't want to hear."

Father Tom asked, "What are you afraid she will say?"

"Whatever she gives as an excuse, it will still boil down to the same thing. I wasn't enough, I failed her. True or not, it's what she believes or she wouldn't have — you know."

"Nick, trust me, the fear is worse than the pain. You need to let go of your anger; you're knotted up inside and that is a loose thread. The first step is to put everything in the open."

"I'll try."

"Good, and my advice would be to do it sooner rather than later. So, other than dealing with the breakup, how are things?"

Nick Shrugged. "Fine, I guess."

"You look thin; is your appetite good? Are you eating okay?"

"Yeah," said Nick, "I suppose."

"How about sleep? You look a little haggard."

"I'm fine, mother."

Father Tom held his gaze. "I am not making idle chatter. How are you sleeping? Is there insomnia or nightmares?"

Nick let out a breath. "Alright—yes, I have had trouble sleeping the last few months. I think it's because my new place doesn't suit me."

"How many hours do you sleep?"

"Four or five most nights, Sometimes more, sometimes less."

"What are you doing for fun?"

"I read a lot."

"That's it? Any social activities?"

"Not so much. What's with all the questions?"

The priest leaned back in his chair. "Just trying to get a picture of your new lifestyle. Nick, do you feel blue a lot?"

"My wife cheated on me. I am living in a crappy trailer, and I'm probably going to lose my job. So yeah, I get to feeling sorry for myself now and again, but I'm not depressed if that's what you're getting at."

"Are you drinking more than you used to?"

"I don't have a drinking problem," Nick said.

"Good, that's good. You won't have any problem quitting. Until I say otherwise. I'd like you to avoid alcohol altogether."

"Why?"

"Alcohol is a depressant; it alters mood and metabolism. Until we understand what's going on with you, I'd prefer you weren't self-medicating."

"Like I said, I don't have a drinking problem."

"Again, good," said the priest. "You won't have a hard time stopping. It's important, Nick. I need you to stay away from booze and any mood-altering medications."

"Fine."

"Do you ever feel angry or anxious for no particular reason?" asked the priest.

Nick shook his head, "No—not really. These questions are making me a little uncomfortable though."

The priest noticed that Nick's eyes darted upward and his lips pursed before answering the last question. Both gestures suggested a lie. "One last question. Do you ever feel like you want to hurt yourself or others?"

Nick's face reddened, and his fist knotted. "You're kidding, right?"

*He deflected the question. That's a big red flag. Enough for today,* he thought. "Nick, I know this is hard for you, but it's important. I want to see you again next week. Let's say Thursday."

"Honestly, Father, I don't see what else we have to talk about. I see what you mean about me and Becky—we should talk. Maybe I didn't deal with the split very well, I get that. I can fix that. How about you consider just sending a letter to the chief saying that I got stressed out over a personal issue and that I'm fine to go to work?"

Father Tom stood up, indicating the session was over. "Sorry, Dominick. Like I said earlier, you're dealing with Becky is a beginning, not an end. We need to talk more about why you reacted the way you did. One more thing, I've got some homework for you. I want you to schedule a daily physical activity. Every day, you need to get out; golf, go to the gym, take a walk — I don't care what, but something around other people would be best. Whatever it is, make it a regular routine."

Nick sighed. "Okay."

"One last thing. I want you to think about something. If, six months from now, your life was perfect, what would it look like? Make some notes, I'm going to want to talk about that."

"You're kidding right? Is that something you learned at *shrink* school?" asked Nick.

Father Tom guided Nick towards the door. "It's how I justify my exorbitant fees. Stop by Nancy's desk on your way out and have her set you up for an appointment for Thursday."

Father Tom had just started dictating some notes into his voice recorder when Nancy entered the room. She said, "I see you wanted to meet with him again. How is Dominick?"

"I'm afraid storm clouds have gathered above the house of Adler."

Nancy shook her head dismissively. "I'm not surprised, considering what his wife did to him. Cheating is bad enough, but what she did was just shameful."

"Oh, and just what have you heard about that?"

"Well, I'm sure that I won't be repeating it. Let's just say that she acted disgracefully."

The priest frowned and admonished her. "Indeed, you would do well not to repeat it. You would, in fact, do well not to listen to gossip in the first place."

Nancy protested, "I am just saying — what she did…"

"Judge not, lest ye be judged. Matthew seven, verse one. See, I *do* read the Bible once in a while."

A wry smile crossed Nancy's face. "I stand corrected. As penance,. I'll give you that coffee now."

"After the morning I've had, bourbon would be more worthy of the task."

"You'll settle for coffee," said Nancy. As she closed the door, she added, "Although, wait until 5 o'clock; I'll try to round up a little something. I may even join you; my back's been bothering me all day and it might help."

# Chapter 13

Becky waited impatiently. She felt the urge to act quickly, to do something - anything. For months, she had hoped against hope that Nick would reach out; wishing he would come home, or call, even send a text- anything. She needed an opportunity to explain, to ask for forgiveness, to maybe rebuild their life together. Now the thing she had once so desperately wanted broke her heart.

It was a simple text message, abrupt and to the point. It said, *We need to talk. If you're off work next Saturday morning, meet me at the park where we used to go hiking... 10 AM?* She had replied with an equally simple, *Okay.*

Over the last few months, it became hard to dismiss the inevitable; still, she clung to a sliver of hope. But now, after the god-awful episode at his trailer, she knew it was over. The unthinkable had really happened. Nick wasn't one to sleep around. She knew there could be only one explanation for his wanting to talk now; he found someone new and wanted a divorce.

Seeing that naked woman with him struck her like a punch to the gut. Shock became panic, then an immense and heavy sadness. Before she had driven halfway home, the sadness gave way to a sense of betrayal. She knew jealousy wasn't fair, not after what she had done with Racheal and Sly - and then with Travis. Still, seeing him with someone else hurt – incredibly so. Adding insult to injury, the little slut was young, much younger than herself; and gorgeous. She had nearly talked herself into going back to Nick's trailer and confronting the woman who stole *her* man, but knew that was foolish. So, she did what she could do – cry.

Over the next few days, her more rational self realized that she couldn't be angry with Nick, or even the woman, for that matter. Yet her pain and anger deepened. *Sure,* she told *herself; I screwed up, but if given the chance to tell Nick in my own way and at the right time, we could have worked it out. No, it was that bastard posting that video that ruined everything. Nick's hate for me, my humiliation, Rachael's pain- everything. It's all on Sly.*

Like a mantra, her mind came to focus on a single, near obsessive thought; *That monster must pay.*

"Finally," she said.

Becky watched as Racheal bounced down the steps of the shelter. She looked better, more like herself. The swelling in her face was down, and the bruises were fading. Becky smiled as she noticed Racheal wearing one of the outfits she had lent her. *It was cute on her;* she thought.

As Racheal opened the door to the car, she said, "Your text was a surprise."

"Yeah, it surprised me too," said Becky. She put the car in drive, then asked, "How are things going?"

Racheal shrugged as she fastened her seatbelt. "Better I guess, a little. Where are we going?"

Becky replied, "I thought we would grab some lunch and talk. I decided I am all in with helping you deal with Sly. I'll do anything I can."

"Really?  What changed your mind?" asked Racheal.

"The more I think about it, the more I realized he needs to pay for what he did. I don't want him to get away with it."

Racheal's brow furrowed. "Yeah, we need to talk about that. Oh, and make the restaurant cheap, something like McDonald's. Money is still pretty tight."

"Don't worry about it. I'm buying."

They had grabbed fish tacos from one of the food wagons in Hempstead Park and were sitting at a nearby picnic table. Racheal said, "Man, these are awesome, the food at the shelter is pretty bleak."

"Do you need more cash, or anything? We can run by a store later."

"No, I'm good for now. Besides, you've done enough already. More than I would expect, given the circumstances."

"I'm happy to help. By the way, sorry I was so hard on you before. I was upset, I thought you and Sly…"

Racheal took Becky's hand. "No, really, I understand. This is nice though; I miss hanging out with you."

An unexpected wave of warmth came over Becky. This was really the first time that she and Racheal had been together and talked since *that* night, at least talked normally. The feeling of Racheal holding her hand triggered an odd realization, one that Becky avoided until now. *I actually had sex with this woman. It seems so unreal now.* The memories she long pushed away came flooding back in vivid detail; Racheal's gentle kisses, the softness of her skin - her taste. *My god, I really did that — and enjoyed it. How is that possible? Would I do it again? Would she?* Becky shivered and admonished herself, *Geez Becky, get a grip for Christ's sake.* She said, "Yeah, me too. So, what can I do to help you deal with Sly?"

The change of subject disappointed Racheal, she had more she wanted to say to Becky. She wanted her friend back in her life. Instead, she asked, "Did you talk to your husband about getting a copy of the video?"

"No," replied Becky. "I haven't had the chance yet. Don't get your hopes up, though."

"I don't think it will matter anyway."

Becky sat her taco down. "Why? I thought you said you needed proof."

Racheal let out a sigh. "Here's the thing, Becky. I talked to my lawyer, and she said that the whole website thing will help my divorce case, but she didn't think the district attorney would do much about criminal prosecution. The website is down, I checked. Sly videotaping us and posting it is illegal, but not the same as if he took videos of nude strangers. It would be hard to prove we didn't consent. According to her, the D.A. doesn't care much about this kind of stuff; he's all about violent crime."

"That's bullshit," Becky growled.

"I know. But I still filed the charges. The cops were sympathetic, and they said they would lean on him pretty hard. But they also hinted the same as my lawyer; don't expect the district attorney to push it very hard. If he does anything, he'll plead it down, and Sly will get a fine or probation."

"So, the son of a bitch is going to get away with it?" asked Becky.

"I don't know — maybe. Be prepared for it, though; Sly always seems to make out."

Becky looked across the park toward the entrance to the walking trail. *Why did I come here? This is where Nick wants to meet.* She had such fond memories of the two of them wandering the trails together, talking about life, the future, about nothing at all sometimes. It hurt that Nick had picked this, of all places, to end it — to end *them*. She felt a wave of nausea at the thought. With it came the anger of being robbed. She wanted justice, or at least vengeance. She said, "Maybe we can sue him, bleed him dry?"

"Maybe," said Racheal. "But he doesn't have much, and he is about to have less. I guess the good news is that my lawyer petitioned the court to have Sly removed from the house, and to return the money he took. So, he'll be on the street in a few days. That's something."

Becky shook her head. "It's not enough."

"I know. I thought I'd call the spa where Sly works and tell them he is going to be charged with a sex crime. But my lawyer says I shouldn't."

"Why not? He's a predator. They should know."

"She doesn't want it to look like I am on a vendetta. Plus, if he's unemployed, and it's my fault, I may have to give him support."

"That's ridiculous," said Becky. "What if I call them?"

"Leave it be. If he gets charged, they'll find out on their own. If you want to do something, talk to Nick and see if he has the video. Your suing Sly would expose him; that would be good."

Becky cradled her face in her hands. "I'll see Nick in a few days."

"Good, ask him for it then."

"I'll try, but he's going to ask me for a divorce. It won't be a good time to bring it up."

Racheal squeezed Becky's hand. "Oh, Becky, I'm so sorry. I know you don't want that."

Tears welled up in Becky's eyes and she sobbed. "It's not fair. That asshole ruined us, and he's going to get away with it. I hate this — I hate him."

"Me too," Racheal said. "and it's not just that. I'll be looking over my shoulder for the rest of my life. I tell you, he's a vindictive, petty man. We haven't seen the last of him, I'm afraid."

"What do you mean?"

"The other day I found a typed note on my windshield. It said something like; *it would be too bad if someone sent the videos to your family. Let's pray that doesn't happen.* It was unsigned, but it came from Sly. He's going to blackmail me sooner or later; maybe you and the other women too."

"Jesus Racheal, what did the police say about it? Can they trace it or something?"

Racheal sniffed and said, "No, that's just TV bullshit. I didn't give it to them. There is not much more the cops can do but dust for prints. He is a cunning bastard. I am sure he didn't leave any. Like I told you before. He won't go down without dragging everyone down with him. He is going to hurt me somehow. Maybe you too, if he thinks you're helping me. Warn your husband to keep his eyes open too. Sly is a coward, but anything he might do wouldn't surprise me."

Nearly sobbing, Becky said, "I wish he were dead."

"If only wishing made it so," said Racheal. She again took Becky's hand. "Becky, I am sorry I got you into all this, about getting you tangled up with Sly."

Becky let out a deep sigh. "That night was my fault not yours. Sly is a sociopath and he deserves to go to hell. Still, I have to own what I let happen, and I'm paying the price."

Racheal lightly stoked the back of Becky's hand with her thumb. "That night that we… well… I regret Sly was involved, but that's all I regret. I miss you."

A flurry of conflicting emotions welled up in Becky. Fear, confusion, guilt and excitement all competed for dominance. "Racheal, I won't lie. That night… you and I… together… It was one of the most erotic experiences I ever had. The thing is, I still haven't figured out I feel about it. But, I know this much; I love my husband. I'm losing him, but I still love him. I'm depressed about that, and angry at Sly, and feeling shitty about myself. I am not anywhere close to being ready to get into anything with anybody, and I don't think being involved with another woman would ever feel right for me."

Racheal smiled. "Becky, I'm not in love with you or anything. Yes, being with you was incredible. Given the right circumstances I would do it again, but that's not what I am looking for. I miss you, I miss what we had – as friends. My life has been torn apart, I am alone and a little scared of what comes next. And I am scared of Sly. I think you're in the same boat. We could both use each other's support. I want you back in my life.

There is some chemistry between us; I think we both feel it, but we can deal with that. I just don't want it to make things weird, or to keep us from being friends… just friends if that's best."

Becky squeezed Racheal's hand. "Just friends? That I could do. The truth is, after the anger faded, I started to realize I missed you too. You're the only one who has any real idea what I'm going through, I could use a shoulder to lean on. But Rache, don't expect more than friendship, I can't deal with anything more right now."

*Right now?* Thought Racheal, *Interesting choice of words.* "Good, it's settled. Now, what to do about Sly…"

# Chapter 14

Sly chugged the last of the six-pack. "Fuck you, Racheal," he growled as he threw the bottle against the wall. The day started badly and went downhill from there. He woke up to a text from Carol; she couldn't see him anymore. Then work called; some big, angry guy showed up looking for him. He guessed the stupid bitch had confessed everything. She had warned him to stay away for his own safety.

At noon, he got served with divorce papers, a restraining order, and a court order to depart the premises within 24 hours. Then came the pièce de résistance. The police showed up at his door with a search warrant. They said they were investigating an unlawful surveillance complaint. They did the bad cop – bad cop routine on him; called him a pervert, and told him they would love to film him getting passed around in the shower at county lock up. One of them even asked if he only hit women, and would he like to take a swing at one of them. He had to admit, they scared him. They searched the house, fortunately, he had taken his video equipment and laptop over to his friend Jimmy's house. That bought him some time. He knew they would be back. He was terrified of going to jail, he knew what they would do to him there.

*Well*, he thought, *if she wants to play rough, we'll play rough.*

Sly grabbed the last of his boxes and carried it to the garage where his Dodge pickup waited. He didn't want nosey neighbors watching him pack. Looking at the small stack, he wondered if he had missed anything. He intended to travel light, but there would be no coming back for a while. It took some arm twisting, but he convinced Jimmy to let him use his fishing camp to lie low for a few days. When things settled down, he would drive to Montana.

Just looking at the boxes fueled his anger. "That fucking bitch wants the house; well, let her have it," he muttered as he slammed the tailgate. *Unbelievable,* he thought as he walked towards the house. *A divorce? It's ridiculous. So I screwed a few women, so what? It's not like I wouldn't let her fool around with some guy for a video. I mean, who gives a shit? She's always been a self-righteous priss.* A smile spread across his face as a notion occurred to him. *Maybe Jimmy was right. Maybe I could make some money off the videos after all.* He always figured Jimmy for a wimpy little bitch, but the guy was smart. When he told Jimmy about how he was going to send the videos to Racheal's dad, Jimmy suggested she would probably cough up some cash to get the originals - maybe her friend Becky, too. *There's no way Racheal had the guts to call the cops on her own. It had to be that Adler bitch behind it. Her and that fuckin asshole husband of hers needed to pay.*

He walked through the kitchen to the bedroom. Surveying the large pile of clothes on the bed, he smirked. "Fuck them all, this is just a warm up. I'll be back, and when I am, they'll all be sorry they fucked with me."

He opened the dresser drawer and pulled out all of Racheal's socks, bras, and underwear and threw them on the heap of her other clothes. He looked around the room, searching for anything else to include. After a moment, he snapped his fingers as if something suddenly occurred to him. He moved to the closet and pulled two photo albums off the top shelf. One went on the pile of clothes, he opened the other. Lingering a few moments over the snapshots, he wistfully said, "It didn't have to be like this, honey."

Sly tossed the remaining photo album on the bed, then picked up the five-gallon gas can that had been sitting on the floor. After dousing the bed and clothing, he poured a trail of gasoline out of the bedroom, down the hall, and into the living room. Noticing their wedding picture hanging over the fireplace mantle, he threw it on the floor and broke it under his heel. He closed the drapes to the two living room windows, then soaked the drapes, sofa, and two upholstered chairs with the flammable liquid. Finally, he made a trail of gasoline from the couch and chairs to the center of the room, where he splashed a large puddle on the carpet. He admired his work momentarily; confident it would get the job done. He chuckled and said, "Enjoy what's left of our house, sweetheart." He fished a box of matches out of his pocket, and added, "Too bad you're not on the bed too."

The footstep behind him made him jump. Turning, he said, "What the fuck? You…" Sly took a step toward the intruder; but stopped in his tracks. He never saw the taser, he only felt it. The 50,000 volts seemed to explode in his groin and radiate through his body. The pain in his testicles was excruciating.

Falling back in the room, he only barely clung to consciousness, his body and mind seemed disconnected, he couldn't move. Seconds later, the sensation of a cold liquid being poured on him brought him back to his senses. He looked up in disbelief as the glowing match arced towards him.

Vision and hearing abandoned him the moment the match landed. Sly's entire world became only heat and searing pain. Reason was gone; animal instinct demanded he stand and run – run from the unbearable agony. As he tried to gain his feet, a world of fire exploded around him. He tried to scream, but the air he inhaled scorched his nose and throat like a hot poker. His windpipe seized, locking his screams in his chest. He didn't hear the door slam behind him. Collapsing, he attempted to crawl away – anywhere away from the pain. He was dead before the car outside pulled from the curb.

# Chapter 15

An angry Detective Frank Miller slouched in his car, surveying the scene. He hated being on call; and he hated getting dragged out of bed in the middle of the night. Mostly he despised fire calls. *What a circus,* he thought. *It's a small house and barely burnt, and they have half the fire department here. There's three, no, four trucks parked out front, and there must be at least 15 of them wandering around. Typical; they're like crows. If you see one, you see a dozen.* He chuckled to himself; *I wonder if they hold hands when they take a leak?*

He rolled down his car window and pulled a cigarette from the pack above his visor. Lighting the smoke, he thought, *for the life of me. I don't get what people see in these clowns. We're the ones getting shot at, and all they do is squirt water at fire — big deal. Yet, the public absolutely adores those guys. Hell, women practically drool over them.* His ex-wife had married a firefighter, he suspected it was out of spite. Miller thought the guy was an asshole. *But then, they're all assholes.* He grumbled, "It's a fucked-up world, Frank."

Miller hated working fire deaths. He didn't like dealing with firefighters; the burnt buildings were always a wet, filthy mess, and the bodies were plain hideous. He could handle blood and guts; shotgun to the head-no problem. But a burnt body gave him the willies, and the smell… the smell was god awful. He pulled out a digital voice recorder and noted the time, date, and address. Getting out of the car, he surveyed the scene, this time more closely, making notes of the house's general appearance and the apparent damage. He would have the crime techs photograph all of it when they arrived. Slowly walking around the house, Miller looked for anything unexpected or out of place. Noticing a burnt pile of debris and a mattress laying in the backyard made him groan. He complained, "Damn it, do they go out of their way to fuck up evidence?"

Arriving back in the front yard, he noticed a patrolman leaning on a tree by the driveway. "Looks like you're doing a fine job of holding up that tree," said Miller.

The officer stood up straight and replied, "Oh, hi Detective. I didn't notice you come on scene."

"Nice job of keeping eye on things. So, what do we have here?"

The officer stiffened. "The fire department got a call for a structure fire shortly before 11 PM. They found the body inside."

"And…"

Puzzled, the officer said, "And what?"

"Anything else? Have you talked to witnesses? Who called it in?"

"No," said the patrolman. "That's what I got."

"Well, thank you for that detailed report, Sherlock." Miller said dryly. "Keep up the good work and you'll be a captain in no time." He then moved towards the front door, annoyed at having to step over all the tools and hoses, and around the horde of firefighters. As he walked away, he heard the patrolman mutter, "Asshole." For the first time since he arrived, he smiled.

Inside, the stench of burnt flesh and smoke assailed him. The fire department's portable flood lights sat on the floor. They were incredibly bright, but cast strange shadows throughout the devastated room. A pall of wispy blue smoke hung in the air. To Miller, nothing seemed so desolate as a burnt out building in the middle of the night. The utter destruction caused by even a small fire was staggering. Near the center of the room stood a large man in blue coveralls putting plastic bags in a bin. Miller asked him, "Are you the lead investigator?"

"Yeah, Max Ross."

Miller glanced at the body on the floor. To his surprise, the coroner himself was examining the body and not an assistant. To the fire investigator he said, "So Max, you got a fire fatality. Why am I here?"

"We will call this suspicious until the samples come back from the lab. But this fire was lit deliberately. There're multiple fire sets and trailers. Hell, there's even a gas can by the body. As you know, anytime there is a fatality associated with a crime, it becomes your deal."

"What's your best guess?"

"The victim is a guy named Sylvester Roberts. He lives here, we are trying to track down his wife. His stuff is packed in the pickup truck in the garage, and we found her clothes piled on the bed. If I was a betting man, I would say that Mr. and Mrs. Roberts were calling it quits, and he decided to burn down the house and all her stuff before leaving town. I'm guessing the dip shit got careless with the gas and managed to light himself on fire when torching the place."

Miller nodded and parsed what he just heard. Then said, "I suppose that heap of smoldering debris in the backyard was the evidence from the bedroom, huh?"

Ross frowned. "Yeah, the crews needed to get the mattress out of the bedroom; it was one of those foam numbers. They're stubborn bastards to put out."

"That kind of fucked up the evidence, don't you think?"

"Relax, the company officer documented everything with video before anybody moved anything. You got your evidence."

Pointing at the body, Miller said, "Is this where they found him, or did somebody move the body?"

"Oh, shit. Me and the boys rolled him around a while for fun. We just didn't know any better. After all, I've only been doing this for a short 15 years."

Miller put his hands up defensively. "Okay-okay, don't get your knickers in a knot. I have to ask." He scanned the room closely, and asked, "Did you talk to the first arriving company?"

"Of course. They're still here, if you want to talk to them."

"I will, later. Did they notice if the door was open or closed when they got here?"

Ross replied, "They said it was closed - locked, actually. The burn pattern confirms it. There is no char on the door edge or jam."

Looking at the door, Miller noticed an orange plastic evidence marker by a box of matches lying just inside the door. He then looked at the body again, measuring the distance from it to the door. "Hmm," he said, "Why would the guy lock himself in before setting the fire?"

Ross said, "I thought about that too. It's not a dead bolt or thumb lock. He would just have to turn the knob to get out."

"I'd expect he would have left it open, stood by the open door and tossed a match in. Why is he closer to the middle of the room?"

Ross shrugged. "Can't say for sure. It's possible he lit the fire by the door. When he caught, he stumbled into the room."

"Carrying the gas can?"

"No. I would assume he left the can in the room, went to the door, and lit the fire. When he caught fire, he panicked, dropped the matches, and tried to escape and made it to there."

Miller ran his hand across the back of his neck. "Maybe. Still seems off, though. Another thing, why leave your truck in the garage? You would think he would have pulled it out into the drive with the motor running before he lit the fuse."

"That would have been smart," said Ross. "But then smart guys don't light themselves on fire. Hell, they don't burn down their own house to begin with. Stupid people keep us both in jobs."

Miller couldn't shake the feeling that something didn't seem right. "I tell you what, I wouldn't be surprised if we find out this guy got killed, and the fire is a cover up."

Ross shook his head. "That doesn't explain the packed boxes. And why mess with the wife's clothes then? Seems like a weird detail to stage."

"I don't know," said Miller. "Maybe the perp had a hard on for both the husband and wife. She may have got lucky by not being home, or she could be tied up in some basement somewhere."

"Well, you got lucky in one regard, detective. Fortunately, whoever set the fire didn't know what he was doing. All the windows and doors are closed, and he used a crap load of gasoline. The place took off instantly, but the fire couldn't breathe. It burnt itself out fairly quick. Had he left the door and a bedroom window open, we would be standing in a pile of ashes having this conversation. And there wouldn't be much of Mr. Roberts left for the coroner."

Miller looked at the coroner, who had been listening to the conversation as he worked. "So, Coroner Patrick, what the hell are you doing here at this ungodly hour? How come a deputy ghoul isn't doing this?"

The coroner, Jerry Patrick, was squatting next to the body. "The on call ghoul, as you so graciously call us, has the flu; so, here I am."

Miller liked Patrick, he was a pro. "Don't get all sensitive on me, Jerry. What can you tell me about the crispy critter there?"

"Max is right. We caught a break. The victim has pretty significant surface burns, but the body is more or less intact."

"Can you nail down cause of death? I especially want to know when he died and if he was dead before the fire."

"I can't say for sure until I get him on the table, but I don't see any injuries that would've caused death other than the fire. There aren't any apparent bullet holes or stab wounds. We'll take a good hard look at him though, and see if there are any other injuries or signs of restraint."

Miller pinched his nose shut, trying to abate the stench. "Do me a favor, run a complete blood panel on him too. I want to know if there are any drugs or alcohol in his system."

Patrick smirked. "Wow, there's an idea. Why didn't I think of that?"

"Sorry." said Miller. "It's just that my guess is that this isn't what it appears. I don't want anything missed."

"Don't worry, nothing will get by us, Frank."

Miller turned back to Ross. "How long before your tribe is out of here?'

"We're about done now," answered the fire investigator.

"Good, my lab boys will be here any minute. Be sure and send me a copy of all the fire reports when there're filed."

On the way back to his car, Miller told the patrolman to interview everyone on the block. He wanted to know if anyone saw or heard anything unusual, and if anyone was close to the owners. At his car, he pulled some antacids from his pocket and tossed a couple in his mouth, then lit another cigarette. He made some additional notes, then called the station and briefed his lieutenant. He also requested any and all records regarding both Mr. and Mrs. Sylvester Roberts. Finally, he slumped in his car seat and prepared for a long night.

# Chapter 16

Nick sat at a picnic table, waiting. To distract himself, he again read the note Haley had left on his windshield.

*Nick,*

*I am on my way back to Iowa. Even though we have only known each other for a short while, I will always remember you. It may sound weird considering we have only been together twice, but I feel a connection to you. Maybe another time, we could have had something special. Nick, you're a good man with a good heart. You deserve some happiness. Please stop hiding in the dark.*

*Love Haley*

*Stop hiding in the dark*, he thought. *Sorry, Haley, it's not that easy. Still, you brought a little sunshine with you. I owe you for that. I hope you find what you're looking for.*

With a dry mouth and pulse pounding in his temples, he looked at the park entrance again. He knew he had no reason to be nervous; it was only Becky. Still, the anxiety threatened to trigger one of his *episodes*, as he sometimes called them. Marco, Haley, and Father Tom all said confronting her would be good for him; he had doubts.

*How will it go? Will she cry and beg me to take her back? Will she call me a loser because I couldn't make her happy anymore? Does she hate me because of Haley — do I care?* He wasn't sure what he wanted to say to her, or what he hoped to hear. Except for that fiasco a few nights earlier, he hadn't seen

Becky in so long, and so much had happened; anything was possible.

Thinking about Becky and the future confused and frustrated him. He didn't see how they could fix things, but the idea of actually walking away forever seemed almost too bizarre to be real. *What can we do, Becky? I can't get what you did out of my head, but I can't live like I am. What can you say to make things better? Nothing, probably. What do I even want to hear? Tom says I need closure. Maybe I want a reason to believe we have a chance? I hope you have a better grip on this than me.*

Nick hurriedly slid Haley's note in his pocket as Becky's car pulled into the lot. He stood and watched her slowly approach; head down, hands in her pockets. She wore a white, flowing, gauzy dress. He remembered it, although he hadn't seen it in years. It was casual, but a little sexy too. He once told her it was his favorite, but she hardly ever wore it; "too flirty", she had said, "a little breeze and I'm flashing the world."

*I wonder if she dressed up for me, or if she dresses like this all the time now?* He wished he'd chosen something better than his faded jeans and T-shirt. She had changed a little; her hair looked shorter, and she had lost weight — maybe too much. Still, as if seeing her for the first time, he marveled at how beautiful he still found her. *It's funny how you stop noticing after a while*, he thought.

When they came together, they did not hug, both noticed it, both wondered if they should have. An awkwardness filled the space between them that neither would have dreamed possible not so long before.

Not knowing what else to offer, Nick said, "Thanks for coming."

"Sure, no problem." A slight smile traced itself upon Becky's lips. Nick recognized that smile, he'd seen it before. It was her attempt at a brave face when trying not to cry. Nick always found it sadly endearing. She cleared her throat and said, "I am surprised you asked to meet here, though," she said.

"Why?" asked Nick.

"I don't know, this was our place, we have a lot of wonderful memories here. It just seemed like a surprising choice, under the circumstances."

*Circumstances?* he thought. He hoped she would be happy to see him; she didn't look it. He wasn't sure what he expected from her, but subdued sadness wasn't it. His own feelings were unexpected as well. The nerves were still there, but something else emerged too, something odd. He knew her so well and they were in a place he visited hundreds of times. It was all familiar, yet off at the same time. He felt disconnected, displaced. Most surprising, the anger that weighed so heavily on him for so long had somehow become thin and inconsequential. In all their months apart, he harbored nothing but bitterness and resentment toward her. But now, with her standing there… regardless of what she had done, he just couldn't bring himself to hate her.

He said, "It's a nice day. I figured we could take a walk like we used to. I kinda hoped it would make things less awkward."

"Okay," she said. They walked side-by-side down the asphalt walkway that led underneath the tree canopy. After a few minutes, Becky said, "You look tired, and you've lost weight. Are you taking care of yourself?"

Nick shrugged and replied, "I could say the same thing about you. I guess both our lives have sucked lately."

"Yeah, you could say that," Becky said. "Hey, I heard what happened. I hope you're not in too much trouble at work."

"I don't know. Time will tell, I guess.

Becky Patted Nick's arm. "Thank you."

"For what?"

"For punching that son of a bitch out. He deserved worse. I hope everything turns out okay for you."

Nick grimaced and said, "Don't worry about it. I enjoyed it, and if they fire me, they fire me."

"Bull," she said, "losing your job would be the worst thing that could happen to you."

"Trust me, I've been through worse."

Becky didn't miss the implication. An awkward silence descended upon them as they walked. The tension became unbearable for Becky, and she finanly broached the subject she so dreaded. "Look, Nick. I know why we're here, and I won't make it hard on you. We can be civilized about this."

Nick stopped and looked at her. "I'm not sure I follow."

"I'm talking about the divorce. That's why you wanted to talk, isn't it? You want a divorce."

"No," said Nick. "That's not why I asked you here. I just wanted to talk; lord knows we both have things to say. Why? Are you wanting a divorce?

The knot in Becky's stomach relaxed some, but she had to fight the urge to hyperventilate. Tears of relief welled in her eyes. "No — No, I *don't* want a divorce. Not at all. But when I saw you with that woman, I guessed maybe you wanted to…."

"I'll be honest with you, Becky. I have no idea what I want. I guess that's why we need to talk."

"She's very pretty. Is it serious?"

"Is what serious?"

"You and that woman. Are you two in a serious relationship?"

"No, and her name is Haley."

"She looked pretty young. Where did you meet?"

Nick sighed; not sure what Becky was getting at. "She's 26 — I think."

"Have you been dating long?" asked Becky.

"Uh -uh. It was our first and last time together. What's with all the questions? Why do you care?"

"My husband is banging some little hottie; I have a right to ask a few questions, don't you think?" She regretted saying it as soon as the words came out of her mouth.

Nick stopped walking and turned on Becky. "Really? Are you fucking kidding me?"

Reflexively, Becky's hands covered her face. "Oh God, you're right. I'm so sorry."

Nick said, "You got no right to…"

"I know, but seeing her standing there naked with you was — it was a shock. It ripped my heart out."

"Yeah, I'm familiar with the feeling," said Nick. "Maybe I should have sent you a video of us having sex. Then you would understand what having your heart ripped out feels like."

"I know — I know. And I'm so sorry. I shouldn't have said anything. I have no right to be jealous, but I am. But knowing you were with another woman broke my heart. I guess I know what you went through now."

Nick fixed a hard glare on her. "No. I don't think you do. To understand what I went through, you would have to watch me with her. Watch me do things with her I never did with you… hear me scream her name. You would have to see me lust after someone else more than you. Then Becky — then you might *begin* to understand how I felt. What I saw damn near broke me, Becky. I mean it, I almost…"

"Oh, Nick, I am so –so sorry. I get that what happened to you was worse. I realize I hurt you, and I swear I never wanted to. You have every right to hate me, but I promise you I hate myself more than you do. I would do anything to take it back. What I did was selfish and stupid. Honestly, I don't even recognize whatever version of me did that. It's not who I am, you know that."

"I'm not sure who you are anymore, I thought I did but then… Why? Why did you do it?"

"Do you really want to get into this?" said Becky.

"I didn't, but now that you took us here… Yeah, I do. More than anything else, I want to understand how you could have done it. Let's hear your explanation."

"I don't want to." said Becky. "If I try to explain why, it will sound like I'm blaming you or making excuses, and I'm not. You were struggling, and I got lonely. I did something weak and foolish. I know I let you down. Let's leave it at that."

"Becky, we were good together. I need to understand. I know you, it's hard to imagine you as a liar and cheat. I can't get past this without understanding how we ended up here. What was it about him that made you do it? Why choose him over me?"

"Jesus, Nick, never think that. I *never* put anybody ahead of you. I never would. It had nothing to do with him, or them. I don't remember even finding him attractive. It was about us— well, me. We were good together, and then somehow, we weren't. Nick, sweetheart, we were together — but not, do you understand?"

"No, I don't," replied Nick.

"You went somewhere inside yourself. For a long time, you rarely spoke to me. We didn't do anything together. Hell, you did nothing at all, with or without me. Before that night that I — you know, we hadn't made love for months. I'm not making excuses for what I did, but I fell into an awful place. It got to the point where I suspected you were seeing someone else. You pulling away hurt, and I felt abandoned and depressed. It's not an excuse, but that's where my head was at."

Nick remembered Haley's explanation for why she cheated. A lump grew in his throat at the memory of how he treated Becky. "So, you're saying I drove you to it? Tell me the truth, were you going to leave me?"

Becky shook her head emphatically. "No-No-No, nothing like that at all. Racheal and I became friends. Sometimes, we got together after work. We got close, I guess it just felt good to have somebody to laugh with. After a while, we started hanging out at her house, and her husband was there most of the time. The three of us kind of became friends. It was all innocent."

"Innocent? What I saw was your idea of innocent?"

"Of course not. Jesus, this is hard to talk about. The thing is, Racheal always kinda flirted with me, Sly too, after a while. I won't lie; I liked the attention. It sort of made me feel alive again. Anyhow, one night we all got drunk and high and she started coming on to me. Her and I started making out. It felt like a goof at first, sort of showing off for Sly, I think. I'm not sure how, maybe it was the taboo, or that I was high, but suddenly it wasn't a goof anymore, it got real. I guess because it was a woman, not a man, I didn't feel like I was actually cheating. It got intense and I — well, lost control; you saw the rest."

"Uh-uh Becky. Making out with a girl out of curiosity is one thing; screwing him is another."

"Him? You mean *them*, right?"

"Okay, whatever, *them*."

"You don't get it, do you? When you talk about it, you keep focusing on *him* — about what I did with *him*. But for me, it was about her. She seduced me, he didn't. Being with her felt so sexy and thrilling. Nick, I never would've had sex with just him. I wouldn't have even been alone with another man. Somehow, being with her… I can't explain why being with her seemed okay, but it did. She and I were together, and things somehow escalated, and I just went along with him being involved too. But I tell you, it wasn't about him."

Nick glared at her. "It sure as fuck didn't look like you were *just* going along."

"The truth is, it was almost all Racheal and I. The asshole edited the video to show what he liked, what made him look good. He wasn't that big a part of it."

"BULLSHIT! I saw what I saw, Becky."

"What do you want me to say, Nick? Yes, I had sex with both of them. I let *him* have me. Is that what you want to hear? Yes, in the moment it was nasty and erotic. I've never done anything like a threesome before, and it was fucking thrilling. Your wife lost control and acted like a little slut. Are you happy now?"

"No goddamnit, nothing about this makes me happy." Nick growled, "But at least you finally admit that you wanted it."

"No, I didn't — not before that night, anyway. I mean, yes you're right, when it happened I liked it. But I never- never intended to cheat, I wasn't even thinking about it. And I regretted it immediately. Listen to me, Nick. It was just an hour of stupid, drunken sex. Nothing more. They were nothing more than actors in some sort of real-life dirty fantasy."

"Be honest Becky, how many times did you see them? How long did you sneak behind my back?"

She took both his hands and stared into his eyes. "Nick, I swear to you, it only happened that one night. When it was all over, I realized what I had done and the guilt practically crushed me. I swear, I ran out of there as soon as I could. I felt so dirty; on the way home I pulled over and threw up. Every time I looked at you, the shame made me ill."

"Not ashamed enough to tell me."

Becky said, "I wanted to. I should have. But you are already in such a deep dark hole, and we were not doing well together. I just couldn't bring myself to tell you. I intended to, when things got better. You found out before I got the chance."

"FUCK THAT! You cheated on me. I didn't deserve that. To make matters worse, you let a worthless piece of crap use you like a cheap… You humiliated me, you lied to me by not telling me. I didn't deserve that either. If you had trusted me and did the right thing, we may have gotten past it. You say you love me, but you stuck a knife in my heart."

Becky was stunned, Nick had never raised his voice at her before, not like that. Timidly she whispered, "I tell myself the same thing every day. It kills me knowing that."

Nick looked at her for several moments, breathing hard. He turned and started to walk again. Becky stood and watched him walk away, unsure if she should follow. He beckoned for her. They walked for a few hundred feet before Nick finally spoke. "Was it really so bad, those last few months?"

"Nick," Becky said, "I am not sure what's going on with you, but yes, it was like you were drowning. And sometimes it seemed like you were pulling me down too. I feel horrible about that night, I truly do. But what I really regret is that I abandoned you. Whatever's going on with you has gotten worse, and that may be my fault. That's hard to live with."

"Father Tom seems to think that making peace with what you did is important. He says I need closure. If it makes a difference, I realize I could have been a better husband."

Becky sniffed and wiped a tear from her cheek. "I don't expect you to forgive me, but I hope you can stop hating me."

"Becky, I don't hate you."

She wiped away another tear. "Yeah? You treated me like garbage that you could simply throw away. How could you walk away without saying a word? Even I didn't deserve that, not after everything we've been through together. I would've preferred you hitting me to what you did."

Nick took Becky's hand as they walked. "Becky, I could never hit you, you know that. And I don't hate you. Lord knows I've tried, but I just can't. For a long time, I was angry, it almost consumed me. But I'm getting so tired of that; it's exhausting. I feel bad about the way I left; I just couldn't face you. And I am sorry about my outburst earlier. I needed to vent, to let you know how bad you hurt me."

Becky leaned her head against Nick's shoulder. "I know I broke your heart. And you broke mine too, every single day for the last eight months, the year before that too. Can't we just call it even?"

Nick sighed and said, "It's not that simple."

Becky sniffed. "Tell me what you feel. When you look at me, do you only see the woman in the video? Do I disgust you?"

"Of course not. That's ridiculous; you could never disgust me."

"Does knowing that other people saw me do those things — knowing they all think I am some kind of sex crazed tramp embarrass you?"

"Yeah, it does. Knowing the guys at work saw the video is mortifying, but I could never be ashamed of you, if that's what you're getting at."

"Then why can't we at least try again?"

"Becky…" Nick's phone rang. He pulled it out of his pocket and checked the caller's ID and let it go to voicemail. "Like I was saying, it's not that simple. You and I need to…" The text message chime on Nick's phone went off.

"She's persistent," said Becky.

Nick shot her a look that said, *enough*. "It's Marco."

Nick showed Becky the message: *Nick, call me ASAP… Urgent.* He said, "Marco's got a bug up his ass. Do you mind if I call him?"

She said, "He has some shitty timing, but go ahead."

Nick punched three on his speed dial. Marco answered on the first ring. "So, Marco, what's the problem?"

Marco replied, "Sylvester Roberts, that guy you punched out. They found him dead at his house."

"No shit? What happened?"

Marco chuckled, "The asshole tried to set his house on fire and burned himself up."

"Can't say I'm sorry. He was a worthless waste of blood and bone."

"Yeah, well, the cops may be wanting to talk to you.'

"Me? Why?"

Marco said, "I talked to Max Ross; he was the on-scene investigator. He said the crime scene detective suspects it wasn't an accident. I'm just giving you a heads up. Be careful."

"What's any of it got to do with me?"

Marco said, "You put him in the hospital not long ago — just saying. You can bet they will want to talk to you."

"Yeah, okay. Thanks." Nick ended the call.

Becky asked, "So, what did Marco have to say?"

"It looks like your boyfriend got himself killed."

"What? Who?" asked Becky.

"What do you mean, who? Sylvester Roberts. Just how many boyfriends do you have?"

"None. And that's a crappy thing to say."

"Okay, sorry. I guess Roberts was trying to burn down his house, and managed to set himself on fire."

Nick watched Becky's jaw set, and her eyes narrow. She said, "Good. I hope the SOB burns in hell. So, they are saying it was an accident? That's good."

"I guess, but the cops got it in their heads that somebody might've killed him. Why is it being an accident good? Why would you give a shit? Did you off him?"

"Very funny — of course not. But I am okay with him being dead. It's just good that the cops aren't hassling anybody over that waste of a human. I'd hate to think maybe they suspected Racheal. She was divorcing him, and she was terrified that he would come after her. She even said he might try to hurt us, especially you. The world is better off without him."

"Oh really, Racheal told you that? So, you two are still seeing each other then?"

Becky replied, "She and I…" It took a moment for her to realize what Nick was actually suggesting. "Oh, God no. We're not *seeing* each other, if that's what you mean."

"Hey, you said it was all about her. I guess I get it now. All that crap about it being a onetime thing isn't all true, is it? You and her are still…"

"NO! Nothing like that is going on. It *was* a onetime thing. The day after I was — with them, I told them to never contact me again. After I found out about the website, I confronted her. It turns out she didn't know anything about it either. She and I were in the process of filing criminal charges against him. We talked a couple of times about that. That's it."

"So," said Nick, "you and her aren't… you're not in a relationship?'

"Jesus Nick, listen to me. I messed up and had a stupid one-night thing with a couple. I am fighting like hell to save my marriage here and I am practically groveling trying to get you to forgive me. What's it going to take for you to get it through your head? I love you—only you, dammit. I am not a lesbian, and there is no one else—man or woman. It happened. I am sorry, but there is nothing I can do about it."

"Well, excuse me for being a little insecure. You had a steamy threesome, but hey, it's all okie dokie because it was all about her, not him. Then you tell me she seduced you and it was, how did you put it? Oh yeah, thrilling. Now I hear you two are still spending time together. Are a few suspicions really so out of line?"

"Okay, I get it. But, listen to me, that night was what it was, a terrible onetime lapse in judgment, nothing more."

Nick said, "I need some time to wrap my head around this. I've known you forever, and this whole going nuts over another woman thing seems bizarre. Why didn't you ever tell me you had a thing for women?"

"I guess I was afraid to talk about it. Maybe ashamed. And it wasn't something I thought about a lot, just sometimes."

'Do you still think about it?"

"Nick, it's not a thing. I was curious, that's all. It's over, let it go."

"Okay, if you say so. I'll just let it go… my wife has a threesome -no big deal at all. Let's change the subject. Did you say you were going to get him arrested?"

"Yeah, we even talked about me filing a civil suit against him too. That's why I came to your place the other night. To see if you had a copy of the video."

"That was pretty ballsy of you. A lawsuit would have brought out the whole sordid mess."

"I didn't care. He fucked me over, and Racheal said he was going to do his best to screw you too. I wanted his ass to pay. I guess it doesn't matter now, huh?"

"No, I guess it doesn't," said Nick. They walked around a curve and came up to Lake Tucker. It was a small lake, only about 5 acres, but it was as picturesque as any lake could be. It was spring fed, and the water was clear and cold. That and the shade of the trees made sitting by it cool even on hot days. It was a favorite spot for meditation, tired runners, and lovers.

Becky pointed to a nearby bench. "Look, there is *our special* spot. Can we sit for a bit? Before Marco called, we were talking about trying to salvage our marriage. I want to say something, and I need you to listen. What I did hurt you, a lot. And I know that finding out about it the way you did must have been devastating. You feel betrayed, and you should. Your pride got wounded, and on top of all that, the guys at work seeing the video had to be humiliating. God knows it is for me. I messed up bad, and if I could take it back I would; but I can't."

Nick said, "Becky…" She put a hand on his arm to stop him.

She continued, "There is no reason to forgive me, but I want you to ask yourself something; are you better off without me than with me? I love you; I always have. Yes, I fucked up, but you know that's not who I am. You know me, deep down, do you imagine it will ever happen again? Nick, if you can somehow get past my mistake, if you can somehow figure out a way to live with it, I will spend every day making it right again."

He looked out over the water, picked up a stick, and threw it in. "Becky, I don't know if I can. When I look at you, I'm reminded of that video. That may not be fair, but that's the way it is. Images of you and them together keep flashing in my mind."

"I understand, really I do. Images of you and that woman together really mess with me and that's just my imagination. You shouldn't have had to see what you did – no one should.But understand this, you might as well be jealous of my vibrator. They — *him* were  never what any of this was about. It was about the idea of *what* was happening that seduced me. Nick, believe me when I tell you, you're the only man I want, or ever wanted. I did what I did, I can't change that. But please, don't make it into something bigger than what it was. I'm not saying that it should mean nothing to you, but ask yourself this; was your being with Haley something that should change the way I look at you? Did it change how you feel about me? I know it's not the same thing, but it's really not so different either. We both had sex with other people. Why does that have to define who we are to each other? I had no right to do what I did - maybe *you* did - but we did the same thing. The question isn't about who screwed who, it's about if you can ever trust me again — and if you still love me."

Nick said, "That sounds like some major rationalization."

"It's not. I've said it a dozen times, six different ways. I did a horrible thing. There are no excuses for it. I only ask that you focus a little less on what I did, and a little more on who I am, and what we had."

Nick flashed back on something Haley had said on their date… *bad things happen to good people and we have no control over some things. But we can control how we feel about them and how we react. Happiness is a choice.*

Nick said, "I didn't expect our talk to go anything like this. I'm a little overwhelmed; let me do some thinking. I'll say this, Father Tom will be happy we talked about all this. He said I needed it; I guess he was right."

"About that," said Becky. "Full disclosure, I visited Father Tom yesterday."

Becky saw a look of surprise, then anger on Nick's face. "Why? Did he give you tips on what to say today?"

"Of course not! When Jazz told me the department sent you to him, I wanted to — well — give him some background, I guess. I thought he needed to know some things if he was going to help you."

"I wish you hadn't done that. What did you tell him?"

"I told him what I did to you, and about the video — talk about humiliating. I also told him about how you were struggling before that. Mostly, we talked about me. I gotta admit, I've been pretty messed up lately myself."

"Yeah," said Nick. "There is a lot of that going around nowadays. Still, I wish you would have left me out of it. I'm fighting for my job here, and I'm trying to convince him I'm okay to work. You telling him I'm messed up in the head won't help."

"Jesus, Nick, I would never tell him anything like that. And Father Tom's been good to us for a long time. You don't honestly believe he would do anything to hurt you. Give him a chance; he's only trying to help. So are Marco and Jazz, and me too, for that matter. For Pete's sakes, let people help you."

"I'm tired of people telling me I need help."

"No, you're not," said Becky. "This is me you're talking to. I know you better than you know yourself. You're not upset with people suggesting you need help. You're not blind, you *already* know you need it. No, you're just too stubborn to admit it, and you're too proud to accept it."

"It's not that." said Nick. "If it gets out that I can't hack it, I could lose…"

"…Lose what, Dom? Your friends? Your health? Your marriage? Look at yourself sweetheart, how much more will you let this thing you're going though take from you?"

"I was going to say my job."

"You make it sound like your job isn't already on the line. How long before it takes that from you too? You know it will, one way or the other. Stop being a wuss and face this thing."

Nick scoffed. "You, and Marco too, think you know me, that you've got it all figured out."

"I do know you, and I love you; choose to believe that or not. I have no idea what's going on with you, but I know it's eating you alive. I also believe Father Tom can help you if you let him."

"You know, you're not always right," he said.

"No, I'm not always right. But we both know I'm not wrong right now."

Nick wiped a single tear from his eye. He hoped Becky didn't see it. "You know what pisses me off most about all this? With all the crap you put me through, I still miss you — miss talking to you like this. You were my anchor, the one person I could depend on without question, my best friend. I miss that most of all."

"I could be again, if you let me," said Becky.

Nick whispered, "I am not sure we could ever get that back again."

"That's up to you, isn't it?"

Nick sat quietly for a few seconds as he digested it all, then leaned over and nudged her with his shoulder. "Hey, get a load of this. I got a cat now. Who'da thunk it?"

Becky grinned. "Yeah, sorry about that. I kind of put Jazz up to that as a joke. I didn't think she would actually do it. Sorry."

"It's okay, I kinda like her." With that, Nick stood, and the two of them finished their walk. They talked about work and life in general. He asked if she remembered to have the lawn sprayed for weeds. She asked about what was happening in the fire station. He told her about what happened with Jenkins.

She gave him a playful nudge. "Defending Charlie's honor, huh?"

"What's that supposed to mean?"

"I'll tell you something, but don't laugh. She always made me feel a little jealous. I thought you two would be dating by now."

"That's crazy," said Nick.

"Is it? She's young, pretty, and she's a fellow firefighter, and she adores you. It's kinda hard to compete with that."

"Come on Becky, she's like my kid sister."

"Don't get me wrong, I never suspected anything between you two, and I like her. But I always wondered if there wasn't some chemistry there."

"No, there is not. Besides, between the two of us, she would be into you before me; if you catch my drift"

Becky grinned and gave Nick a nudge. "Hmm, there's a thought. She's cute, maybe I should call her."

"SAY WHAT?"

Becky laughed. "Too soon for jokes?"

"Little bit." He gave her a light, playful slap on the fanny.

The banter continued as they approached their cars. The tension didn't leave entirely, and there were bothersome questions left unasked and unanswered. But the awkwardness lessened as the conversation meandered to the mundane.

When they parted, Becky worked up the courage to give Nick a hug. When his arms wrapped tightly around her, she found it hard not to cry again. "Thank you for this morning," she said. "It has meant everything to me. It's all I've wanted since the day you left me."

He replied, "I dreaded doing this, but I am glad we did. It was good seeing you. I mean that."

By the time they got in their vehicles, they both felt better than they had in months. As they drove their separate ways, Nick smiled and turned up the radio. He sang along to Margaritaville by Jimmy Buffett. Becky wiped tears away as she dialed Jazmine.

# Chapter 17

Frank Miller settled into his chair, set his coffee down, and opened his email application. His pulse quickened when he saw the message from Jerry Patrick, the chief corner. For reasons he didn't fully understand, he *wanted* this case to be more than it looked like. He chided himself. *Relax Frank, stay objective, look at it for what it is.* Patrick's note read:

*Detective Miller,*

*Attached is the autopsy report on Sylvester Roberts. A general summary of the results are as follows: Sylvester Roberts was a 34-year-old white male in good health. The victim died of suffocation subsequent to laryngeal edema induced by inhalation of super-heated air. This, and low-levels of carbon monoxide in his blood system, indicates that the victim was alive when exposed to the fire, but died shortly after. A gross inspection of the anatomy revealed second and third degree burns over the entire body surface. There were no other signs of trauma. Per your request, indications of possible restraint were looked for, and found absent. The victims' blood alcohol level was .09. This would indicate moderate intoxication, with likely at least marginal impairment of mental acuity and motor function. I found no other drugs in the blood stream.*

*Note: Inspection found a chemical liquid (likely accelerant) on clothing remnants beneath the body. Waiting on lab results for conclusive finding.*

*In summary, Mr. Roberts was a healthy individual, moderately intoxicated, but functional; who died as a result of being trapped in a fire.*

*Let me know if you have questions*

Miller read the report twice, then opened and printed the official autopsy report. A half page in, Detective Manny Rivera leaned over the wall of his cubicle and said, "Hey, Frank, Jabba wants to see you in his office."

Miller let out a sigh and said, "What's he want?"

Rivera shrugged. "Probably to bust your balls about something. Take him a bagel, it helps."

Jabba, more precisely, Jabba the Cop was the nickname the detectives had given Captain Joseph Johnson. Johnson was a big man, not tall, just big. He weighed well over 300 pounds, most of which he carried in an impressive gut. Red-faced, and always a bit sweaty, he looked to be a heart attack waiting to happen. His slow, ponderous movements belied a quick and agile mind. Johnson liked conversations short and to the point, he hated idle chatter, nor did he need to hear anything twice. Miller liked that about him, although that was about all he liked.

Miller entered the open door to Johnson's office and slid into the chair closest to the desk. Johnson sat perched on an office chair that looked overmatched by the load it endured. He pulled out one of the lower drawers to use as a footstool. The pose reminded Miller of a caricature someone had drawn and posted on the bulletin board; a walrus dressed as Henry VIII. The cartoon was well drawn and got a ton of laughs, but no one dared claim credit.

Johnson said, "Frank, what's going on with the Anderson sexual assault case?"

Miller replied, "It's about buttoned up. The DNA came back conclusive, and the arrest warrant for the neighbor should be ready this afternoon."

"Good, we can get that one off the board, we're getting backed up. What about that arson fire over on Cyprus Court?"

"I'm not sure," said Miller, "but I'm beginning to think there's a lot more to this one than we thought."

"How's that? Didn't the fire investigator say the dumbass killed himself committing arson?"

"Yeah, the arson part is a lock. The lab hasn't got the evidence samples analyzed yet, but there's no doubt that accelerant got used. Hell, they found a gasoline can in the living room."

"Okay? So, what's the problem?" Miller could tell that Jabba was already getting impatient.

"At the surface, it looks like a classic domestic disturbance. Husband and wife are splitting up; he packed up all his stuff getting ready to bail. On the way out the door, he threw all her stuff in a pile and tried to burn the place down. That's the way the fire department reads it anyhow."

Johnson crossed his arms. "And…"

"And it's too damn convenient. These two, the husband and wife, are at each other pretty good. I pulled the records, and we were out there on a domestic disturbance call shortly before it went down. They put each other in the hospital; hell, he knocked her out. She put a restraining order on him right after, and a few days after that, she swore out a criminal complaint about his posting of revenge porn or something. For all we know, he might have been pulling a disappearing act over that. I have to look into it."

"So, you think she had it in for him?" asked Johnson.

"Maybe… it's worth looking into, anyway."

"Any evidence she was there?"

"No, not yet. We found her at a shelter for battered women the night he died."

Johnson asked, "How does she subdue him? He isn't going to just stand there while she sets him on fire. Any sign she tied him up, or hit him on the head?"

"No, nothing like that. The coroner says the body is clean. Maybe she held him at gunpoint."

Johnson pinched the bridge of his nose. "If she had a gun, why not just shoot him? You're saying that this poor little battered wife, who put a restraining order on the man who beat her, somehow overpowered her husband and burned him alive?"

"I'm just saying she may have had motive. She had reason to want him dead. It seems coincidental is all."

"It doesn't work," said Johnson. "It's a lot of work to pack all his stuff up. Plus, if she had criminal charges on him, she likely would have gotten the house. Why burn down her own house and all her own stuff? Maybe she wanted him dead — maybe not. Either way, there is no upside to killing him that way. If she had a weapon, she would have used it. Not burn down the house just to get him."

"Maybe she is trying to hide the crime," Miller wondered aloud.

"Doubtful," said Johnson. "I read the report. The crime scene is too complicated; it would take planning and premeditation. If she were planning it, there are better ways to do it. Right now, you have nothing but a thin motive, and no evidence to support it. It's not worth wasting time on. We have other cases…"

Miller persisted. "…It isn't only motive. The crime scene doesn't look right either. Let's say the guy is going to burn down the house, he pours the gas all over the place and then leaves the gas trail to the door to light it off from — right?"

"Yeah, I suppose," said Johnson.

"Well, our guy is in the middle of the room with the gas can next to him. And the matchbox that he supposedly used to light it is over 6 feet away."

"What's the fire inspector say about that?" asked Johnson

"Not much. He seems confident that Roberts accidentally lit himself on fire, and ran into the house in a panic."

"That works too, doesn't it? Why not believe the expert?" asked Johnson.

"I suppose," said Miller, "but I don't like it. It smells hinky. Another thing, the firefighters found the door locked. Who closes themselves in right before lighting a fire? And here's what really bothers me. The guy's truck is in the attached garage, with all his stuff — and the door is down. Who lights a house on fire before getting their truck out of the garage?"

Johnson drummed his chubby fingers on his stomach. "I'll give you that — it's odd. Still, remember Occam's Razor; the simplest answer is usually the right one. The simple solution here is that Roberts is pissed at his wife, and burns down the house rather than letting her have it. He's drunk and stupid and lights himself on fire. Or have you considered he did it on purpose? He wouldn't be the first husband to off himself over a split. Maybe the Mrs. had a boyfriend."

"Maybe. I still think I should run down a few loose ends."

Johnson huffed, then sniffed. "Okay fine; spend a few hours on it. Talk to the wife. But don't make a hobby case of this, we're backed up. See if there is anything solid to build on. If not, let it go, and report to me in a day or two. Personally, I think you're chasing windmills?"

"Chasing windmills? That doesn't make any sense. Since when do windmills run?"

"Read a book once in a while, dip shit. Now, shut up and get out of here. And remember, don't go off on this. We got a crap load of cases backed up."

Miller returned to his desk thinking, *It's tilting at windmills from Don Quixote', dumb ass. But you got a point. There are too many loose ends.*

Miller collapsed in his chair, lost in thought. He heard Rivera say. "Let me guess. Jabba wanted you to hurry up and close your cases. I bet he said, *'We got a backlog of cases, downtown is on my ass.'* Am I right?"

"Something like that," said Miller.

Rivera shook his head in disgust. "He doesn't care a damn bit about police work, just clearing cases, so he looks good. I told you to take a bagel, it smooths him out."

"Yep, he's a lot of things, but a detective ain't one of them." answered Miller. Pulling out a sheet of paper, he started making what he called *a free association list* of questions and problems. He used it to help put a case in context. The trick, he knew, was not to analyze, just write what came to mind, almost like brainstorming. He wrote:

1. Evidence suggesting he likely intended to light fire = stuff in truck, her clothes.

2. Evidence against = Body location, truck in garage.

3. Did he accidentally set self on fire? Maybe not?

4. If not, how did he get burned? He wasn't drugged, injured, or restrained. Surprised? Had partner?

5. Signs of suicide? Poured gas on self? Why matches 6 ft away?

6. If killed, who wanted him dead? Wife? Why burn down house? The wife's location at time of fire? Motive? What about opportunity? Why burn down own house?

7. Was he fleeing town? Why?

To Do:

1. Talk to on scene patrolman at domestic call. What did wife do to put him in hospital?

2. Talk to the officer who interviewed her about revenge porn.

3. Crime scene report, Any sign of struggle,

3. Talk to wife- Alibi? Boyfriend? Boyfriend = partner in murder?

4. Check financials of both wife and victim.

Miller tapped his pencil against the sheet of paper and waited for another idea to surface. When nothing came to him, he picked up the phone and called the lab. He requested they send the crime scene report and all pictures. Next, he logged into the department server and pulled up three reports. The first was the domestic disturbance report, followed by the complaint report filed by Racheal Roberts. Finally, the report filed by the officers who investigated Mr. Roberts. He had read them once, to see what was in them. Now, he read them to see what wasn't.

# Chapter 18

Father Tom found Nick sitting in the study's overstuffed leather chair. He appeared more relaxed than when they last met. Better rested as well. "Dominick, my boy. How goes it?"

"Hello Father, it goes well."

The priest had no sooner sat than Nancy came in with a tray. On it was a coffee carafe, a small cup of cream, and some sugar packets. There was only a single cup and saucer. The priest looked unhappily at the lone cup and then at his secretary. He sighed and shook his head. "Thank you, Mrs. Holthouse."

He turned his attention to Nick. "So, Dominick, I must say that you look considerably more alive than the last time I saw you."

"Yeah, I've been sleeping better the last few nights. So you know, I also put a pause on the drinking, like you suggested."

"Good, that's fine," said Father Tom. "I believe I also asked you to change up your routine some, try to get out more, maybe go to the gym."

"I haven't started back…" The sound of a gentle knock on the door interrupted Nick.

Father Tom called out, "Yes?"

The door cracked open enough for Nancy to stick her head through. "Can I interrupt for a moment?"

The priest chuckled. "By all means, considering that you already have."

The woman entered the room with a coffee cup and a smug smile. "Are you sure I'm not interrupting? I *can* come back later."

Smiling broadly, and again chuckling, the priest replied. "Nonsense. You come bearing gifts, and blessings a hundred-fold shall be yours."

The woman shook her head as she set down the cup. "Oh nonsense. Would a simple thank you be so hard?" The woman turned to Nick. "Dominick, can I trust you to make sure he only drinks one cup? The man has the self-control of a beagle puppy."

Nick tried to disguise a laugh behind his hand. "I will do my best, ma'am."

In a poor imitation of an English lord, Father Tom declared, "Leave us now, woman. We men have weighty affairs of state to ponder."

With a dismissive wave of the hand, Nancy turned her back on the men and moved towards the door. "Lord help us," she said.

From behind her she heard a sincere, "Thank you, Nancy."

Nick said, "You do like your coffee, don't you?"

The priest smiled as he filled his cup. "Alas, I am helpless against its call." He sat back and added, "You were saying…"

"I said that I have not gone back to the gym yet. But I have started taking daily walks in the park – working my way back to jogging."

"Good, that's good Dominick. I think it's important that we change some behaviors."

"What does that mean?" asked Nick.

"We will get to that in a minute. I believe I gave you a few other tasks."

Nick leaned forward in the chair, his elbows propped on his knees. He looked relaxed, but engaged. He said, "I met with Becky."

"Outstanding! How did that go?"

"Really well. It was good. We talked over a lot of things; things got said that needed to be put in the open."

"How do you feel about what was said?"

"You were right about my meeting with her. It did me — both of us — good, but I am not entirely sure how I feel. It got pretty heavy. We both kind of put everything on the table, and I haven't worked through it all yet. I guess I feel — I don't know, a bit overwhelmed, but mostly relieved, I guess."

"Relieved?"

"It's hard to explain, Father. I almost feel like a weight has been lifted. I'm lighter if that makes sense."

"It does. Emotions, especially suppressed ones can be heavy burdens, " said the priest. "Tell me about feeling overwhelmed. It's an interesting choice of words."

"Seeing her brought up a lot of feelings; some were unexpected, confused might be a better word."

"Explain that, Dom."

"At first, seeing her, and hearing her explain about her – her *fling*, made me angry. I expected that. But, as time went on, I felt more — I don't know — empathetic? Maybe even a little affection, I guess. I feel all jumbled up inside. I shouldn't feel anything but resentment; what she did was unforgivable, but yet… it's just so damned confusing. I don't know what to do with that."

"What to do with what?'

"Look, Father, my wife cheated on me. She disrespected me, and it got out — it's common knowledge, and that's humiliating. I should be furious. I have every right to be. Any guy would tell me to kick her to the curb. That makes sense to me. But, I find myself rationalizing it some. She says she loves me, and I believe her. She says it was just the one time, and it was just sex; that she got caught up in a moment of weakness. That's crap, and I know it, but I want to forgive her. And that's messed up."

"No, it's not messed up. You feel what you feel, Dom."

"You're a priest; of course you think I should take her back. Catholic law doesn't allow divorce, now does it.?"

The priest sighed. "Oh Dominick, it's not that simple. You're right, the church doesn't condone divorce. As a priest, I think you need to do everything you can to make your marriage work. As a follower of Jesus Christ, I think you should forgive her whether you stay together or not. It's the Christian thing to do. Speaking as your counselor, I think you need to stop worrying about what you *should* feel and focus on what you *do* feel. You have to ask yourself whether continuing with Becky will be a positive or negative influence on your emotional well-being. Only you know if you can trust that relationship again."

"That's not much help," said Nick.

"It's the best I got. I will say this though, you are going through some things. Your marriage problems are a symptom, not the cause."

Nick sat back in his chair and crossed his arms. It was a defensive posture, and it didn't escape Father Tom's attention. "Meaning?" asked Nick.

Father Tom poured another cup of coffee and gestured the cup toward Nick. He shook his head-no. The priest shrugged and put a splash of cream in the coffee. He sipped it, and said, "Meaning things were not going well between you and Becky before the affair. More precisely, they were not going well for you." He waited for Nick to respond, he got nothing so he continued. "Becky came in to see me the other day."

"Yeah, she told me." said Nick.

"She said that for a while before you broke up, you seemed to be struggling."

"I was under some stress, and maybe I wasn't my best self, but it wasn't that big a deal."

"Why were you under stress?"

"Nothing special, just work stuff, maybe some husband-wife things too. But again, nothing special."

"What did you mean by *not your best self?*"

"I admit, I was a bit grumpy for a while, maybe a little inattentive. What else did she say? Did she talk about us?"

"Look Nick, this is a bit ticklish. I owe her confidentiality the same as you. I can discuss what she reported regarding *your* behavior, but I can't divulge anything about how she felt, or what she is going through now."

"That doesn't seem fair."

"Fair or not, she has a right to privacy, just as I wouldn't divulge details about you. Besides, if you two talked you likely know more about what she thinks than I do. If you have questions, talk to her some more, or come in together."

Father Tom took another sip of coffee, then set the cup down. "Now let's get back to you. Becky described you as more than just grumpy. She said you were sullen, withdrawn, and defensive. She also said you were having a lot of bad dreams. That you would wake up in the middle of the night in a cold sweat."

Nick shook his head. "She's exaggerating."

"Oh?" asked the priest. "Marco said about the same thing. He also said that you have lost interest in most of your old hobbies. And that you seem to have isolated yourself from your friends. I'll add that Becky said that you are constantly on edge, and restless. She also says that unexpected noises startle you. Does any of that sound accurate?" The priest studied Nick's face closely as he spoke. Tension was clearly building in the man.

Nick paused for a few moments before speaking. "Look, I get everybody's trying to help but, this is all just…"

Father Tom interrupted him. "Nick, before you answer, I want to remind you that anything you say here *stays* here. Your safe here. I remind you I have known you for 20 years- I don't suspect you're struggling — I know you are. It's as obvious the sun on a cloudless day. I'm here to help you, but I can't do that if you don't cooperate. I am asking you to trust me."

Nick buried his face in his hands. In a raspy voice, barely above a whisper, he said, "You don't understand. I am losing everything; all I have left is my job. If you tell the chief that I can't hack it, that I'm not fit — I got nothing. Sure, I've been dealing with some stuff, but I swear to you I can handle it. Getting right with Becky was a big load off. I am telling you I can do this."

"Son, my report to the chief only answers two questions; were there extenuating circumstances that contributed to your altercation with that man, and do you appear emotionally fit for duty? I'll put it to you plainly. If I wrote that report today, I'd tell the chief that you hit that man because you're having problems with self-control. I would also tell him that as you sit here right now, I don't think you should be working. I think you are hanging on by your fingernails and it wouldn't take much for you to become a danger to yourself or others. If you were to go back to work, I promise you that within a matter of weeks, you will end up in trouble again, for one thing or another. Dominick, my friend, you are not even close to being able to handle anything."

Nick's eyes met Father Tom's, and for the first time, he could see that Nick's defenses had fallen. The mask had been stripped away and the pain and desperation were as obvious as the tears gathering in the man's eyes. Nick whispered, "Then I'm lost."

Father Tom laid his hand on Nick's shoulder. He gently said, "You're not lost, you're just groping in the dark. If you want to save your job; if you want to reclaim your life, stop hiding from this, and face it. Nick, I promise you — you can get better. You only have to stop denying something is wrong, and bring it out into the light. Stop hiding in the dark."

Nick's eyes snapped open, and he stared at the priest. "What? What did you say? Where did you hear that?"

"I said, stop hiding in the dark. I didn't hear it anywhere. Why, does that have special meaning to you?"

"No – no. It's just that someone else said that not long ago."

"Well, they were right. Nick, we can do this if you work with me. Can you do that?"

With tears streaming down his face, Nick nodded yes.

"Okay, let's start again. The symptoms that Becky and Marco described, how long have they been going on?"

Nick leaned back in his chair and looked at the ceiling. "I am not sure exactly when they started. Maybe a year and a half ago. Maybe before that."

"What about the nightmares? When did they start?"

"I guess at about the same time as everything else. It sort of sneaks up on you. It wasn't like I just woke up one day and felt like shit."

"I understand," said the priest. "Tell me about the dreams. Do they have similar themes? Do you remember them when you wake up?"

"Shrinks and dreams," said Nick. "You all get worked up about them."

"Stop being elusive, Nick. Tell me about them."

"Yeah, they're mostly the same, sometimes a little different, but not much. At first, it was always just a house fire and I would be trying to rescue a little girl. And she would die in front of me, and she blames me for it. After Becky and I split up, the dreams changed some. Besides the little girl, I was also trying to save Becky. Everybody ends up dying."

"Do you die?"

"I don't know. I always wake up when the little girl falls apart."

"What do you mean, the little girl falls apart?"

"Just before she dies, she grabs me, or I grab her. Then she just crumbles into a pile of ashes. But she always tells me — she says — it's my fault. Becky blames me too."

"Becky blames you for the little girl?"

"No – maybe. It's all kind of jumbled up. I think she blames me for her…"

"Her what?"

Nick choked back a sob. "Her affair — she blames *me* for the affair. Becky says I abandoned the little girl, just like I abandoned her. She calls me a coward — she says I'm weak."

"Nick," said the priest, "do you have any idea why Becky would say such a thing?"

Nick took in a deep breath and blew it out to compose himself. "No. not at all."

"No idea at all?"

Nick shifted his weight onto one hip, the priest noted the obvious unease in his Friend. "I suppose, it's because she must think I am weak. Deep down… maybe she had the affair because she doesn't see me – this thing– maybe I am weak."

"Has Becky ever said anything like that?"

"No."

"Have any of your coworkers questioned your firefighting ability?"

"No, not that I know of."

"Then why do you feel like Becky and the little girl are blaming you?"

"I don't know," said Nick. "I think about it all the time – it eats at me."

"How often do you have this dream?"

Nick said, "At first, it was only once in a while. But as time went on, it got more frequent. Lately I've been having it a lot." Nick paused, he sniffed, and rubbed his eyes. "Father?"

"Yes?"

"Sometimes, lately, I see images of the little girl when I'm awake and close my eyes. It really scares me. I think I'm losing it."

"Do you think she's real?"

"No, of course not."

"Does she speak to you, or interact with your environment?"

"No," said Nick, "she just appears like a mental flash in my head."

"Then you're not losing it. It's not unheard of; sometimes people fixate on imagery from particularly vivid recurring dreams. It's almost like getting a song stuck in your head, only it's an image. You'd need a psychiatrist to explain why the brain fixates. But I assure you, you're not losing your mind. Have the other symptoms gotten worse as well? Especially lately?"

Nick said, "Yeah, I guess they have."

"Tell me about what happened at the fire a few weeks ago."

"What? What fire? What do you mean?"

"Dominick, I think you know what fire I mean. You were at a fatal fire not long ago. I understand that something happened. Tell me about it."

Nick began fidgeting with a button on his shirt. "It wasn't a big deal. We were fighting a basement fire, and tactics got screwed up. Charlie, Marco, and I almost got toasted, and I mouthed off to the Battalion Chief and Captain. I shouldn't have, but in fairness, we almost got killed."

"That's not what I meant. What happened when Marco asked you to help move the body?"

"Marco told you about that, huh?"

"What happened, Nick?"

Nick let out a big sigh. "Sometimes. I get something like… I guess you would call them panic attacks. I don't know why, but I had one. I just couldn't bring myself to pick up that body."

"Tell me about what happened."

"This — this is hard. When I saw her…" Nick took a sip of water, "She was burnt badly, and bloated. The stench was… have you ever smelled a burnt body?"

"No," said the priest. "I am grateful to say I have not."

"It's a sickly sweet smell, almost overpowering. Seeing her like that, knowing I had to touch her, freaked me out. I mean, I've handled dead people before, more than a few times. This was different; I got really dizzy and saw little floating lights in my eyes. Then I got short of breath and I felt a tightness in my chest. I am ashamed to admit this, but I wanted to run, to get away. I had to."

The priest asked. "Do you remember what you were thinking?"

"No, not specifically, anyway. I just remember thinking, don't touch her; whatever you do, don't touch her."

"How long have you been having these attacks?"

"A few months now," said Nick

"What brings them on?"

Nick stood up and began moving around the room. Not pacing, more like wandering. He feigned interest in small items in the room. "I am not sure — different things, I suppose. Sometimes, when things startle me, or I get stressed. Sometimes, they just happen."

"Are they occurring more often lately?"

Nick now had his back turned to the priest. He was pretending to inspect the diplomas and pictures on the wall again. He said, "Yeah, they're happening more often, and they're getting worse. The last one almost made me pass out."

"They scare you, don't they?" asked the priest.

Still looking at the wall, Nick replied, "Of course, wouldn't they you?"

"Nick, sit back down." Father Tom waited for Nick to return to his chair before continuing. "I mean, they bother you more than the other symptoms."

"Here's the thing Father. You can't be a firefighter if you pass out every time you see a dead body, or hear a loud noise. This is a career ender. You wanted to know why I didn't come see you earlier, and why I don't want to talk about all of this now? Well, there it is. The truth of the matter is - *I* - have real doubts whether I can do the job anymore. Now you know."

"Balderdash!" said the priest.

"Excuse me?"

"Nick, what if I told you that those panic attacks are a common physical response to what you're going through? We can address them."

"Okay," said Nick. "I guess that's the million-dollar question. What am I going through?"

"Have you ever heard of post traumatic stress disorder?"

"Sure, combat soldiers get it. I haven't been in Afghanistan for nearly 20 years. It's a little late for it to show up now, don't you think?"

"Maybe. Maybe not," said the priest. "But you should know that firefighters get it too."

"So, just like that, you talk to me for 30 minutes and you think that's what I have."

"Nick, my boy, I suspected it before we even met last week. I was sure of it pretty quickly. You're knotted up so tight you don't know which way to turn. Frankly, I'm surprised you haven't cracked months ago. I wish you would've come to me last year, or at the very least, when you and Becky split. We could have saved you a lot of grief and pain."

"So, what now? asked Nick. "Drugs?"

"I am not a medical doctor; I don't prescribe drugs. They may help a little, but they won't address the underlying issue. However, the first step is to have you visit a doctor. It would be wise to make sure you have nothing going wrong under the hood. I'll talk to the chief; he will make arrangements with the company doctor. She may prescribe an antidepressant to take the edge off."

Nick said, "If it's all the same to you, I'd rather use my GP."

"No, it should be Doc Fetter. Trust me, it's in your best interest for the department to know what's going on here."

"I doubt that's in my best interest at all."

"Don't be daft son. Hiding an injury – physical or emotional – from the department is foolish. It's partly why you're here now."

"Okay, I hear you. Then what?" asked Nick.

"Then we figure out what's at the bottom of all this. You say that the symptoms started about a year and a half ago, is that right? Did anything remarkable happen prior to the symptoms?"

"Yeah, a year and a half ago. What do you mean by remarkable?"

"A particularly bad call, or maybe something in your personal life that was shocking or disturbing."

"I'm a firefighter/medic-, dealing with disturbing things is pretty much in the job description. But no, nothing stands out. I don't remember anything in particular that got to me."

Father Tom stood and said, "Well, we will talk about that more next week. Here's what I would like you to do in the meantime. First, I will make that appointment with Dr. Fetter. I also want you to make a point of re-engaging in more normal activities. Keep up with exercising daily. And listen, you need to make an effort to be around people, even if you don't want to. I also want you to do some research on post traumatic stress disorder and cognitive behavior therapy. You can prepare a list of questions for me if you have any. Finally, I want you to think more about any events that might stand out as being particularly disturbing to you over the last two or three years. That's important."

Nick nodded and said, "You're quite a stern taskmaster."

"It's not so much. And Dominick, it will help. I want you to understand and believe that things *can* get better. You will get through this."

Nick shook Father Tom's hand and turned to leave. He paused for a moment and then turned around. "Father, thank you. I want you to know that I really appreciate what you're trying to do for me."

The priest watched Nick leave. Under his breath, he said, "Good, this went well." He then returned to his office and sat down to take notes. A few minutes later, Nancy came in with a glass of water. "What's that for?" he asked?

"Did you remember to take your pills this morning?"

"Oh," said the priest. "I did forget, thank you. Leave the water, I'll take them in a moment."

The woman held her ground. She set the water down in front of him, folded her arms, and stared at him impatiently. Finally, the priest understood and grunted. He opened his desk and retrieved his pills. After taking them, he said, "Are you happy now, Madam Whipcrack?"

The woman sniffed, "Whipcrack, hmm? That's gratitude. You would be dead in a week without me. Goodness knows, you would forget to breathe if someone didn't remind you."

The priest nodded. "I am sure I would survive at least a few weeks, but point taken. And your help is greatly appreciated."

She blushed, but waved off the compliment. "How did it go today?"

"Today was a good day. I think I can help him."

She bestowed upon him one of her very rare smiles. "If anybody can help him, it would be you. God gave you a gift."

"God, and the University of Notre Dame."

She scolded, "Knowing a thing and doing a thing are not the same. Don't belittle the gifts of God."

The priest smiled. "Sometimes, I think *you* should be a priest."

"Maybe someday, the church will give women the opportunity to serve. For now, I am content to help you as best I can."

He patted her hand. "And I am better for it."

The remark made her blush thoroughly. "Oh, go on. Now, do you need anything before I leave?"

"Yes, Nancy, I would like you to do something for me. Put together a packet of information briefly explaining the signs and symptoms of post traumatic stress syndrome. I think there is some resource material in one of my files. Also, put together a packet on critical incident stress debriefing, and look up some organizations that can be training resources for our fire department."

She replied, "Is this for you, or am my putting this together for someone else?"

"It's for the fire chief. I think I want to have a discussion with him about being more proactive regarding protecting the emotional health of our firefighters."

"Good," said Nancy. "I'll take care of it right away."

"Oh, one more thing," he added. "Call over to the chief's office and ask him to send over all the station reports for calls that Dominick worked."

"How far back?"

"Let's say three years," he replied.

"That will be a lot of reports, I would think. Do you want them to apply some search criteria? What are you looking for?"

He shrugged. "I am not exactly sure. But I will know it when I see it. Let's start with fire calls involving injuries to children."

# Chapter 19

He had intended to surprise her by knocking on the door. However, the pain in the ass desk clerk doggedly insisted that, absent an emergency or a warrant, he needed to call up to her room before giving out the room number. Rather than send him up, she told him she would be down shortly. He wanted to see where, and how, she was living, to get a sense of the woman. But this was a voluntary interview, and he needed to be gentle with her. He didn't want her to clam up, or worse yet, lawyer up. So, he was doing it her way. Apparently, Racheal Robert's way meant making him wait. And so Detective Frank Miller cooled his heals in the lobby of the Dunbar Residence Inn.

This was yet another frustration in what had been an exasperating morning. He had gone to the Mercy House Shelter looking for the widow Roberts, only to find she had moved out. Roberts had left a forwarding address to a local hotel, but they had no record of her. A dozen phone calls finally led him to the Dunbar.

He impatiently slapped his hand on the armrest of the leather club chair. The noise reverberated through the otherwise quiet lobby. Miller noticed that this drew an irritated glance from the desk clerk. He smiled and nodded at the clerk; *Good*, he thought, *I hope it annoys the crap out of you; you little putz*. As he waited, Miller considered how best to play it with Roberts. The more he dug into the case, the more complicated it got, and Mrs. Roberts was certainly in the middle of it somehow. He just couldn't figure out how.

The evening before, he had met with the two patrol officers who had responded to the domestic disturbance call at the Roberts home a few weeks before the fire. They verified that Mr. Roberts had roughed up his wife during an argument. Apparently, she got knocked out when he hit her. When he pushed the two about why Mr. Roberts ended up at the hospital, they got a little circumspect. With prodding, they admitted that Roberts got punched out by one of the responding firefighters; a guy named Dominick Adler. It was a detail they left out of the report.

When asked why they didn't arrest the firefighter, they hinted they considered it some street justice and let it go as professional courtesy. They added both Mr. and Mrs. Roberts seemed adamant that they didn't want to pursue any charges. Miller found that detail curious – something to look into.

The conversation with the two officers had fired up the synapses of his brain. He loved a good hunt, and he definitely smelled something afield. Miller sensed an important piece of the puzzle had just fallen in his lap; he just wasn't sure how it fit. As he waited, he rolled the information around in his head. *One thing is certain: there has to be a connection between Racheal Roberts and Dominick Adler. A love triangle of some sort? Maybe something else; he had to have a reason to punch the guy. Was Adler the reason for the Roberts' big fight? And what about the sex tapes? How did that figure in? Was Adler part of that too?*

Miller's phone conversation with Danny Martin earlier that morning further reinforced his suspicions. Martin was the vice detective who was investigating Racheal Roberts's complaint. He learned the wife accused her husband of running some sort of pornography website. According to her, Roberts had used hidden cameras to capture and post several explicit videos of her, as well as himself with numerous other women; all without their consent..

To Miller, this information strengthened Mrs. Roberts' motive, but he still wasn't sure how it tied into the firefighter. He thought, *They are hooking up and the victim's whole revenge porn scheme seems to fit, but not perfectly. Either way, a firefighter involved in a death by fire was awfully coincidental. I need to play this right; let her tell the story; just add a nudge or two here and there. When the time is right, I'll throw her a curve ball and see if she swings. One way or another, I'll find out how this porno thing ties into Roberts' death. And I will learn what the wife and Adler are to each other — and if it's enough to get hubby out of the way. One thing fits for sure; most murders always come down to money, jealousy, or revenge. This one is starting to fit all three.*

The ding of the elevator interrupted his thoughts. Out walked a woman he assumed to be Racheal Roberts. She was petite, likely around 5'4" and couldn't weigh 110 pounds soaking wet. She was pretty, but her posture, her clothes and even her hair all seemed intended to avoid notice. The word *mousy* came to mind. *She doesn't look capable of murder*, he thought. *But then, they never do.*

He rose and extended his hand. She returned a timid hand shake. He showed her his badge and said, "Hello Mrs. Roberts, my name is Detective Frank Miller. I am investigating your husband's death; would you mind answering a few routine questions?"

"I am not sure how I can help you. My husband died trying to set our house on fire. I don't know any more than that."

"I understand, Mrs. Roberts. May I call you Racheal?"

Apparently ignoring the request, she said, "Let's go in here to talk."

She led him into an adjoining room. For lack of a better description, it impressed Miller as an attempt at a formal sitting room. Light green paint sat atop oak wainscoting. Knock off paintings of Englishmen on a fox hunt were scattered on the walls. Plush carpet and an imposing stone fireplace completed the look. There were three furniture groupings, each featured an overstuffed couch, coffee table and two comfortable looking wingback chairs. It was mid morning, and the room was empty. She closed the glass panel door behind them and moved to one of the overstuffed chairs. Miller sat on the couch, facing her. He said, "Mrs. Roberts…"

She interrupted, "You can call me Racheal."

Miller gave the woman in insincere but practiced smile. "Racheal, let me begin by offering my condolences for the loss of your husband. It must have been a shock."

She nodded, and said, "Thank you, it was. We were not getting along, but I never wanted … it was just terrible."

Miller noticed that the woman in front of him had both hands in her lap; she was squeezing her right hand with her left. He also noticed that her eyes were moist. "You said just now that your husband died while trying to set your house on fire. Any idea why he would do that?"

Racheal gazed at her folded hands while answering. "My husband was a petty and vindictive man. We had just separated, and I was filing for divorce. I was going to get the house; it would be just like him to burn it down rather than let me have it."

"You two were having trouble, then?"

A wry smile crossed Racheal's face. "You could say that."

Miller added, "I saw in the reports that you and your husband had a pretty nasty fight not long before the fire. I understand he hurt you — you ended up in the hospital. Is that right?"

"Yes," she said.

"Can you tell me what happened that night?"

She looked less scared and more perturbed. "I already told the officers there that night. What does this have to do with the fire, anyway."

In his most sincere tone, Miller reassured her. "It's important that we understand why your husband did what he did. It's in your best interest to help us — You know, for insurance purposes. If it looks like he was burning down the house for an insurance claim to split between the two of you, that could be a problem. If, on the other hand, it was just an act of spite — well, then, that's a different thing altogether."

Miller expected his veiled accusation to rattle her. To his surprise, she barely reacted at all. She said, "Insurance claim? That's a joke, right? I mean, we barely had any equity in the house at all. Even if the insurance company pays off, I'm sure I'll be in the hole. No, Sly, I mean Sylvester, got served that afternoon with a court order to vacate the premises. I promise you; he did it for spite."

"The night he put you in the hospital, you had a big fight. What was that about?"

"I found out he was having an affair, several of them, actually. I confronted him and he got mad."

Miller said, "That's not the whole truth now, is it? You filed criminal charges on him for running a pornography business using illicitly gained videos. You told the detective that he filmed women without their knowing it. That was why you fought, wasn't it?"

"Yes, that's right. There were videos of him and several women — They were awful."

"What makes you think they didn't consent to be in the videos?" Miller asked. He noticed tears forming in the woman's eyes.

"You could just tell."

Miller gently said, "I hate to ask this, but I have to. Are the videos of you?"

Tears were now flowing freely. Racheal sniffed, "Some, not all. There were… Jesus, this is humiliating. There were at least 3 other women, maybe more. Again, what does any of that have to do with the fire?"

Miller ignored the question. "Racheal, I've been around the block a few times. Believe me when I tell you that nothing shocks me, and I swear I won't judge you. But I need to know the truth. Were you and your husband working together, making videos? I understand fan sites can be lucrative."

"Of course not!" she said. "I would never … I had no idea. I was furious when I found out that he filmed me without me knowing it. It was mortifying, and I am absolutely sure he did the same thing to those other women too. My husband was a pig."

*And there it is*, thought Miller. "Okay," he said. "Your husband must've had a computer to do what he did. Did the two of you share a computer?"

"No, we each had our own laptops."

"When the police searched your husband's house for the laptop and his video equipment, they couldn't find anything. Also, the night of the fire, no computer was found in the house. Do you have any idea where he might have hidden it?"

Racheal let out a sigh. "I have no idea. Why are you asking?"

Miller persisted, "Is it possible someone burned down the house after they took the computer? Could somebody else know about the videos, and perhaps wanted to get rid of them?"

"The awful things were on the Internet. Anybody who saw them would know about them. I don't see how getting the videos on his computer would help anything."

"The videos aren't on the net anymore; he took them down."

Racheal nodded. "The night we fought, I threatened to call you guys about the videos. It's what got him so angry. He pulled them down because of that."

Miller asked, "Is it possible he was blackmailing somebody? Could there be other videos that hadn't been posted."

"Maybe, if he needed money, he'd do something like that. Why are you asking about blackmail? You said he set *himself* on fire." Racheal's eyes went wide with realization. "Oh, my God, you think somebody killed him."

Miller casually shrugged. "Perhaps, perhaps not. We haven't concluded anything yet. That's why I am here; to eliminate possibilities. It's how we determine what happened; it's a process of elimination."

"Sorry detective, I can't help you with who might have wanted to hurt him. He was one of those kinda guys who could charm the pants off of you, but he was a schemer, and he left a lot of hurt feelings in his wake. He played me for a fool. I had no idea what he was into."

Miller felt it was time to lob the grenade; the all-important question. "Speaking of hurt feelings; an odd thing happened the night you went to the hospital. One of the firefighters punched your husband. What was that about?"

Miller noticed the tiniest tensing in the corners of Racheal's eyes. She said, "I heard that. Can't say I'm sorry. I am not sure what happened. I was still kinda shook up."

"The guy's name was Dominick Adler. How do you know him?"

Racheal said, "I don't. I've never met him."

Miller leaned forward so as to close the gap between the two of them. He wanted to intimidate her by invading her personal space. To his surprise, she held her ground. He said, "So, you have never heard of him?"

"I didn't say that," she said. "I know the name. I work with his wife; she and I are casual friends. But I've never actually met him."

Miller propped his elbow on his knee and then his cheek on his fist. "Really? I have it from pretty good authority that you and him are friends. In fact, it's my understanding that the two of you are *more* than friends."

Racheal's eyes found Miller's and held them in an icy gaze. "I am sorry, detective. You've got some bad information. I wouldn't know the man if I saw him on the street. And for the record, I have never had an affair — with anyone — ever."

Miller deliberately put an ominous tone in his voice when he slowly said, "Racheal, having an affair is not a crime. But lying to me *will* get you in trouble. Think carefully before answering. Are you denying you had an affair with Dominick Adler?"

Miller noted that Racheal never blinked or flinched at the threat. Gone was the timid-looking Mrs. Roberts. The woman before him now looked combative. She said, "Detective, I said before, I've never met the man. And tell your witness, if there is one, that they are full of crap."

Miller leaned back in his chair. "Well, I'm sorry. I guess I got that wrong. I'll check with my source and see what's going on there." His inner voice said, *Well, that didn't work. She is either telling the truth, or she is one cool and calculating liar.* He said, "So, if you two aren't at *least* friends, why do you suppose he punched your husband?"

"I have no idea. Why don't you ask *him?* Is there anything else, detective?"

Miller asked, "Yeah, when we searched the house, we didn't find your husband's gun. Any idea where it might be?"

Miller noted the look of genuine puzzlement when she answered. "I didn't even know he owned a gun. It would surprise me if he did. He never showed any interest in guns. My husband was a schemer, but he wasn't a hard-core criminal. Really, he was a bit of a coward."

Miller stood up, she remained sitting. He said, "I have to ask, just a formality, you understand. Where were you around 10 PM on the night of the fire?"

Racheal Roberts let out an exasperated huff. "You really should read your own police reports. Your officers found me at the Mercy House shelter on Maple Avenue."

Miller smiled; there was a chill in it. "I *did* read the report, Mrs. Robert's. It tells me where you were at 1 AM, not at 10 p.m. Are you saying you were there at 10 PM as well?"

"Yes, Detective Miller. That is what I'm telling you. You can check the records. They track who comes in and out, you know, for security."

As Miller was walking towards the exit, he said to himself, *Yes, Mrs. Roberts, I will most certainly be checking on that.* Just before he opened the door, he said, "Oh, one more thing. You said you had a laptop as well. We didn't find it in the fire either. Do you know where it is?"

"I do. My laptop is in the back of my car."

"That was a lucky break," said Miller. "You know, that it wasn't in the house during the fire."

Racheal replied, "Not really. It's hardly ever in the house. I take it to work with me, to do homework for my online classes during my breaks and lunch hour. It's in the car most of the time."

"That's very good. Unfortunately, I am afraid I'm going to have to take it to the station and have our techs go through it. Don't worry, it's just a formality and you will get it back soon."

Racheal stood and crossed her arms. "I need the computer, and it has personal stuff on it. I do not want you rooting around through my files. So, unless you have a warrant, you're not taking it anywhere."

"Mrs. Roberts, I'll be blunt. I want to see the videos…"

"… Oh, really? And why is that?" The look on her face made it clear that she thought his interest wasn't entirely professional.

A bit flustered, he replied, "For the case. I-I need to see who else may be in them." Regaining his composure, he went on offense. "If those videos had anything to do with the death of your husband, then the people in them may have had motive. As it stands now, we only know about you. You can see why helping us is good for you, right?"

"Detective, my husband set himself on fire. The videos had nothing to do with his death. Even if they did, I don't have a copy of them."

Miller shook his head. "You filed charges on him for making them, it stands to reason you would have made copies — for evidence."

"I told you. He took them down, I never had the chance.'

Miller tried a bluff. It almost always worked. He said, "So you told me. Really, it's better if you cooperate. I can get a warrant if you insist, but it will look like you're hiding something."

Racheal glared at him. "I will be happy to cooperate once you bring me a warrant."

"As you wish. Racheal, if you're protecting someone, say a boyfriend, you're not playing this smart."

She huffed. "Back to that again? I think you should leave now."

"Very well," said Miller. "But I may have more questions later– I'll be in touch soon. Thank you for your help."

Racheal watched the detective leave the room. As the door shut behind him, her hands covered her face, then wiped away tears. A few moments later, she reached for her phone, and with trembling hands, she dialed a number. "Hello, Becky. I just had a detective here and…"

As Miller walked to his car, he said to himself, *she's certainly not the timid little thing I made her out to be. And it's damn certain that she knows more than she's telling, especially about those videos and this Adler guy. I think I'll head over to the fire station and see what I can dig up. I also want to find out just who is in those videos.*

# Chapter 20

Nick sat reading. Cat had perched herself on the back of the chair with her paws on his shoulder. Since Haley's visit, Cat had become much more affectionate. Nick guessed she had concluded that he was indeed human. "Are you comfortable, your highness?" Cat purred in response.

The book was getting good; the detective had just thrown his captain through a window. *I can relate to that,* he thought. His phone interrupted him; it was Charlie. "This is a surprise," he said.

"Hey Nick. How would you feel about some company?"

"Sure, that'd be great. Did Marco put you up to this? Maybe his version of a wellness check?"

"No, Marco has nothing to do with this, and I'm not checking up on you. We need to talk — It's important."

"Are you okay? What's going on?"

"I am fine, it's you… I'll be over in about an hour, see you then."

*I wonder what the hell that's about? Whatever it is, I bet Marco is involved somehow, he just doesn't want to admit it.*

Other than the brief call about Robert's dying, he and Marco hadn't spoken since their argument at his hearing. Nick guessed his friend was giving him space. He regretted the way he had left things with Marco. Jazz too, for that matter. Becky was right, they just wanted to help.

He started regretting a lot of things lately. It felt like a fog was lifting, and the view wasn't very pretty. *I'll call them tomorrow, maybe head over to their place and hang for the night. Hell, I haven't seen the kids in months.* He and Becky were godparents to Marco's kids. It wasn't just an honorary position; they loved those kids.

Guilt washed over him, *I shouldn't have disappeared out of their lives; I've neglected a lot of people and things lately.* Watching Marco's kids grow up is what inspired him and Becky to talk about finally trying for some of their own. He wished he hadn't put her off and wondered, *would things be better if we had kids… or worse?*

He did his best to straighten up Casa Del Crapo, and even threw a blanket over Cat's nasty couch. He regretted not having any beer or liquor in the house, but he had gotten rid of it all when Father Tom had told him to stop drinking. He had to admit he felt better, but it seemed weird to not have anything in the house to offer a guest… not that he ever had any.

Nick heard footsteps on the gravel drive and opened the door to greet her. He watched as she walked towards the wrought iron stairs. Nick always found it odd to see her out of uniform, it happened so rarely. The day had been hot, and the swelter of the afternoon lingered into the evening. Charlie had dressed for the weather, wearing a loose-fitting blouse that exposed her abdomen, and a skimpy pair of shorts. *She's showing a lot of skin,* he thought. Then chastised himself for appreciating the view. He also scolded himself for liking that she was carrying a six-pack of Negra Modelo.

When he met Charlie at the bottom of the steps, she threw her arms around his neck and squeezed him in an enthusiastic hug. It was followed by a brief kiss. She said, "It's good to see you. I've missed you. The whole station house has."

Nick extricated himself from the awkward embrace. *What the hell was that?* he thought. "Good to see you too, Charlie. Are you sure you're not checking up on me?"

"No, of course not. Well, maybe a little. I have to say, you seem better than the last time I saw you. You look rested."

"Yeah, I'm doing a little better. A lot better, actually."

Charlie looked at the door of the trailer. "So, this is the rat trap I've heard so much about. Are you going to invite me in?"

*She is acting weird, maybe I shouldn't.* He nodded towards the beer. "Well, since you come bearing gifts, it seems only polite. How'd you know I like Modelo? Let me guess, Marco…"

A brilliant smile, with perfect white teeth, graced her face. "Oh, hell no. Marco doesn't know I'm here. This is what you call a clandestine meeting." Charlie's smile vanished. "Seriously, let's go inside. We have some stuff to talk about."

They made their way up the steps and into the trailer. Charlie lingered by the door and looked around. "Geez," she said, "this is one depressing shit box. Is this where unicorns come to die?"

"Nice. You come to my lovely home and insult my decor. And I just had the place redone."

Charlie twisted the top off of one of the beer bottles and extended it to him. He waved it off and said, "No thanks. I'm on the wagon for a few weeks."

Concern snuck into Charlie's expression. "What's that about? Are you on some meds? Is something going on with you?"

"No, nothing like that. The department sent me to Father Tom for an attitude adjustment. It was his idea." Nick motioned for her to have a seat at the kitchen table. "I'm glad you came Charlie, but you didn't come here to critique my decor. What's on your mind?"

Charlie took a swig of beer, set it down, and then began absentmindedly peeling the label off of the bottle. "Nick, I think you're in trouble, *big* trouble. A detective was snooping around the station yesterday. He was asking a lot of questions about you. Stuff like what kind of temper you have, and what happened that night you slugged that Roberts guy. He was also asking if you ever talked about Roberts or maybe threatened him."

Nick shrugged. "Don't worry about the cop too much. I never said anything to anybody about that guy and I've nothing to hide. I hit the guy; it stops there."

"Yeah, that's the problem. It doesn't stop there." Charlie took another swig of beer. "Jenkins threw you under the bus big time. From what I hear, he told the detective all about Becky making porn videos with that guy and his wife, and that's why you and Becky split. He made the whole thing sound really sleazy. The jerk also said you have been erratic ever since, and violent — that you attacked him. He even told the cop that you are on suspension because the chief pegged you as unstable. According to the guys on B shift; Jenkins made you sound like a total psychopath."

"Well," said Nick, "that sounds like Jenkins. Still, he can shoot his mouth off all he wants. I had nothing to do with that guy dying, and the detectives won't find any evidence that says I did."

"Dammit, Nick, you need to take this seriously. This detective is determined to make a case, and he's got you in his crosshairs."

Nick said, "Take a breath, Charlie. He hasn't even talked to me. Even if he believes I did it, there's nothing I can do about it."

"He hasn't talked to you yet because you're the prime suspect. It's like musical chairs, and you're the last one standing when the music stops. You need to be ready for when he comes for you."

*Sorry, Padre.* Nick reached over and grabbed a beer. As he twisted off the top, he said, "I'll be ready if he comes."

"Oh, he's coming. Count on that. Do you have a lawyer?"

"No," said Nick. "I'll get one if they arrest me."

"By then, it will be too late. You need to get ahead of this. Get a lawyer now."

Nick smiled. "How come you know so much about all this? Have you been binge watching Law and Order?"

Charlie said, "This ain't funny. One of my friends is a lawyer, and I talked to her. She will represent you if you want."

"Thanks, Charlie, but you're overreacting. As I hear it, the fire investigation team is calling it arson gone wrong, not murder. It'll be okay. I wasn't near the place."

"I am not overreacting, Nick. You need help. Can you *prove* you were not there? Can somebody provide you cover?"

"What do you mean, provide me cover?"

"I mean, can someone provide you with an alibi for the time of the fire? Were you with somebody?"

Nick replied, "No, I was home alone."

Charlie took a deep breath and exhaled slowly. "I figured. I am about to suggest something you won't like, but hear me out. When the detective asks you where you were that night –and he will – tell him you were with me. Tell him we were both here together well past midnight."

Nick's eyes widened in disbelief. "Are you out of your mind?"

"It's not as crazy as it sounds. We could sell the cops on it. Heck, more than a few of the guys at work already suspect we've got a thing going. Even Marco has dropped subtle hints about-the dangers of in-station romances."

"Charlie, I'm not dragging you into this, and I am sure as hell not letting you go to jail for perjury."

"Nick, you're like my big brother. I never would have made it at the department without you. I won't stand by while some asshole cop takes you down for something you didn't do."

Nick patted her hand. "Thanks, really. It's sweet of you to want to help, but it won't work anyway."

"Of course it will. I was home that night with Kelly, she will back me up. No one else can say where I was or wasn't."

"Charlie, they will check the story out. They'll ask around. No one will buy it."

"Sure they will — Marco will back us up. He just has to say he suspected something. That's not so far from the truth."

"Yeah, and what happens when they find out you're a lesbian? It's kind of common knowledge."

Charlie laughed at that. "Nick, I am not a lesbian. Jenkins started that rumor when I shot down one of his advances. I never denied it because having the guys believe that is easier than having them hit on me."

Nick said, "And what about Kelly? I thought you two were together — like, together, together."

"Nah, just friends," said Charlie. "Hey, if you want, we can just claim to be friends, and we were just hanging out. That works too. They won't believe it, but let'em think what they will."

Nick took a swig of beer. "Faking being gay? Man, how do you put up with all that nonsense at work? Jenkins shouldn't get away with that crap."

"It's called being a woman in a man's world. I'm used to it. What about my idea?"

Nick said, "No can do."

"Why not?"

"One, because cops aren't stupid, and you might get in trouble, and I won't have that. Two, the rumors will set you back at work. You work hard to earn their respect; I won't let you throw that away by giving the idiots reasons to trash you — and they will. And finally, I don't need an alibi. They have no evidence; because I wasn't there."

"Look, maybe you don't need my help — yet. But when it comes down to crunch time, say it. I'll be okay. Promise me you won't let yourself be some dumb ass martyr just to save my reputation. Promise me."

"Okay, Charlie. I won't be a dumb ass martyr. But I tell you, I won't need your help."

"Good, now we are going out, and you're buying me dinner. Then we're coming back here and I'm spending the night."

"The hell you are."

Charlie laughed, and said, "Oh, relax. I'm not coming on to you. It's only because you're probably being followed. I want them to see us together. Why do you think I dressed like this? And by the way, you should have seen your face when I kissed you – priceless."

Nick shook his head. "I kinda wondered why you look so… Anyway, you watch too many TV shows. I promise you I am not being watched. We'll order pizza, and you're welcome to hang out for a while if you want. Then you're going home."

A sly smile found Charlie's lips. She teased. "Look so what? What were you going to say?"

"Never mind."

"Oh, my god you're blushing. You were checking me out."

"You're a brat."

"So, have you ever thought about it?"

"What?"

Charlie teased. "You know what; you and me …?"

"No, of course not."

"Liar, you're a guy. Heck, *I've* thought about it. Sooner or later, that stuff crosses everybody's mind. Don't get me wrong, no way could it happen. It would be a huge mistake and it would make work completely weird. But you have to admit…"

"I thought I was like your big brother?"

"You are, sorta. I am just saying it's not so farfetched." She laughed, "Can you imagine… Becky would kill us."

"No, I can't imagine it, and let's not tell her," said Nick, "or anybody else for that matter. Now change the subject, please."

"Wow, it doesn't take much to rattle you, does it, grandpa? What kind of pizza sounds good?"

Outside, a police officer was noting Charlie's license plate number.

# Chapter 21

"Nancy," said Father Tom, "Dominick will be here in a few minutes. We are not to be interrupted today; no calls — nothing. We may go past the scheduled hour. If so, cancel whatever else I have."

"I understand. Do you need anything?

"Perhaps a couple bottles of water in the study. Call me when he arrives." *Today*, thought the priest, *will be a tough session for Dominick, but it's time to prod him a little. I think he's ready.*

Nancy called and said that Dominick was waiting for him in the study. Father Tom found him sitting in the overstuffed chair, legs crossed and looking pensive. Nick spoke first. "Father, how's your world today?"

"My stars are aligned, and a fair wind is at my back. How are things with you?"

"I am doing pretty good, all things considered."

"That sounds ominous. Is something going on?"

"This is awkward. The guy that Becky — you know — messed around with, well, he got killed trying to burn down a house. Somehow, the cops have got it in their heads that someone killed him — me."

"Gads. What would inspire such foolishness?"

"He was the guy I punched out. I guess they figure because I hit him that maybe I wanted him dead."

"At our first meeting, you got fairly angry when talking about him. Is there more to it? Other than the fight, do you two have a history?"

"No," said Nick. "I kinda see their point, though. I have a pretty good motive. I wouldn't be the first jealous husband to kill a guy. Heck, once upon a time it would have been called justifiable homicide. I could have called him out at dawn with dueling pistols. Those were the days."

"Witch burning was once common too. We have evolved."

Nick shrugged, "Have we? You think we are more civilized nowadays?"

The priest cleared his throat. "It's an age lacking grace and decorum, but yes, we're less barbaric. Dominick, I am your priest. Remember, anything you say under the seal of confession is *Sub Rosa*. That's an absolute, recognized by both church doctrine and the law. Do you need to make confession?"

Nick smiled and waved off the suggestion. "I have a lot of sins to account for, but I assure you that murder is not one of them."

"Thank God!" The priest blushed. "Sorry about that. I forget myself sometimes."

Chuckling, Nick said, "You are absolved."

"If I may ask, how did you react to hearing about his death?"

"Honestly, a little gratified. But not much more than that. When I first found out about Becky, I wanted to kick his ass, but I got over that. I was madder at Becky than him. Maybe it was his making those sleazy videos, or beating his wife, that got to me. I suppose I would've smacked him even if Becky wasn't involved."

"Really?" asked the priest. "You would have risked your job over a stranger. I doubt he was the first wife beater you've come across."

"I see your point. The truth is, I needed to hit somebody, anybody. He was a perfect choice."

Father Tom leaned forward. "Explain what you mean by 'I needed to hit somebody.' Why?"

"I can't explain it. It goes back to what we talked about in our last meeting. I felt so, I don't know, twisted up. I needed release. When I hit him, I didn't even know I was doing it."

"Do you still feel twisted up?"

"Still? Yeah, but not as bad, or as often. It's better, but it's still there."

"Do you regret hitting him?"

Nick thought a moment before answering, then said, "No, not really, but I regret losing my self-control. Looking back, it's hard to believe I was in the state I was. I am not sure how I got along as well as I did. But that night, it just seemed to overpower me. Had we been alone, I might have really killed him. I think I wanted to."

"I see," said the priest. "And now? Do you still get feelings of rage?"

Nick shook his head. "Not so much. Now, it's more like, I don't know, something like a gnawing…or, a tension — I guess? And maybe a touch of sadness. But the fear I am going to fly apart is mostly gone. I feel more—like me."

"Does the police investigation set you on edge?"

"A little, but honestly, I find it hard to get worked up about it. In the grand scheme of things, that just seems sort of distant."

"The grand scheme of things? Please elaborate."

Nick shrugged. "My job, Becky, getting well, I got a lot going on."

"So, would you say your stress level has increased?"

"No Father, if anything it's maybe better. Since we have been meeting, I am more grounded somehow. I guess that's why the whole cop thing isn't so bothersome. It just feels good not to be so miserable."

"Glad to hear it. How are you sleeping?"

"Better," said Nick. "Only one nightmare lately."

"Good. So, Nick, last time we met, I asked you to do something. I wanted you to recall any events in the last few years you found especially difficult. Anything come to mind?"

"I gave that a lot of thought, Father — I did. But really, I couldn't come up with anything."

*That's unfortunate. I was hoping he would get there himself.* The priest said, "What about the Bentley fire?"

"The Bentley fire?"

"Yes, the Bentley fire. On Baker Avenue, a little over two years ago."

"I don't really remember much. Since then, I have had a lot of calls.

"No Nick, I believe you remember that call very well. Remember, I told you that honesty was important in this process. I understand it's uncomfortable, but I need you to tell me about it."

Nick straightened in his chair and folded his arms across his chest. "There isn't much to tell."

Father Tom opened his bottle of water and took a drink; on cue, Nick followed suit. The priest said, "There was a fatality, wasn't there?"

Nick pulled on the collar of his shirt. "Yeah, I guess. It happens sometimes."

"This was an unusual one, though, right?" asked the priest.

"I guess. The mother had put her two kids down for a nap. One was seven, the other was four. She claimed she walked down the street for some coffee with friends. She's a known meth head, and the friends were two itchy looking tweekers known for dealing. So, I'm guessing they weren't having coffee and bunt cake. Anyway, the four-year-old wakes up and throws his blanket over a cheap space heater. When the thing catches fire, he panics and runs out of the house. The seven-year-old didn't make it."

The priest said, "Walk me through how the fire went."

"Like I said, there's not much to tell. The place was a typical meth head shit hole — trash everywhere. The fire started in the kids' bedroom and spread through the rest of the house. We knocked it down pretty quick, but the place got gutted."

"No, Dominick. Walk me through what *you* did at the fire."

"What do you want? Like I said, it was a fire. I did what I always do. Let's move on."

Father Tom noticed that Nick's face had reddened, and that his jaw muscles flexed. He watched Nick's agitation grow. The priest pushed ahead. "All right. So, walk me through it."

"Why is it so damn important?"

"I don't know," said Father Tom. "Why are you so reluctant?"

Nick snapped, "Okay, fine. I fucked up. Is that what you want to hear?"

"What happened, Dominick?"

"When we got on scene, the mother was screaming about her kids being in the house. Just as we were advancing the hose line to the door, the four-year-old wandered up to his mom, crying. Some cop yelled they found the kid, and I took it to mean they had found both. We still did a search like we always do, but it didn't seem very — urgent. Anyway, the girl was still in there, but we didn't know. We didn't find her."

"Okay," said the priest. "Walk me through that. You're at the door with a hose line, what happened next?"

Nick was plainly restless; his foot was tapping, and he was continually shifting weight in the chair. "I told you, we didn't find her. It happens."

"Nick, stop avoiding this. Tell me what happened, it's important."

"Alright, this is just … Anyway, me and Tommy got the hose line, we're moving down the hall. The fire was cooking and the smoke level was about a foot off the floor. We couldn't see shit.

There was even some rollover, you know, flames rolling around above our head. They were coming out of a bedroom. So, I opened the nozzle and worked a stream across the ceiling. It steamed up and pushed the smoke to the floor. Everything got dark and hot. Then, BOOM, the whole freaking roof is coming down on our heads. It rattled me; I decided we should pull out. The house was empty, right? No reason to risk hurting somebody. I was — (sniff) wrong."

Tears were streaming down Nick's face, and he was making a conscious effort not to sob. The priest said, "The roof fell on you, pulling out made sense."

"That's just it, Father." moaned Nick. "The roof didn't collapse; the house had a cheap suspended ceiling. Those tiles didn't weigh a pound a piece. When I hit the ceiling with the nozzle, I knocked them out of their track. The fire had gotten up above them and when they fell, it seemed worse than it was. I bailed on that little girl for no good reason. It was a rookie mistake. She died because I freaked out. It's my fault that little girl died - I -I- let her die."

Dominick held his face in his hands. Father Tom waited for a few seconds, then gently said, "You're doing fine Dom, now finish the story."

Dominick whispered, "I did finish."

"No, son, you didn't. What happened later?" Nick shook his head emphatically. Then came minor trembling in the hands, followed by the beginnings of hyperventilation. The priest said calmly, "Relax Dominick. Breathe in deep, then hold it for a second." He waited, then said, "Now exhale slowly." The priest watched Nick complete the breathing exercises for several seconds. When Nick seemed to regain his composure, he handed him the bottle of water. When Nick put the bottle down, the priest said, "Go on now, finish the story. You can do this."

"No, I can't, I've never told anyone about this." whispered Nick.

"Go on, Dom. You're almost there."

Nick closed his eyes and took a deep breath. In a shaky voice, he said, "The cops were scouring the neighborhood looking for the little girl because the boy had said his sissy had been with him. I guess he got confused or scared. So, after we knocked down the fire, we were doing mop up. The fire started in the bedroom, and the damage was pretty bad there. Anyway, I was pulling debris out of the closet when I — Oh God — I..." Nick began sobbing, almost uncontrollably.

"Go on, Nick. What happened?

"I -I was pulling debris out of the closet. I - I tried to yank something out of the closet. It wouldn't come, so I pulled harder. Father, it just popped out."

"What popped out Nick? What happened?"

"It was so fucking careless of me. I wasn't really paying attention; she must've crawled into the closet to hide from the fire before she died — before I left her to die. I grabbed (sob) I grabbed the little girl without knowing it. She was burnt so bad; she was falling apart. I didn't know she was there. I just didn't know..."

"What? Go on."

"God forgive me, it was her arm. I- I can't."

"Yes, you can Nick. Finish. Let it out."

"Oh God, I- pulled her arm off." Nick collapsed out of the chair and onto his knees. "Don't you understand? I let her die, then I tore her apart. I ruined her — I ruined that precious little child." The priest kneeled down beside him and wrapped him in his arms. He cradled Nick while he sobbed. They stayed like that for a long while.

In almost a whisper, Father Tom said, "Dominick, you made an honest mistake. It's one that anyone could make. You're a firefighter, people die at fires and you can't save them all. It's a bitter pill to swallow, but you know it's true. She was gone. Her body was nothing but an inanimate object; her soul was safe."

With tears streaming down his rugged face, Nick looked the perfect picture of utter despair. "Father, I understand that. I've even told other firefighters that same bullshit. But the truth is, sometimes we screw up, and people die. My head tells me it's just part of the job. But in my gut, I can't let go of it. I can't be that callous. I can't just shrug it off as a bad day at the office. I try to push the memory of her down, but it never goes away, at least for long. Even when I'm not thinking about it, it's there, right below the surface, waiting. You don't have to tell me; I know. The little girl in the dream is her — she haunts me. She wants me to pay."

Nick's breath hitched as he fought to control himself. He continued. "After the fire, that drugged out excuse for a mother screamed at us, accusing us of letting her child die. She blamed all of us, but it was on *me*. When that realization hit me, it felt like I sank into the earth. I'll never forget that sensation; of sinking."

Tenderly, Father Tom stroked Nick's hair. "You took a big step towards getting better today, Nick."

Nick shook his head. "Father, this has been eating at me for two years. There is no getting better. There is no forgetting."

Father Tom said, "Nick, you're right in that you will never forget. But you're wrong about there being no getting better. You suffered through a horrible experience. All of your misery; the anxiety attacks, the depression, the anger, loss of sleep, all of it, are your body's attempt to process an extraordinarily horrific experience. You've been trying to bury those memories, to hide from them, and that's unhealthy. Your mind won't let you get away with it. Getting better isn't about forgetting, getting better is about perspective and acceptance."

"No offense, Father, but that sounds like New Age mumbo-jumbo."

The priest groaned and sat back in his chair. "Let's get off the floor, Dominick. I'm too damn old for kneeling. As far as the New Age mumbo-jumbo goes, it's really pretty straightforward. Take another swig of water, settle yourself, then I want you to close your eyes and tell me about a happy moment, one where you were completely at peace with the world."

Nick sniffed and said, "Your kidding, right?"

"No, I am not. Try."

"A happy moment, huh? That's hard."

"It shouldn't be," said the priest. "Take your time."

"Years ago, Becky and I rented a beach house. One night, a squall blew in from the ocean. The power went out, we lost the lights and the air conditioner. So, we threw the windows and terrace door open. It was mostly dark, but I remember that I could barely make out the white curtains billowing in the breeze.

She and I laid together on the bed, listening to the surf pound on the beach and the wind blowing through the trees. You could smell the rain; do you know that smell?"

"Yes," said the priest, "I do."

"I love the smell of a summer storm. I remember one of those buoy bells ringing every once in a while. We laid there, holding each other for the longest time, just listening, and enjoying that muggy breeze blowing on us. I don't remember ever being so content."

Father Tom patted Nick's hand. "That sounds like a beautiful moment, a defining moment for the two of you. Ask yourself this Nick, why should that memory be any less powerful than the tragic memory of that fire?"

"I don't know, ugly is more powerful than beautiful, I guess."

"No," said the priest. "A memory is only a memory. We give them weight and substance by expending mental and emotional energy on them. Both your memories are equally real, and neither will leave you. How much power each has is up to you. You *can* control what you choose to focus on."

Nick flashed back to Haley's words. "You're talking about Locus of Control."

The priest smiled. "Well, aren't you full of surprises then. Yes, something like that."

Nick said, "It's easier said than done."

"True, it is anything but easy but it can be done. I asked you to read some articles about cognitive behavior therapy, did you?"

"I looked it up on Wikipedia," said Nick.

"Saints protect us. Had you put some real effort into the task, you would be the wiser for it. What we will do in the following weeks is work on changing your perspective regarding those negative events. We will also change your response behaviors when events trigger those memories. That starts with an awareness of what is happening to you, recognizing episodes for what they are and asserting positive coping strategies."

"Sounds daunting," said Nick. "I can't be off work for months. If I go back at all."

Father Tom smiled. "It will take time, probably 10 or 12 more sessions, perhaps more. That's the bad news. The good news is that you have already taken the two biggest steps. You've acknowledged the underlying issue. It's denial and avoidance that causes all the cascading symptoms. Also, you have already started changing coping behaviors; not drinking is an important one. Forcing positive changes in routine is another: working out, socializing, doing things you enjoy. It's called asserting normalized behavior,  we will work on that, too. I want you to tell your doctor that you are in therapy for PTSD and that you have had panic attacks. She may prescribe an antidepressant if the symptoms don't get better. But. I expect you will see some improvement in how you feel fairly soon. Dom, we have work to do, but you're on your way, you *can* do this."

"What about the report to the Chief?"

"I'll tell him the truth. You are undergoing treatment for PTSD. I'll also report that it was an important contributing factor to your incident with the citizen in question, and that with ongoing therapy, you can return to work. I'd like you to take another week off. Your nerves are still pretty raw, and I want you to avoid triggering events for a while. I wouldn't oppose temporary assignment to the training or inspection divisions though, if that's what the Chief wants. I expect you will hear from the department in a few days."

Nick wiped a tear away from his eye. "Look at me crying like a little kid. Do you believe I can get back to normal, eventually? You know it's only a matter of time before there is another fatality. I can't avoid it forever."

"We'd all be better off if we cried more and punched less. As far as firefighting goes, I believe you will make it back, but I make no promises. That depends on you. You may find handling bodies to be a permanent trigger. You will need to learn some coping strategies. Immediate venting is very helpful. I'd suggest you talk to someone you trust as soon as an event occurs. Emotions can be stubborn gremlins, they don't like to be ignored. Talking about your feelings helps with gaining that sense of control I talked about. I also want you to come see me right after every fatality call or a call with badly hurt kids, even if you think you're okay. Now, let's talk about those panic attacks some more. Are you familiar with the serenity prayer?"

"Yeah, sure, it was from Saint Francis." said Nick.

"That's a common mistake. It's actually credited to Reinhold Niebuhr." Father Tom handed Nick a small card. "I want you to memorize this. A few minutes ago, when one of the panic attacks was coming on, I had you do some breathing exercises. They should help. If they don't, discuss it with your doctor. For right now, if you sense an attack coming on, I want you to do those breathing exercises, and in your mind, I want you to recite this prayer as you do it. Breathe in with the first line, pause, then breathe out with the second line. Pause and then breathe in again with the third line. Keep that up until you've repeated the prayer three times. It's a good way to control your breathing and relax anxiety. Plus, the message is reaffirming. You would do well to keep it in mind. Do it with me now.

"Breathe in as I say; *God, grant me the serenity to accept the things I cannot change.*" Breathe out as I say: *Grant me the courage to change the things I can.* Now breathe in again as I say: *Please grant me the wisdom to know the difference.* Now breathe out slowly, and repeat."

"I take it there is a message you're giving me here," said Nick.

Father Tom stood up, signaling the session was ending. "Indeed, there is. It is this; you are a man doing a tough job. I talked to your coworkers, and I've read your file. By all accounts, you're as good a firefighter as there is. But you're still only a man. My friend, you have a lot less control than you would like to believe you do. You've got more than enough courage to make a difference. But you need to cut yourself a break when you can't. Could things have gone better at that fire? Perhaps. But you did as well in that situation as anyone else would, and that's all you can ask of yourself or anybody else. Remember that, and hold on to it the next time you wake up in a cold sweat, and sooner or later, you will find peace."

As they were walking out the door, he added, "One more thing, Dominick. Of all the behaviors you need to change, the most important is your urge to isolate yourself. You need to summon the courage to reengage. Believe it or not, doing normal things helps you feel normal. You're surrounded by people who love you. They want to help you. Let them."

# Chapter 22

Nick's lungs burned, and each stride jarred his back and knees. Still, running again felt good. He only managed three-quarters of a mile before he had to take a walking break, but it was a start. He was confident it would come back quickly. Coming up from the lake and out of the tree canopy, he spotted a man leaning against his truck. Nick didn't recognize the guy, but was sure why he was there. He jogged the rest of the way to the parking lot.

The stranger was pudgy and had thinning hair. A cheap sport jacket, slouched posture and slack expression suggested lazy stupidity, but not the eyes, those were sharp. They were the eyes of an agile mind. "Are you Dominick Adler?" the man said.

"Yeah, who are you and why is your ass leaning on my truck?"

The man held his hands up in contrition as he pushed away from the fender. He produced a badge. "I am Detective Frank Miller. I need you to come with me."

"Why?"

"I need to ask you some questions. Let's go."

"Am I under arrest?"

"Not yet, not if you cooperate."

Nick said, "I just finished a run, and I need to cool off. We can talk here."

"That's not how it works." said Miller. "Get in the car Mr. Adler, trust me, you're better off cooperating."

"Cooperate with what?"

"You know very well what," said Miller. "I am looking into the death of Sylvester Roberts."

Nick shrugged. "I heard he killed himself trying to burn down his own house."

"Uh-uh. I think somebody killed him."

"What's that got to do with me?" asked Nick.

"Let's stop dancing, Adler. You had some serious issues with the guy; you put him in the hospital. If you had nothing to do with the guy dying, great. Let's go to my office and straighten it out. I'll help you get out from under it."

Nick wiped his face with his t-shirt. "Yeah, let's stop dancing. You're not the least bit interested in helping me. You wanna talk, fine. But here is the deal. If you want me downtown, arrest me. I'll call my lawyer, and you two can figure it out. If you want to talk, then you're going to have to take a walk with me while I cool off — otherwise go pester somebody else."

"Okay, tough guy, we'll talk here if you want," said Miller. He walked over to the nearby park bench and sat. Nick walked by him and nodded toward the hiking trail. "Oh, for fuck's sake," growled the detective as he got up and followed. A smile snuck on to Nick's face. Miller couldn't see it, but knew it was there.

To Miller, this was more than an annoyance; Adler was messing up his plan. It was straightforward enough; he heard the guy was unstable and had an explosive temper. He intended to get him in an interrogation room, push him hard, make him lose his temper and slip up. If he could catch him in a lie, he might be able to squeeze out a confession. It had to be on video, though. Miller now decided to go with Plan B instead; push the guy and try to get enough for a warrant. If he got lucky, maybe Adler would swing on him. Then he could book him for assault and grill him.

The detective pulled up alongside Nick and said, "I hear you are on suspension from the fire department."

"That's right. What else do *they* tell you?"

"They tell me you got suspended for punching out Sylvester Roberts. Is that right?"

"Yep. That's right."

Miller asked, "Why did you do it?"

Nick looked at Miller for the first time since they started walking. "If they told you why I got suspended, I'm sure they told you why I hit him."

"Pardon me for being so blunt, but I heard it was because he was fucking your wife. Seems unfair they would suspend you for that. I mean, it seems justified."

Nicked smiled at him. "Maybe you could tell the chief that. You know, put a good word in for me, seeing how you want to help me and all."

Miller watched Nick's reaction closely. He had thrown his first verbal punch; apparently, it didn't land. He tried again.

"You must have really hated the guy, right? I mean, he was a real dirt bag. Hell, he was not only banging your wife; he made a video of it for the Internet. That's pretty shitty all the way around."

Nick again ignored the bait. Miller tried again. "I hear tell, that's how you found out about them. You saw the video. Wow, that must have hurt. One of your buddies who saw it said it was one hell of a show. What's your wife's name? Becky? Yeah, that's it, Becky. I find this hard to believe, but your buddy says Becky not only did the guy, but his wife had a turn with her too. Pretty kinky stuff."

The detective saw Nick's face redden, but he said nothing. Miller went in for the kill. "He said that your wife couldn't get enough, that this Roberts guy fucked her into a quivering mess. That must have been hard to watch. Hell, I'd want to kill somebody too."

Nick felt the knot in his chest tightening. *That fucking Jenkins…* He took a deep breath. "Detective, I'm not sure who this *buddy* is, but they are exaggerating."

Miller replied, "Really? That's all you got to say? Hey, do you suppose I am reading this all wrong? Maybe you couldn't do it for her anymore, and she needed another man to step in. So, you went along with it. Or maybe you just get off on being humiliated. Some guys are like that. I know a guy who actually gets his jollies watching other guys plow his wife. She goes out and finds some young stud and then sends him pictures of them going at it. I believe they call it cuckolding. Tell me, Nick, are you a cuckold? Did you get hot and bothered watching Roberts pound your wife, or did you man- up and take him out?"

Nick said, "Detective Miller, I see what you're trying to do and you're an asshole for doing it."

"Oh, sorry if I upset you. I mean, I wouldn't want to be *insensitive*. Did you keep a copy of the movie? Do you watch it sometimes to, you know — get inspired?"

"You're a sick little puppy, Miller," growled Nick.

"Me? This whole thing is sick. Roberts, his wife, your wife, the videos. Then there's you, the helpless victim. Standing there with your dick in your hand while the three of them make a fool of you. Admit it, you hated the guy, and the two little bitches too. They laughed at you, they humiliated you. That's why you haven't talked to your wife in eight months, and why you punched Roberts out — and burnt down their house. Who could blame you? That's why you killed him, to regain your manhood, to stop being a little bitch. Isn't that right?"

Miller watched, almost shocked, as his target stood there, eyes closed, breathing deeply, lips moving like he was praying or something. He asked, "Are you alright? Are you freaking out or something? Are you losing it, like you did with Roberts? Are you going to swing on me?"

Calmly, Nick said, "Detective, you are mistaken.

Frustrated, Miller tried a different approach. *Let's see who he throws shade on.* "Okay, help me out then," said Miller. "I talked to Roberts's wife. She tells me he made those videos without anyone knowing it. She said there were a bunch of women. Maybe she went nuts and killed him. What do you think?"

"I have no idea. I've never talked to her."

"That's not what she says. She says you two know each other – pretty well, in fact."

Nick replied, "Again, you are mistaken."

"I talked to your wife too. She seemed to hate the guy. Some sort of lover's spat, maybe? She's pretty pissed about the video going public, blames him for your marriage going south. Do you suppose she could have done it?"

"No, I don't, she doesn't have it in her," said Nick. "Just curious detective, what makes you so sure anyone killed him? Why don't you believe he set himself on fire trying to torch his own house?"

Miller pointed to a bench. "Can we sit? I need a break." Nick stood while Miller sat. "That's one theory." Said Miller, "But I don't buy it. Too many people have reasons to do this guy in, and low and behold, he has an *accident*. I don't like coincidence."

Nick said. "I understand there will be an inquest. You're accusing people of a murder, that might not even get ruled a murder. Accidents *do* happen, you know."

"Trust me Mr. Adler. They will rule the thing a murder, and we both know who did it."

"Do we?"

"You hated Roberts for sleeping with your wife, that's reasonable enough. Then you found out he was blackmailing her. You went to his house to confront him, also reasonable. He was setting the house up to burn, and you took the opportunity to do him in. His computer with all the sex tapes is missing. That's what this was all about. Look, the guy was a slimeball; considering what he did to you and all those women, no one would blame you for what happened. Hell, maybe it was an accident. He could have had the gas already poured out, and a candle got knocked over during a scuffle, right? You were protecting your wife. Get her to back you up about the blackmail and I bet you get a slap on the wrist, nothing more. But you got to stop this hard ass routine and fess up. You also have to give up who else is involved. I suspect you were helping either your wife or his — or both."

"I'll give you this Miller, you have a hell of an imagination. In the last five minutes, you've thrown out three different crime theories, and none of them really work, do they?"

"Okay Adler, you tell me. Where were you that night?"

"None of your business." said Nick.

"That sounds like a guilty man talking. If you have an alibi, let's hear it. Were you with someone? Let me guess — Racheal Roberts."

"Again, none of your business."

"By chance, was it the woman you were with the other night?" Miller noted a slight flinch at the question. "Who is she?"

Nick said, "Miller, this is getting us nowhere."

"You work with her, don't you? Maybe I need to chat with her?'"

Nick shook his head in disgust. "You're a piece of work, aren't you? She is a friend and nothing more, and I wasn't with her that night. That's all I am going to say."

"I would hope you would want to help us find the guilty party, unless, of course, it's you."

"You don't even know if there is a guilty party."

Miller stood up. "Oh, yes, I do. We will talk again soon."

"I look forward to it."

Miller sneered. "You shouldn't. Next time I'll cuff you."

As Miller was walking away, Nick called out. "Hey Miller, you're not the cop who was married to Sandra Miller, are you?"

"Yeah, what of it?"

Nick shrugged. "I hear tell she had a fling with one of our guys — ended up marrying him. Having a firefighter raising your kid has gotta burn, right?"

"Fuck you, Adler."

"Sorry detective, *I didn't mean to be insensitive.* I guess you couldn't do it for her anymore. Tell me. Do you think about killing the guy a lot? You know, because they humiliated you. I guess we are both kinda little bitches, huh?"

"Funny, Adler. My guy is breathing, yours isn't. Like I said, I'll see you soon."

Nick sighed and watched Miller walk out of sight. He then sent Charlie a text: Police will talk to you. TELL THE TRUTH!

# Chapter 23

Nick stood at the door, mouth dry and palms sweating. His first meeting with Becky had gone better than he expected. To his surprise, their visit ended almost pleasantly. But Becky had been cryptic when she invited him over, and whatever she wanted, he gathered it was serious. His encounter with Miller had rattled him, and he had a few tough days. He called Father Tom, and that helped, but he wasn't at all sure he was ready for any drama.

It seemed strange *visiting* the house – his house; he had avoided it for so long. A squirrel running up a tree in the yard caught his attention. A memory of him and Becky planting the tree came to him; *It seems a lifetime ago;* he thought.

The place mostly looked the same, except… It took a moment to grasp the difference. The flower garden by the mailbox was empty, so were all the other flower beds. *Weird,* he thought, *planting flowers each spring was a big deal to her.* He remembered being dragged to the greenhouse every April, and impatiently following her around as she looked at every flower in the place. His disappointment at her not planting anything caught him by surprise. He didn't care about flowers, but losing the ritual disappointed him; it said something about Becky, about how she was doing.

She opened the door and graced him with a broad smile, one of her real ones, not one of the polite versions. They shared a clumsy hug. She was still in her work scrubs. *Odd,* he thought, *she's usually home, showered and changed by this hour*. "Come in," she said. "You look great."

"You too," he said.

Becky pulled at her scrubs. "I'm sorry about the way I'm dressed; you're a little early and I got home late. I'll go change."

Nick waved off the suggestion. "Since when do you have to apologize to me for how you're dressed? You look fine."

She shrugged and gestured him in. If approaching the house had seemed strange, walking into the family room was almost disorienting. An incredible sense of nostalgia washed over him. Nothing had changed, not a picture moved, or pillow displaced – nothing. His breath caught a little when he saw his cheap reading glasses still sitting on the table next to his favorite chair. He had the distinct feeling he was standing in a museum.

"The old place looks the same." he said.

"Pretty much, I repainted the powder room."

Not sure what else to do, Nick put his hands in his pockets. "Yeah, I remember you saying you wanted that done. The place looks good, you're doing a good job of taking care of it. Am I sending you enough money — you know, for expenses?"

"Thanks, yeah, it's enough."

"I noticed the lawn needs mowing."

Becky chuckled and said, "The guy comes every other Saturday. But go for it if you want. I bet you remember where we keep the lawn mower."

Nick nodded subtly. "No, I'm good."

"Ah huh, I figured. Come on back to the kitchen, I was about to make us supper."

Nick's gut tightened, and little floaty lights started dancing in the corner of his vision. He wasn't ready for this, for reconciliation. It was too soon. "Oh, I – I can't stay for supper." Nick lied. "I have a thing to go to later, sorry."

She said nothing, but her head slumped ever so slightly. She gathered the groceries that were sitting on the counter and stuffed them in the refrigerator, not paying attention to where they landed. Nick knew her well. There was no missing the disappointment or anger. It dawned on him then, she hadn't changed and showered because she stopped at the market on her way home. *Well, I'm a jerk*, he thought. "Hey sorry Becky, go ahead and cook; no reason for you not to have dinner."

"Don't worry about it. I'll nuke a frozen dinner later. Do you have time for a beer? You can take it with you if you need to make a quick escape."

"Becky, don't be like that. I'm sorry. I am happy to see you — really, I am. It's just — I'm not ready."

"For dinner?'

"You know what I mean. I need time."

Becky nodded in agreement. Nick knew it was halfhearted. He watched her inner gears shift; the softness of her expression hardened. She said, "So, do you want the beer or not?"

He nodded, and she tossed him one; maintaining her distance.

Becky said, "Has that awful detective talked to you yet?"

"A couple of days ago. He is a piece of work."

Becky leaned back against the counter, wiping her already dry hands with a dishtowel. "The guy grilled me pretty hard. Mostly about you; he wanted to know if you have a temper. He asked a lot of questions about how you reacted to finding out about my — mistake. Somebody gave him all the sordid details. I am pretty sure he thinks that my… *behavior*… drove you to kill Roberts. He kept asking if you ever threatened me, or threatened Sly or Racheal. That seemed like a big deal to him."

"What did you tell him?" asked Nick.

"I told him the truth. You left me without saying a word, and we hadn't seen each other or talked ever since. He didn't believe that — but then neither do I, really."

"Lets' not get into that again. I know I should have handled things different," said Nick.

"Yeah? You think so? How does that happen? After all our years together, you simply disappeared, no tears, no questions, no fight, nothing. You ghosted me. I am your wife, not some tinder hook up. You don't ghost your wife."

"There were tears, there were questions," he said.

Becky wiped her eyes. "How would I know? You wouldn't talk to me."

"I know, and I'm sorry. Like I said before, at first, I was too hurt and angry. I didn't trust myself around you. Then it just seemed too late. I didn't want to confront you — to end it — but I couldn't let it go either. So, I sat, and I wallowed in self-pity. It was wrong. I know."

"You were afraid of hurting me? Nick, even if you had it in you, and you don't, hitting me would have been better than what you did."

Nick said, "Maybe it wasn't you I was afraid of hurting."

"What? What does that mean?"

"Nothing, let it go. I handled it badly. Let's leave it at that."

Nick saw a look on Becky's face he couldn't decipher. That was rare. After a few seconds, she said, "Well, that cop thinks you lost it, and had something to do with the fire. You need to watch out. That guy is after you."

"Yeah, he made that pretty clear. I wouldn't worry about it too much, though. He doesn't have any evidence, only a wild ass theory and a motive. From what I hear, I have a lot of company when it comes to motive. A bunch of pissed off women and jealous husbands had reason to hate the guy too."

"Yeah, I'm one of those women. I'm pretty sure he suspects I'm involved somehow too. I talked to Racheal, his wife. She says the same thing. We both got asked a lot of questions about that damn video."

Nick asked, "Did he ask you about that guy's missing computer?"

"Oh, yeah. He was all worked up about where it was. I told him I didn't know."

"Good," said Nick.

"Actually, that was a lie. I do know where it is."

"What? How? Why did you lie?"

"Racheal told me about it. She was terrified of the police having it. Could be there's something bad on it. Sly got mixed up with something scary. That cop was pushing so hard, I just panicked."

"Becky, Miller said that guy was trying to blackmail you and his wife. Is that true?"

"No, he wasn't. But after he died, a friend of his, some guy named Jimmy, got a hold of Racheal. He threatened her."

"What about you?" asked Nick

"Not yet, but I'll hear from him eventually. Everybody Sly had on video will. But I don't give a shit anymore. I told Mom and Dad the truth about why we broke up. And it seems like everyone we know has either seen the damn video or heard about it. It's out there somewhere, and it always will be. I'm tired of worrying about it, people who love me will deal with it, and the rest can go to hell."

Nick asked, "Does that include me?"

Becky shrugged.

"So, your mom and dad know. How did they take it?"

"Okay, I guess. They say all the right things, but I can see the look of disappointment on their faces. They don't know about the video though; it would kill them if they saw it. I guess I'll have to warn them that somebody may send it to them. I trust they won't look at it, but having to tell them about it will just dredge it all up again." Fighting back sobs, she added, "It seems like this nightmare will never end."

Nick pulled Becky close and hugged her. "Beck, I really am sorry you're going through this. You don't deserve all this crap."

"No, I don't. And I have just about had it with this whole damn mess. I fucked up and paid the price. Sly was a dick. He's dead. I'm glad. Story over. But no, now we got cops chasing us, and some sleaze ball threatening blackmail. When does it end, for Christ's sake?"

Nick said, "It may not seem like it, but sooner or later, this will all clear up. Some kinda normal will come back."

Becky stepped back from him. "I wasn't going to get into it tonight; I was hoping you and I could just have a nice dinner together, try to reconnect a little. But since that's not happening, we may as well talk about it. About getting normal."

"Becky, like I said before, I'm not ready. I need time."

"That's just it, Nick. It's really all about time. Since you and I talked last, I have been doing a lot of thinking. Honey, we're both stuck in limbo, we can't seem to get back to where we were, and neither of us is moving forward. It's unhealthy, and it's making us both miserable."

"Look, Becky, if this is about my not staying for supper…"

Becky sniffed, "It's not.  Well, maybe it is, sort of. We've been apart for a long time, too long. If we were going to find a way back, we would've done it by now. I realized that the other night when I went to your trailer and you had a girl there…"

"We talked about that Becky. Haley and I are not a thing. Don't put more into it than…"

"No Nick, hear me out. It hurt when I saw her, but I came to realize that its possibly a good thing. You're healing, moving on now. I should have told you the other day, but I — well, I did the same thing a few weeks ago. It meant nothing, but I wanted  – no – needed to do it. I felt so damn guilty afterwards. That's why I didn't tell you."

Nick growled. "You're with a new guy now?"

"No. it was one night, same as you and that girl."

Nick pushed her away. "All that talk about loving me, about wanting to get back together — and you're out getting…"

"Cool off. Until a few days ago, you were gone, out of my life, and I lost hope you would ever talk to me again. Everything I said about loving you was true – it still is – but yeah, I got lonely. So did you."

"Then why did you act the way you did the other day — about me and Haley?"

Becky said, "Nick, that's what I am saying. After our talk, I got to wondering why, after all this time, we both just now had one-night stands. Don't you see? We are both tired of being stuck."

Nick sighed, "I guess you shouldn't feel guilty, but…"

"But that's just it. I'm tired of feeling guilty. I've been beating myself up for so long, and I can't do it anymore. Even if you can't forgive me, I'm going to forgive myself. I've been sitting around putting my life on hold waiting for you, hoping you would reach out and I can't do that anymore either."

"What? We just started talking again. The other day, you sounded like you wanted to make things work?"

"I did — I do —  I meant what I said."

"So, what are you saying? What changed?"

Becky said, "I came to realize that I've been stuck because of the way we ended it — the way *you* ended it. I had things I needed to say. Our talk the other day gave me closure. I'm done paying penance. Nick, I still love you; I always will. But I have a life to live and I'm going to do it, with or without you. I don't see I have a choice."

"Becky, neither of us chose this, but…"

"That's the thing, Nick. We *are choosing* it; we choose it every day. You choose to hold on to your doubts, and I chose to believe that you would eventually get past them. Now, I'm choosing to look for happiness. You're going to do what you're going to do. I have no control over it. But I can't keep hanging on forever waiting to find out. Heck, you can't even eat supper with me. That says something, doesn't it? And let's face it, we can't be buddies. Without hope, seeing you breaks my heart. And I am guessing your seeing me brings up bad memories. It's time to get on with our lives, one way or another."

Nick's throat tightened, and his stomach seemed incredibly light, almost as if it could float up into his chest. "So, that's it? You're saying you want to split?"

"No," said Becky. "I am saying we already split; it's just time that we deal with it."

Nick sniffed. "That's your decision?"

"Sweetheart, you're not listening. It's *your* decision. I am just done pretending that you're going to change your mind."

"And *you're not* listening to me. I don't know what I want, Becky. Maybe we can work it out, maybe not. Father Tom has helped me put things into perspective. I get I was less than a husband, and I realize I played a part in how we ended up in this mess. This thing I have, this PTSD as father calls it, had me twisted up. It's getting better. I'm not sure I'm ready to try us again, but I don't want to give up yet either. I am confused."

Becky's heart broke a little seeing her husband near crying. "Nick, I see you're getting better, and I'm thrilled — I am. You say you're confused about us; I don't understand that. To me, it seems pretty simple; you love me or you don't — you want our old life back or you don't."

Nick said, "It's not that simple. I *do* love you. But, being with someone and loving someone aren't the same."

"That's where we fail, Nick. I don't accept that. You choose to commit or you don't. Stop denying your feelings; for whatever reason you lost faith in us, so find a woman who hasn't hurt you, a woman you can trust. Find something less complicated and scary. And maybe someday I'll find the guy who can be happy with me. We both deserve that, even if we can't be that to each other."

"So that's it? You are giving up. We're done?" asked Nick.

"No, Nick. Well, maybe I am giving up — I guess. But if you ever figure things out, you know where to find me."

"Should we hire lawyers?"

Becky shrugged. "That's up to you. I'm in no rush. Let me know when you figure out what you wanna do. Yeh know, I'm sorta wrung out. I am going to take a shower, and lie down for a while. Feel free to take anything from the house you need; lock up when you go."

After Becky walked out, Nick sat stunned for a long while. Eventually, he grabbed his phone and dialed. "Hey Father, are you busy? … Mind if I come over? … Thanks."

Nick stood, reached into his pocket, and took his house key off the ring. He left the key on the counter and walked out. He cried as he did it; she cried when she found it.

# Chapter 24

He sat impatiently in the back of the small, stuffy room. The light green block walls, tiled floor and harsh fluorescent lighting gave homage to every meeting room tucked away in the basement of every mid-century county courthouse across the country. Frank Miller knew it was here, in these utilitarian little rooms, the *real* and important business of government took place. In rooms like this, boards, commissions, committees and every other breed of bureaucrat deliberated; deals were made, money spent, and fates decided. And here – today – is where the coroner's inquest jury sat.

Inquests were open to the public, but other than the occasional relative, spectators were rare. Miller sat as an audience of one. He had testified early, but stayed for the whole hearing. He knew all too well that cause of death determinations always mattered, so he tried to attend these on all his cases. But the finding of these particular seven jurors mattered more than usual to Miller. This investigation had gotten under his skin. He knew it shouldn't; it was unprofessional, but the case had become personal.

Miller sat alone in the room, the inquest had adjourned for lunch. The quiet afforded him time to think about the case. *Something is going on here, I know it. Roberts was an asshole, he made porn movies with other people's wives… why? Is he a freak, or is it about money? How many women? His wife says there were several, but she could be lying. Maybe there is another player in this game I don't know about. I need to see the guy's video stash. But where is it? On his computer, and where is that? Who took it, and why?... Probably the wife. Roberts suddenly beats up his wife for something... why?... The computer. She would know where it was. Adler punches the guy out the same night... why? Because Roberts slept with his wife?... Sure, but why wait 8 months? No, something changed... Adler and Mrs. Roberts? That makes sense, but I can't connect them. Did the two women have a thing? They did, and they are still in touch, I know that. What does that tell me? What are they into? Did they off the guy? No. They don't have it in them. It had to be Adler, maybe protecting someone. Something triggered Roberts's death; something threatened somebody. Maybe Jabba is right, simple solutions are best; Adler simply got jealous and snapped. But that's not what the crime scene suggests. Give me time,* he thought. *I'll get there. I just need time.*

The sound of people returning to their seats interrupted Miller's thoughts. Coroner Patrick cleared his throat and called the inquest back to order.

Patrick said, "Ladies and gentleman of the jury, we have concluded scheduled testimony. Before I ask you to retire and deliberate, I think it prudent to review the essential elements of this morning's proceedings. I remind you that the de facto cause of death has been established. You are charged with determining the circumstances under which death occurred. Your findings may include; Accidental, suicide, death by the act of another, natural causes, death by misadventure, or circumstance undetermined. I further remind you that although you should attempt to find unanimous agreement, a simple majority is all that is required. Finally, your determination will be listed as official. However, it is non-binding and subject to dispute in criminal or civil courts. Do you have any questions?"

A frumpy looking, gray-haired woman raised her hand. "Please explain the difference between accidental and misadventure."

The coroner replied, "Death by misadventure includes unintended deaths occurring as a result of the victim willingly undertaking a known risk, or illegal activity. Any other questions?"

Hearing none, Coroner Patrick continued the summary. "This morning, you heard me review the autopsy findings. As I said, the de facto cause of death has been established. The victim, Sylvester Roberts, died as a result of thermal injuries. Specifically, suffocation arising from laryngeal edema subsequent to the inhalation of super-heated air. The victim sustained second and 3$^{rd}$ degree burns over 95% of the body. The autopsy indicated no other physical trauma. Blood and urine tests were unremarkable. Toxicology indicated moderate alcohol intoxication. A copy of the official autopsy report is in your packet for review. Questions?"

No one raised their hand. Patrick continued. "Fire Investigator Maxwell Ross testified that the official cause of the fire is listed as incendiary. Supporting that conclusion was the discovery of significant amounts of gasoline throughout the house. Investigator Ross also testified that first arriving firefighters found the house fully involved. All doors and windows in the Roberts house were closed and locked. Ross stated fire crews brought the fire under control within 6 minutes of arrival. Firefighting crews discovered Mr. Roberts' body lying face down in what has been called the living room. They found his body approximately eight feet from the front door. Crews noted a gasoline container lay near Mr. Robert's body. You will find the full fire report, state crime lab reports, and photographs and video of the fire scene in your packets for review. Do you have questions regarding the fire report?"

Again, the frumpy woman raised her hand. "The report calls the fire incendiary. Is that the same as arson?"

Patrick responded, "It is a technical distinction going to motive. Incendiary only denotes an intentionally set fire. Arson specifies an incendiary fire started with criminal intent, or criminal negligence. An incendiary fire may or may not be deemed arson, depending on why it was set."

Coroner Patrick briefly looked at the transcript, then continued. "Detective Frank Miller testified regarding the criminal investigation subsequent to the fire. The house in which Mr. Roberts died was owned by himself and his wife. His wife was not present when emergency crews arrived. Investigation determined that Mr. Roberts and his wife were estranged, and she had taken up temporary residence at the Mercy House Shelter for women. Like the fire report, the police investigation also concludes that the fire was incendiary. Credit card records indicate that Mr. Roberts purchased 4 gallons of gasoline from a nearby service station the night of the fire. Videotape from the station's security system shows Mr. Roberts filling a 5-gallon gas can."

"The crime scene investigation yielded no fingerprint evidence other than that of Mr. and Mrs. Roberts. The detective testified that a court order to evacuate the premises was issued to Mr. Roberts on day of the fire. Evidence showed Mr. Roberts placed his belongings in his truck, which sat in the garage at the time of the fire. Investigating officers found Mrs. Robert's personal possessions and clothing piled on the bed in the master bedroom. The presence of gasoline on Mrs. Robert's possessions has caused investigating officers to postulate that whomever lit the fire, intended to burn those possessions. You have heard testimony by Detective Miller, and confirmed by Mrs. Roberts that she and her husband had been living apart, and that she had recently filed for divorce. Further, she filed criminal charges against him for the creation and distribution of illegal explicit videos of her and others without consent. Mrs. Roberts testified her husband had physically abused her, and that she believes he intentionally set the fire."

The coroner again referred to his notes, took a drink of water, and said, "The reason for this inquest is because the police investigation has indicated some conflicting evidence regarding the circumstances under which Mr. Roberts died. Detective Miller has pointed out some inconsistencies in the physical evidence. Specifically, the position of the body in relation to the door, the presence of the victim's vehicle and belongings in the garage at the time of the fire, and the location of the box of matches assumed to be the ignition source for the fire. Detective Miller also stated concern over the absence of certain possessions, including computer equipment that may or may not have been involved in the criminal activity for which Mr. Roberts was under investigation. These inconsistencies, coupled with the discovery that one or more persons may have had motive to harm Mr. Roberts has caused investigators to entertain the possibility that one or more unknown persons *may* have been present at the time of the fire, and those persons may have deliberately caused the death of Mr. Roberts. As with the other witness testimony, I have included a copy of the crime scene report for your review; as well as a written transcript of all testimony. Does anyone have questions about the criminal investigation testimony?"

A middle-aged man in a golf shirt and jeans cleared his throat. He stood and said, "Yes, I have a question. The officer said several people may have had reason to harm the victim. Yet, there is nothing in the testimony that mentioned any witnesses or evidence implicating specific suspects. Other than what we heard, is their reason to believe others were involved?"

The coroner looked at Miller. "As luck would have it, Detective Miller is still with us. Detective?"

*Shit!* thought Miller. He knew he had to parse his words closely. He couldn't accuse someone in an official proceeding absent evidence, nor could he deliberately mislead an official inquiry, but this juror had touched on the biggest problem with the case. "No. No witness has accused anyone of being involved in the victim's death. Also, at *present* there is no direct evidence implicating any specific person or person's involvement. But… I stress the investigation is ongoing."

The juror didn't seem satisfied. "So I understand. Is there *any* evidence that another person was present?"

Miller paused before answering. "None other than the crime scene seems to suggest the inconsistencies I described."

Miller sat and said to himself, *that could have gone better. And why the hell did Jerry downplay the third-party theory, 'inconsistency of evidence… a potential theory of a person or persons involvement'… what the hell is that? Oh, well, it doesn't matter. I made my point. They get that it wasn't an accident.*

Coroner Patrick addressed the Jury. "Let me express my appreciation for your diligence in listening to the evidence. I ask that you make your judgement based on the facts presented as well as the observations of the witnesses. The evidence excludes death by natural causes. And as the fire was incendiary, accidental death is also precluded. As a result, a simple assessment- should guide your decision;

One, if the evidence convinces you that Mr. Roberts lit the fire and failed to escape, death by misadventure is suggested.

Two, if the evidence suggests the victim started the fire and deliberately took his own life in the process, a determination of suicide is appropriate.

Three, a homicide finding is appropriate if you find sufficient evidence to assert with confidence that a person or persons unknown *caused* the death of Mr. Roberts via the fire.

Finally, if none of those scenarios are compelling, you may also find for cause undetermined.

I now ask you to retire to the conference room across the hall for deliberation. Should you need anything, please knock on the door."

Miller walked out of the courthouse feeling good about the proceeding. A determination of homicide was possible, but a stretch. Still, he made it clear that he had suspicions about Robert's death. Experience taught him that police suspicion was almost always enough for an inquest jury to go with undetermined. He didn't really care all that much either way. Calling it a homicide would put some extra juice in the case, but from a practical sense, either verdict was as good as the other to him.

# Chapter 25

Jimmy Stout wadded up the Kleenex and threw it in the trash. He lifted his hips slightly to pull up his underwear. Getting himself off to videos of his dead friend's widow felt ghoulish, but he had been crushing on Racheal for years. *And Sly would be cool with it,* he told himself. *Soon it will be for real.* Jimmy grinned. *How do you like that, old buddy?* He closed the computer and slid it under the mattress along with the thumb drive.

Jimmy felt pretty good about how things worked out. Sly asking him to stash his stuff was like a golden ticket. When Sly first showed him the videos, he had teased Jimmy that for $500 he could costar in one with Racheal. He knew that was bullshit; not that Sly wouldn't do it, but he knew Racheal would never agree. *But now things are different you prick,* he thought. *You handed her to me on a silver platter. Now I am going to get what I want, for free.*

Jimmy had lied to her, saying Sly had left the videos with him to put up on a new website and send to her family. Then he told her he felt bad about it, and would give her the laptop if she did him a few *favors*. There was no reason to say what those favors were, she understood what he meant. She had cried when he told her the deal; that sorta bothered him at first. But he figured if he gave her a few days, she'd come around. She had no choice. He tried to ease his conscience; *It's just sex, after all. It's not like she hasn't done it a thousand times before. She'll be okay.*

He got out of bed to get a beer and watch some TV. As he made his way to the kitchen, he rationalized, *I'm actually doing her a favor. Sly would have bled her dry. I'm just asking for a little of her time. Hell,* he thought, *the way Sly bragged about how she couldn't get enough, she'll probably like it. The other women… who knows? They may have to be cash deals, but you never know. Lord knows I wouldn't mind tagging that firefighter's wife — maybe give her and Racheal a two for one, like in the video. Yep, that could work out.*

As he stood with his head in the refrigerator, the door to garage exploded off its hinges. Before he could react, two men pinned him face down on the floor. He barely got a glimpse of them, but he could tell they were both big and dressed in black and wore ski masks. One of them pressed something into his back. He assumed it was a gun. The other rammed a hunting knife into the floor right next to his head. A low, sinister voice growled, "Close your eyes and keep them closed. Don't move, don't turn your head, don't flinch, don't even fucking breathe asshole. I am looking for an excuse to end you, got it?"

Jimmy whimpered, "Be cool. I won't give you any trouble. Take whatever you want, just don't kill me."

"Listen close, fuck tart, I am only going to tell you this once. You have something that belongs to us and we want it."

Jimmy said, "I don't know what you're talking about."

A knee crashed into Jimmy's ribs, eliciting a groan. "Wrong answer. Your idiot friend Roberts sold us some special videos. He told us you had them."

"No, you don't understand. Sly is dead."

The ominous voice whispered, "No shit stain, it's *you* that don't understand. We are very aware that he is dead. Before we fried him, he gave you up, he said he gave them to you. And unless you want to end up like your buddy, I suggest you tell us where they are right now. Or I'm going to take this knife and start removing parts of you until you do."

Jimmy felt two horrible sensations. The edge of a knife pressing against the back of his ear, and the spreading warmth of urine under his crotch. He sobbed, "Oh fuck, don't…wait. You can have it. The stuff is under my mattress; I'll get it."

The voice said, "Stay where you are. Jesus, did you just piss yourself?"

"I — I am sorry."

Jimmy heard footsteps moving to the bedroom, then his stuff being tossed around. He didn't dare turn his head to look. Seconds later, the other voice said, "Got it."

The knife pressed harder against his ear; the stinging pain made Jimmy wince. The voice said, "Where are the copies?'

Jimmy pleaded, "Relax man. There aren't any." The knife pressed harder. Jimmy nearly sobbed, "No — Really  — I swear. It's just the laptop and thumb drive."

"I don't believe you."

Jimmy had to swallow back against the rising bile when the warm trickle of blood spread down his neck. "Please stop. I swear, I only have the computer and the thumb drive; there's nothing else. I'm begging man. I didn't know Sly sold it. You gotta believe me."

The voice said, "Listen panty sniffer, here's what's gonna happen. If we find any other copies of our property floating around, we are coming back and you're going to end up like your buddy Roberts. If we hear you called the cops, we are going to come back. You don't want that, do you understand?"

"Yes! Don't worry, I won't give you any trouble. I promise."

The voice warned him, "Stay right here on the floor, keep your eyes closed until we are long gone." With that, the two men took off.

Jimmy lay on the floor sobbing long after they were gone. Eventually, he composed himself enough to get off the floor. To the empty room he said, "Christ Sly, what the hell did you get me into?" Later that same night, he packed a bag and headed for the fishing camp.

*****

The two men in black ran down the alley to their waiting car. Breathing hard, they braced themselves on the hood; listening for an indication they were being followed. The bigger of the two said, "Do you think he will call the cops?"

"No, we scared him out of it. Any chance he has other copies?"

"Nope, he would have fessed up. He ain't no hero."

Satisfied they were alone, both men ripped off their ski masks and stared at each other. Nick broke out in laughter. "Damn, Marco, what the hell was that?"

Marco started laughing too, as much out of nervous energy as anything else. "What was what?"

Still laughing, Nick said, "*Fuck tart- shit stain-* and oh, my favorite, *panty sniffer*. That's some old school gangster there. I was waiting for you to call him a *poopy head* or *stinky butt* any second."

"Hey fuck you," said Marco. "It worked, didn't it?" Suddenly, Marco broke into laughter so hard he had to bend over. "Did you see it, Nick? Mr. Panty Sniffer peed himself."

"We did good brother; I promise you he won't be bothering any women again anytime soon." Nick clapped Marco on the shoulder. "Seriously man. Thank you for this. It means a lot that you would help me and Becky like this."

"Don't worry about it. It was kind of fun. Besides, it was worth it to see you acting more like your old self. I don't remember the last time you laughed."

"Heck," said Nick, "we should do this part time. Maybe work for a loan shark or something."

"Yeah, we can check out Crime Careers Dot Com and see who's hiring. Now, let's get out of here before somebody sees us."

Nick said, "Okay, let's head to the airport and dump this rental."

Marco jumped into the driver's seat and said, "I still think this whole cloak and dagger thing was over the top. We could have used one of our own cars."

"No," said Nick. "I know you don't believe it, but I tell you Miller is following me — better safe than sorry. Besides, what if

Jimmy had seen the car? Gangsters don't drive a pickup or a crappy Honda Civic."

"Gangsters don't use plastic guns either. And don't rake on my ride. I make that Civic look cool. You try supporting two kids who do nothing but eat and outgrow clothes. Let's see what you drive."

"Hey Marco, you should check out having some wood grain decals put on the door panels. Now, that *would* be cool."

"Shut up Nick, and let's go. Jazz will get pissed if I'm late."

"No time for a celebratory beer?"

Marco grinned, "One, that's it — just one."

"Seriously Marco; thanks. I know I've been dick lately. I said some stupid stuff after the hearing; I wouldn't have blamed you if you told me to screw off."

"Never happen man. I always got your back, you know that. Now, buy me that beer."

Marco got home two hours later. To his surprise, Jazz wasn't overly angry, mostly curious. When he finished telling the story, she shook her head and asked. "Are you two idiots out of your minds?"

Marco replied, "I know it was risky. But that slimeball was hurting women. Nick said he would come after Becky too. It had to be done. Listen, you can't talk about this to anybody, especially Becky. Nick was adamant about that. Becky can't know how we got the stuff. What she don't know, she can't be forced to testify to."

After a moment of consideration, a sly smile crept onto Jazmine's face. Marco knew that smile, he *liked* that smile. She said, "Okay, I won't tell Becky. You know, it was kinda bad ass, what you did — protecting our friend and all… and that bit with the knife. How about you go make sure the kids are asleep, then come back and show me how that tough guy handles a woman."

# Chapter 26

"Are you freakin kidding me?" Miller snapped.

Captain Joe, *Jabba,* Johnson put his sandwich down, wiped his mouth with the back of his hand and said, "What the hell did you expect? There is a crap ton of evidence that this Roberts clown intended to burn the place down, and you got nothing that suggests anyone else was even there, much less killed him. Hell Frank, the coroner says it wasn't even close; five voted for death by misadventure, and only two voted for undetermined. Nobody was buying homicide."

"It doesn't matter. The inquest is just a formality. I'll talk to the district attorney…"

Johnson interrupted Miller. "I talked to him this morning. With what you got, and the inquest calling it an accident, he isn't interested. Neither am I, for that matter. You're done; we've got other cases to deal with."

"Look, Captain, this is crap. We've got a solid motive for people wanting to off this guy, especially Adler. I got reasonable evidence that the crime scene was staged, and I interviewed Adler. He's hiding something. Either he killed Roberts or is covering for whoever did. I got a case."

"No," said Johnson. "You've got bubkis. There is firm evidence that Roberts set the fire. That's it, everything else is supposition and theory. For all you know, the guy went up when he lit a cigarette. That's why his truck was in the garage, and why he wasn't by the door. Maybe he decided to do himself in at the last minute… who knows? As for motive, the guy's wife says there were at least three other women in those videos. Even if you had something pointing to someone killing him, we got at least a half a dozen people with the exact same motive as the firefighter, and God only knows how many more-may be out there. And again, none of the evidence points to anyone of them in particular."

Miller jumped to his feet. "Bullshit! I'm telling you this Adler guy…"

Johnson glared at Miller. "Sit down and cool off. Adler punched the guy who banged his wife; so what? You can't prove this is even a crime, and even if you did, you still couldn't prove who did it. Frank, I'm not sure what's up your ass about this case, but you know a dead dog when you see one. I need you on cases that have legs."

"I tell you I'm close. The other night, he went to the airport. He's ready to run."

"Where did he buy a ticket to?"

"He didn't."

"Well, isn't that helpful? I say again, it's over, move on."

Miller turned to leave. "Fine, I'll take another run at Adler and the victim's wife. They're both shaky. I'm sure I can rattle something loose."

Johnson slammed his palm down on his desk. "Sit down and shut up. I'm telling you that you're done. You spent too damn much time on this thing as it is. Plus, we're getting heat from upstairs. The Fire department brass is up the Chief's ass about why his detectives are lurking around one of the fire stations stirring up shit. They want to know what's going on and our chief is not happy that you're interrogating firefighters without him knowing it."

Miller groused. "Since when do I need the chief's permission to talk to witnesses?"

"Cut the crap, Miller. You're not stupid. Our chief felt like an idiot being unable to tell the mayor and fire chief what we were doing. You should've told me first. The thing is this: there is no upside to creating a turf war between the two departments. You don't start a shit storm unless you can nail it down, and you can't. I promise you we can expect blowback for harassing that guy, and that blowback will be on me. Listen close, I'm not taking a hit because you got a hard on for some hose monkey. So, for once in your life, do what I fucking tell you and let it go."

"That hose monkey killed a guy."

"Can you prove it?… No. Will you ever?… Not likely."

Miller dropped back down in his chair. "I'm telling you, give me time and I can wrap this up tight."

Johnson tossed four folders over to Miller. "And I'm telling you that you don't have time. I want you working on these four cases, and only on these four cases. Do I make myself clear?" Miller nodded that he understood. The captain added, "Good, now get out of here."

*****

"Are you here to arrest me?" Nick said to the detective standing on his front porch.

"Not yet," said Miller.

"Then what do you want?"

"We need to talk. Can I come in?"

"I don't think so."

"What's the matter Adler, you got something to hide in there?"

"Yeah, that's right. Haven't you heard? I got Jimmy Hoffa and DB Cooper stashed in my closet."

Miller smiled, it lacked humor. "You're a funny guy. You really should let me in. I don't think you want the neighbors to hear this conversation."

Nick said, "Look at this neighborhood, Miller. I don't think much will bother them. Besides, I don't intend to talk to you. I got nothing to say."

"Okay," said Miller, "then just listen. It's only a matter of time until I tie you into this. You're probably not a bad guy. You just got in the middle of a crappy deal. It's time to get on the right side of this. You can help yourself out right now by telling me the truth. Maybe you did it, maybe you just know who did. Either way, you're making it worse on yourself by playing this game. In the end, there's no getting away. This is your last chance to help yourself."

Nick shook his head dismissively. "Look, Miller, has it ever occurred to you that you're just plain wrong? Nobody but you thinks anybody had anything to do with Robert's death but Roberts. Hell, a buddy from the arson team called me this morning and told me that even the coroner's inquest determined the guy did himself in. Yet, here you are still talking shit. Get this through your head; I didn't kill the guy, nobody else did either. He was a stupid asshole, and he did what stupid assholes do; something stupid. I'll tell you something else; if I wanted to kill the guy, and I didn't, I would never set a fire to do it."

Miller fished a cigarette from his pocket and lit it. "Yeah, why is that? Too obvious?"

"No, because I am a firefighter, and fighting fires is dangerous, bad things can happen. I would never risk the lives of my brothers and sisters. I'll clue you in on something else too, if I had set the fire, that house would be gone. It was an amateur job. By the way, you should lay off those smokes. They're bad for you."

"Have it your way, but know this Adler; time is on my side. Eventually, I will be back with handcuffs."

Nick shrugged, then said, "If you say so. But let's be honest, you don't believe it or you wouldn't be here playing games. Now leave me the hell alone." With that, Nick shut the door in the detective's face.

# Chapter 27

He thought, *and here we go again, round two of what to do with crazy Nick.* Shifting in his chair, he whispered to Union President Stafford, "What do you think? Will I live to fight another day?"

"Beats me. Nick, we've never been through anything like this before. I'll tell you this though, we're probably looking at a precedent. I promise, the union has your back. We will go to the wall for this if need be."

"Great," said Nick. "I just love being a guinea pig."

The Chief's receptionist told them they could go in. It surprised Nick to see only Deputy Chief Stevens and Chief Walsh waiting for them. The chief cleared his throat and said, "Hello Dominick. Good to see you Larry; please sit. I'll get right to the point. We are on new ground here. On the one hand, Dominick obviously violated department policy. He demonstrated a disturbing lack of self-control…"

Larry interrupted, "Chief, clearly there are extenuating…"

The chief cut him off with a wave of his hand. "Let me finish. On the *other* hand, our department counselor reports that Firefighter Adler was suffering from undiagnosed post traumatic stress syndrome resulting from an on-duty incident. Clearly, we must take that fact into consideration." The chief paused and studied Nick. "Dominick, first let me convey to you my sincere wish that you make a full recovery. Father Tom informs me you have made significant progress already and is confident that you can return to limited duty now, and full duty very soon."

Nick said, "Thank you, Chief. I am feeling much better. Father Tom has been incredibly helpful."

"Good," said the chief. "I'll be blunt. This is the first time we've considered emotional state as a mitigating circumstance to behavior, and I am feeling my way through this. While I despise using the 'slippery slope' as an argument, I am not at all comfortable setting the precedent implied here. I can't tolerate firefighters punching out civilians, or starting fights in the station — under *any* circumstances."

Larry said, "Chief, you said yourself, Father Tom reports…"

"I know what Father Tom said, Larry. And I get it, I'm sympathetic. Still, I cannot help but think that at some level, Dominick knew what he was doing, and so must share some culpability. Further, Dominick was aware that he was, how shall I put this, not at his best. He should have sought help, rather than try to hide his symptoms. As a result, I feel I have to impose some degree of disciplinary action, albeit tempered."

Chief Walsh turned his attention directly to Nick. "It is my judgment that Firefighter Adler be suspended for three shifts without pay, beginning with his next scheduled shift day. On the advice of Father Tom, he will report to the training division the following week. After completion of that assignment, he will return to his normal work shift."

Stafford bristled. "Chief, on the one hand, you acknowledge Dominick was ill, and yet you're still punishing him. That is tantamount to punishing someone for spraining their ankle. The union can't stand for that."

"It's not the same thing, Larry, and you know it. If you're unhappy, feel free to appeal it to the commission. If they agree with you, so be it. I'll be okay with that. But as it stands now, I can't give Dominick a free pass."

"Come on Chief," said Larry, "You know that going to the comi…"

Nick interjected, "That's okay Larry. Chief, that's fair. I'll do the three days."

The chief nodded in appreciation. "Dominick, off the record, the department owes you a bit of an apology. We should've recognized your symptoms earlier and been more proactive."

Larry Stafford shifted in his chair, clearly unhappy. He looked about to speak, but remained quiet.

"I don't blame the department," said Nick. "I did everything I could to hide it."

The chief turned to Stafford. "Larry, I've been in discussions with Father Tom. On his recommendation, we're going to add an annual training class on stress recognition and management. We're also going to institute some policies implementing mandatory post critical incident stress debriefing sessions. I am setting up an ad hoc committee to develop those policies. Deputy Chief Stevens will run point. We want the union to take part."

"We will be happy to look at what you're proposing," said Larry.

"No, Larry. I don't need a critique. I need help. The rank and file are going to scoff at the training; and outright oppose mandatory debriefing sessions. I need some support. This is about health and welfare."

"Okay, I'll help sell it and tamp down any blowback. But we won't help write policy, you know that."

"We've been over this before, Larry. I'm not trying to undercut your right to file a grievance. *I'll* write the policy. The committee is for research and advice only."

Stafford nodded in agreement. As they stood to leave, Chief Walsh asked, "Dominick, there's been a detective hanging around asking questions about you. What's going on?"

"It's kinda nuts, Chief. This detective, Miller, has a bug up his ass for sure. It's clear Roberts set the fire; everybody but the detective thinks he burnt himself up. The dead guy and I have some history, he and my wife…"

The chief held up his hand in a stop motion. "I heard."

Nick continued. "Anyway, he's fixated on the idea somebody – probably me – killed the guy. There's nothing to any of the cop's suspicions. He's just fishing. Honestly, I think he's just trying to stir up trouble. He pretty much dislikes firefighters in general, and me in particular."

"Why is that?" asked Deputy Chief Stevens.

Nick chuckled, "For one, his ex-wife left him for Tommy Shoemaker over at station 12. And, well, I may have busted his balls about that a little. Oh, and I may have also invited him to have sexual relations with himself. The guy doesn't have a sense of humor, I guess."

The chief laughed and said, "Tommy Shoemaker, huh? That guy could piss off anybody. Well, screw Miller if he can't take a joke. I had a chat with his chief, let me know if he gives you any more trouble. I don't like cops snooping around my department without permission."

*****

Nick walked out of the building to his truck. As before, Marco stood waiting. Nick said, "Hey gangster, what are you doing here?"

Marco beamed a toothy smile. "Just seeing what's what. How did it go?"

Nick shrugged. "He gave me three days without pay, and I have to pull a week in the training division. Then back to shift."

Marco looked at him sympathetically. "Sorry about the hickey on your record, but you really got off pretty easy."

"Yeah, I'm not complaining."

"Back to shift, huh? Tell me straight; Nick, are you good to go?"

"Marco, are you asking me if I can carry my weight?"

"It's a fair question. You're my brother from another mother, but I got a whole crew to look after and I can't have you spitting the bit. Will you be right when it gets hot?'

"Hey, I'd never put the crew at risk. If I didn't think I could go, I'd say so. I'll be straight with you. I may be a little squeamish about handling bodies for a while, but I am good for everything else. Trust me."

Marco studied his friend, nodded, then smiled. "Good enough. So Nick, I heard about the inquest. Do you think that will be the end of it?"

Nick leaned against the fender of his truck next to his friend. "Miller showed up at Casa Del Crapo, throwing some weak threats around. He's mad as hell, which tells me he got word to move on."

Marco clapped his friend on the shoulder. "That's good. By the way, you will like this. Your old buddy Jenkins got reassigned to first shift *and* transferred to a new station. I hear somebody with a lot of bugles wasn't happy about him shooting his mouth off to Johnny Law."

"No shit? I'll have to congratulate him next time I see him."

"That won't be anytime soon," said Marco. "My intel is that he got sent to shantytown."

Nick laughed. "Are you kidding? He got sent to station 2? He *really* must've pissed somebody off. The mold and asbestos alone could be enough to kill him."

"Come on, I'll buy you a beer to celebrate," said Marco.

"It's not even noon yet, you drunk."

Marco shrugged, "Okay, Susie. I'll drink a beer and you can have tea and crumpets."

Nick said, "I got a better idea. How about I pick up a pizza tonight, and go over to your place? You, me and Jazz can chill, and I can spend some time with your rugrats."

Marco put his arm around Nick. "I would like that, and Jazz will love it. It's good to have you back, my friend."

"Thanks."

"Hey Nick, Jazz told me about you and Becky the other night."

"Yeah, it got a little rough."

"You never should have left it like that."

"She didn't give me much choice."

Marco took hold of Nick's shoulder and said, "Bull, it's time to man up and fix it."

"You don't understand, I …"

"No Nick, you don't understand. Fix it. Fix it now. The window is closing my friend, she is going to move on. A woman like her … men will be lining up. Pull your head out of your ass and go claim her before some guy offers her what you won't. Think long and hard about what you're giving up."

"I'll tell you what I told her, I need to time."

"Time for what?" asked Marco. "Stop lying to yourself, it's pride that stopping you. You love her and you know it. You need her and you know that too. Everything else is bullshit."

# Chapter 28

Becky struggled to catch her breath. She punched the stop button on the treadmill and leaned forward on the console for a few moments to recuperate. She then grabbed a towel, wiped her face, and climbed the steps toward the kitchen.

Just as she was gulping down a glass of water, the doorbell rang. A little self-conscious about only wearing a sports bra and a tiny pair of running shorts that could be mistaken for underwear, she considered going upstairs and grabbing a robe. The doorbell rang again. "Screw it," she said.

Hiding behind the door, she opened it a crack to see who it was. "This is a surprise," she said.

Nick asked, "Can we talk?"

"Of course, come in. It's good to see you."

Nick eyed her up and down and smiled wolfishly. "Well, it's good to see *you too*. Is answering the door half naked a thing now?"

Becky teased, "Hey, I am a single girl now. You never know when a nice looking guy is on the porch. And, as I recall, you opened the door naked when I dropped in on you."

He grinned. "Maybe I knew it was you."

"Nice try, but I seem to remember a naked woman hanging around your living room."

Becky saw an impish twinkle in his eye, one she hadn't seen in a long while. He said, "Like I said, maybe I knew it was you. I hear you're into that now."

She playfully slapped his shoulder. "Funny. Well, you're in a feisty mood, aren't you? So what's up? Did you come to get something?"

Nick said, "As a matter of fact, I did — you."

"Excuse me?"

"I want my life back — with you. I don't want to date, or have you date either. We're married and I want to stay married. Becky, I've done a lot of thinking. It's time I try to be happy, and I can't be happy without you. I was a bad husband; you made some bad choices. We both fucked up, but there is nothing we can't get past if we want to. And I realize now, that I want to. You were right. We are choosing to live the way we live. It's time that I make different choices."

"Nick, I've been wanting to hear you say that for a very long time. But listen to me, you've got to tell me right now that you can get past what I did; that you can trust me again. I can't live in fear that you'll change your mind, or that I have to watch everything I say and do for fear of making you insecure. I told you I'm sorry for what I did, but I am done paying penance. You broke my heart by leaving me. I can't go through that again. I don't want you to come back just because you think you should. Or you're afraid to end it. I want you back because you're ready to start over, that you're sure of it."

Nick wrapped her in his arms. "We have healing to do and, I think the two of us should see Father Tom for counseling, but I'm committed to *us*. I know I still love you, and I want to make it work. I am as sure of that as I am anything. The truth of the matter is, I've missed you for a while now. It's been my pride making me so stubborn. It wasn't just that you had an affair; I couldn't face the truth that I wasn't enough…"

"Nick I never said…"

"… No Becky, you didn't have to. I neglected you, that's part of the reason you did what you did. I knew it before you told me the other day. Maybe it wasn't all my fault, but failing you still hurt. Knowing why you did what you did was as bad as the affair. I realize now that was part of the reason I couldn't face you. You made a mistake, a big one, I made a thousand little ones. Becky, I promise you, Father Tom and I have made progress. I can do better by you. I'm going to keep seeing him until I'm where I need to be. We can get it right again. "

Becky felt tears streaming down her face. "Nick, I love you. I love you so much. I've waited so long…" She kissed him, he kissed her; it was a kiss of joy, of forgiveness, of hope. She said, "Sweetheart, together we can get through anything. We'll get through your therapy, will work out our problems. Together, we'll deal with that stupid detective and all that other crap. We *can* be happy again."

Nick held her close. "I know we can be happy. I am sure of it. Oh, and this may help. The coroner's inquest determined Roberts burnt himself up. Miller is livid, but there isn't much he can do about it. There's nothing for a DA to work with, so Miller won't be bothering us again."

Becky took a step back. A look of amazement spread across her tear-streaked face. "It's over? You're sure?"

"Yeah, I'm sure. He's got nothing. No crime — no investigation. Oh, and that thing about the missing computer, that won't be a problem anymore either."

"What?" said "Becky, what does that mean?"

"Let's just say that the computer and Sly's collection are gone forever."

"Nick, what did you do?"

He shrugged. "It's best we don't get into that. That Jimmy guy won't bother anyone again. Let's leave it at that."

"Nick, you didn't…"

"No, No. But it is taken care of."

Becky wiped away a tear. "I don't know how to thank you."

He reached out and, grabbing the waistband of her shorts, pulled her to him. "I can think of a way."

She kissed him and said, "I am sweaty and gross. Give me five minutes to hop in the shower. Open a bottle of wine and meet me upstairs."

Nick's hands cupped her breasts. "I don't care if you're sweaty. I want you right now, right here. You can take a shower when I'm done with you."

Becky pulled away and took off her bra and shorts. She tossed them to him and walked towards the steps leading to the bedroom. "I've been dreaming of this for a year. You can wait for five minutes. Oh, don't forget the wine."

*****

Becky opened her eyes, and saw that it was 6:30 PM. She relished the feel of the man – her man – next to her. They had made love twice. The first was a little awkward, but sweet and tender. The second time was raw and intense. He had taken her with the brute force of a man possessed. It felt like he was reclaiming her, making it clear that she belonged to him. It was exactly what she wanted and needed. She knew then that she and Nick would be okay. After, they laid exhausted in each other's arms and drifted to sleep.

She slipped out of the bed and put on a robe. Nick roused from his sleep and said, "Where are you going?"

She answered, "We worked up an appetite. I thought I'd go downstairs and whip us up something to eat. Are you brave enough to stay for dinner this time?"

Nick smiled at the reference to their previous fight. "Really? You want to give me grief, right *now*?"

Becky playfully tossed his shirt at him. "Yeah, you deserve it. That was some weak tea, you know. Now get dressed, stud."

Nick replied, "Okay, okay. Yes, I am brave enough to stay for dinner, and maybe breakfast too, if that's okay."

Becky walked over to the bed and kissed the top of his head. "I'd like that."

Nick said, "Hang on a second." He picked up his phone and dialed. "Hey Marco, can we push me coming over back to tomorrow night? I got a thing going on… No, I got a date tonight… Yeah, a cute little blonde. I think you know her…. Yes her, dumb ass …Maybe I could bring her along tomorrow night?"

Nick looked at Becky questioningly. She nodded enthusiastically, then called out. "Hi Marco!"

To the phone he said, "Yeah, we'll see you tomorrow…. As a matter a fact, she is… You better believe it… Later, guy."

"What was that?" she asked. "As a matter of fact, I'm what?"

Nick grinned. "Naked."

"Men! You're all perverts. Do I even want to know what that other bit was?"

Nick looked at Becky, she was practically beaming. He couldn't remember the last time he saw her so happy. "Probably not. Hey, about breakfast tomorrow…"

Her expression darkened. "What? Changing your mind?"

"Uh-uh. Actually, how would you feel if I stayed forever?"

She stared at him for a few seconds, letting what he just said sink in. "Do you mean that? You're staying? You're ready to come home?"

He replied, "Like you said the other night, we've been apart too long."

Becky climbed on the bed and straddled his hips. She kissed him and said, "Welcome home."

"One thing, can I bring Cat?"

She laughed. "You can bring a skunk, if that's what it takes."

She laid on top of him and buried her face in the crook of his neck. He held her tightly as her tears moistened his skin. After a few moments, he felt her grind against him. "Again — really?"

In a raspy voice, she said, "We have lost time to make up for."

They made love again, the third time in five hours, a record for them. When they were done, Nick said, "I need a shower. I'm a sweaty mess; I must reek."

"Don't you dare shower yet. I love the way you smell; I missed it."

"Maybe *you* do, but I feel nasty."

She got up and said, "Oh, alright — if *you* must. You shower and I'll bring us up a snack. I'll meet you back here in ten minutes."

"Ah, sweetheart, I'm done for the night. I'm an old man, you know."

She smiled. "We'll see."

Becky made her way down to the kitchen, grabbed a phone from her purse and dialed. She said "Hi it's me. I just heard from Nick — The police are through with their investigation. They are calling it an accident." She listened, then said, "Yeah, we got lucky. Oh, and another thing. I'm not sure how, but Nick tells me he took care of Jimmy. He got Sly's computer somehow and got rid of it." Again, she listened. "No, he's sure he got all of it." Still listening on the phone, Becky opened the refrigerator and pulled out some cheese and grapes. "Listen, we're good now, but you and I hanging out together will just arouse suspicion. We need to keep some distance for a while." Becky pulled a plate and some crackers from the cabinets. "Me too, Racheal. I really hope everything works out for you."

Becky disconnected the call and put her phone back in her purse. She stopped and listened for the sound of the running shower. Satisfied, she fished a bag from the back of the cabinet below the sink. She removed the taser and hid it under some garbage in the kitchen can.

Nicks voice startled Becky. "I know you did it, I have for a while."

Stunned, she stammered, "Nick, I – I – you need to under…"

He smiled. "I get it. I am okay with it."

"I –we – didn't plan it. We went to the house … we thought he would be out… we just wanted to get his computer. He was there, setting the house on fire. He came at us – Racheal had brought a taser and… you know the rest."

"Yeah, I know the rest. Were you going to let me burn for the crime?"

"God know, believe me, we both decided to come forward if got to that."

Nick smiled, "I believe you."

Tears welled in the corners of Becky's eyes. "Now what?"

Nick shrugged. "Now what? What?"

"What do we – you – do now?"

"Do you have any regrets?" he asked.

"All kinds of them, but not about that."

"Alright, so we go upstairs, and we have cheese and wine. Then we'll see if I can manage another round of sex. Tomorrow, we begin living happily ever after. We both have a lot to forgive and forget, but eventually we will get back to good."

"You make it sound easy."

"Not easy, but we will."

"I love you," said Becky.

"Love you too…." He grabbed the bottle of wine. "…
"follow me upstairs."

Grabbing the cheese plate, Becky bounced up the steps
toward the bedroom– toward Nick– toward a new beginning.

# Authors Note

Dear Reader,

In recent years, suicide has claimed more first responders' lives than on duty deaths. Sobering as that is, the reality may be worse. The Firefighter Behavioral Health Alliance estimates that only 40% to 45% of firefighter and police suicides are reported.

The brave men and women who protect us too often experience unthinkable tragedy; they witness things most can't imagine. For far too many, the stress and emotional scarring can overwhelm. Exposure to death, pain, and loss, coupled with demanding schedules, physical exhaustion, and personal danger, can easily trigger emotional trauma.

Post Traumatic Stress Disorder (PTSD) is a significant and growing problem in the American Fire Service. Research has shown that as many as 20% of firefighters display some symptoms of PTSD, and an estimated 8% suffer significant life deficits as a result.

This novel is a work of fiction, as are all the characters. But the story is all too common in real life. Thousands of firefighters are suffering with undiagnosed symptoms they don't understand, while confused and frustrated family members look on helplessly.

If you are a firefighter, or love a firefighter, the author strongly encourages you to become familiar with PTSD causes, symptoms and treatments. A good place to start is the International Association of Firefighters Center of Excellence for Behavioral Health Treatment and Recovery…   www.iaffrecoverycenter.com

*H. Scott Walker*

H. Scott Walker

To Explore Other Books By

H Scott Walker

Please Visit  His Website At

www.hscottwalker.com